THE HOUSE OF MALACHITE

THE HOUSE OF MALACHITE

rachel blaufeld

This is a work of fiction. Names, characters, places, brands, media, and incidents are either the product of the author's imagination or are used fictitiously. The author acknowledges the trademarked status and trademark owners of various products referenced in this work of fiction, which have been used without permission. The publication/use of these trademarks is not authorized, associated with, or sponsored by the trademark owners.

Paperback ISBN: 979-8-9870516-9-6

Edited by
Julia Ganis, JuliaEdits.com

Cover design by
© Sarah Hansen, Okay Creations, LLC
www.okaycreations.com

Interior design and formatting by
E.M.
TIPPETTS
BOOK DESIGNS
www.emtippettsbookdesigns.com

trigger warning: infertility

Our happy ending was never meant to be.
We were nothing but a threat.

BLURB

With the ability to take away heartbreak, Tulya Vegga learned early how to mend shattered souls. One touch from her palm could make someone whole again. On the magical island of Rubia, it was her gift…and her curse. Bound to her mother's will, Tulya was never meant for happiness—only service.

Donovan Malachite was the opposite: he could inflict pain without lifting a finger. One look could send a zing up anyone's spine. Feared and revered as a ruthless businessman, Donovan was groomed to inherit his father's empire and carry out his mother's calculated plans. He'd never admit his quiet fascination with his innocent neighbor, Tulya.

But when his brother, Magnum, falls in love with a forbidden human, Donovan is forced to accompany Tulya on a mission to "fix" the situation.

They set out to right someone else's wrong.

Instead, they break all the rules.

And maybe…each other.

PART I

CHAPTER
ONE

Tulya

The snow dripped from the sky, softly pinging the great room's bay window. It was so quiet as I sat on my knees, watching the white flakes settling on the ground, forming piles of marshmallow fluff, beckoning me to dive in... But as much as they invited me to come outside, I continued to sit behind the foggy glass, longingly staring at the dusky purple sky, sort of wishing I lived among fewer rules. Earlier, I'd begged Mama to let me go play, but I was already wearing my tulle party dress and tights, and she looked at me with *the look*, and I didn't even wait for her to say no. I'd sulked away to the study.

As legend had it, the island of Rubia was formed by a gorgeous goddess who cried lava, creating barriers between those who hurt her and the heart pounding in her chest. Always seemed strange that she'd crafted this place here and not in a more temperate climate. Most of the time, I didn't believe the legend. At school, we learned every Rubian was special in their own unique way and their powers were meant to be used within Rubia only. These capabilities were gifts, intended to help maintain order and allow our magical island to prosper. If we used them for the good of our people, we were granted more. Why would the goddess hold the ability to only help herself and her own heart?

That seemed silly.

Sulking, I flipped around on the love seat, plopping down on my butt, taking in the room and eyeing the ten-foot Christmas tree in the corner. Glory, our housekeeper, and I had picked it out at the Holiday Market, and it sparkled and twinkled against the dimly lit room. I smiled at that at least, remembering how happy I'd been making the branches shine.

My perfectly decorated tree waited to greet others as a fire burned and a tray full of cookies from Boulangerie Bakery sat perched on the coffee table. Too bad they weren't for me. None of this was. Occasionally, if Mama was tied up with her brother, the powerful Minister, Glory snuck me out on errands and we would stop for a croissant on The Avenue, where all the fancy boutiques and cafés were located. It was a dreamy place, Boulangerie, and I wondered if they had something like it in the real world...

To an outsider, our house was an idyllic scene, brimming with holiday magic. To me, it was torture; I wanted to run free and fancy. After all, I didn't have any purpose or powers yet and only wished I could eat desserts and go play in the snow.

I looked at the tray in ravenous hunger and pondered which cookie I wanted to steal the most. After all, I was only a kid in an adult's world.

"*Ezza! Ezza! Where are you?*" A screeching, raised voice carried through the house, calling for my mother.

Shoving my hands in my lap, I pretended to be busy singing carols to myself and not looking at the treats in front of me. I'd been asked to rehearse for the first-grade holiday pageant, so I did my best to pretend I'd been doing so.

"*Ezza!*" My brother's fiancée, Shelby, skidded into the room, looking disheveled in a sleeveless cranberry-colored dress, her hair wild and appearing as if she'd been yanking on it. I'd never heard her call Mama by her nickname, but now she was yelling it with reckless abandon. "*Ezza!*"

"Hi, Shelby," I said, trying not to startle her.

"Oh, hi, umm, I'm sorry, but do you know where your mother is?" She looked at me, wild-eyed, and I could tell she'd been crying.

My heart and brain did that weird flip-flop thing—pinging or pulsing in some sort of way I didn't quite understand. I knew it wasn't commonplace, and was something unique to me, but I hadn't mentioned it to anyone yet. I had fairly decent reasons.

"Tuvy! Do you know where your mother is?" Shelby snapped at me, and I shook my head. Sniffing back fresh tears, she ran a pale wrist over her nose. She didn't wait for an answer, only turned toward the vestibule and started to yell "Ezza" once again, as my heart and head pumped furiously, a small sheen of sweat forming on the back of my neck.

I ran my slight fingers under my long red waves and fingered the moisture building there, willing it to back off. At six years old, I already knew this was a sign of something greater than me. I wanted powers, but also I didn't.

"Ezza!" Even the tree flickered in disgust at Shelby's nonstop screaming.

"Shelby, quiet down." My mother finally appeared in the alcove, looking formidable, other than the bunch of mistletoe hanging above her stoic face making me want to laugh. "What are you hollering about, Shelby? Tuvy is sitting right there, and you're making a spectacle of yourself, young lady."

She meant Shelby, not me. I was nothing more than an innocent girl, and far from a lady.

"I-I—" Shelby stuttered, standing ramrod straight in front of Mama.

"What are you wearing? That is not what we decided on…together. The guests will arrive shortly." Mama stood, unaffected by Shelby's crying, staring her straight in the eyes.

I imagined Shelby taking in my mother, Esmeralda Falcone, her hair pulled back tight in a bun, red lip perfect as always, and not a sequin out of place on her sparkly black sheath dress.

"This dinner is for you, Shelby," Mama went on to say through gritted teeth.

"Bruno called it off, Esmeralda." She practically spit out my mother's full name, and even I knew that wouldn't be well received. "He said my family doesn't have enough magic in their bloodlines, and he should have known it with my common name, *Shelby*, and my lackluster capability to move objects without touching them. It's so commonplace, was what he said, with disgust. Looking right at me, as if it were an evil word." She barely could get out the last part, and I really wished I was playing in the snow. This was the type of drama my sister Caro and I ran away from when it came to Bruno, our older brother by over a decade and some.

From where I sat, I watched Shelby's back heave up and down and I could tell she was breathing hard. My body started to burn, and I wondered if I was getting sick. Despite the small smirk lifting Mama's mouth at Bruno's decision, I rose off the love seat, my feet carrying me next to Shelby.

"It's probably for the best," Mama said, not missing a beat. "But you'll have to gather yourself and make an announcement to the guests this evening, who are coming to celebrate your engagement. Throw some water on your face and comb your hair back. And for heaven's sake, put on the dress we selected."

"No," Shelby shrieked, falling to her knees. "You wanted this, I know it. Bruno said it—"

"You should have thought of this when you set your sights on Bruno."

Mama didn't waver in her words, but she did slip me a side-eye as I continued to stand next to Shelby, who was on her knees weeping.

Her mood had swung from being frantic and mad to devastated. "You were never going to bless us, and I love him… I'll never love again," Shelby began to shriek.

At the same time as her voice rose, my fingers shook and my palm lifted to Shelby's shoulder. Mama watched with one eye, following my movement as I also fell to my knees, Shelby's aches traveling my own spine as my fingertips met with her bare shoulder. My body swiveled to face my brother's ex-fiancée; I had no clue what was happening or what was driving me to do so, my torso seemingly having a mind of its own. My palm came to rest over Shelby's heart and something fizzed and shocked between us, Shelby's eyes opening wider than earlier. Heat raced up my legs, traveling my spine and back down again.

"What are you doing, Tuvy? Get up right now," Mama demanded, but I couldn't move.

A force I didn't know was willing me to stay put, kept my knees planted, my hand drawing all the heartache out of Shelby, locking it away somewhere—I wasn't quite sure where.

"Get up. I demand it, Tulya." Mama resorted to my full name.

I felt my head shaking no... *I've found my power*, I started to think and then I worried. Panic joined the warmth in my veins.

After a few more beats, Shelby moved my hand and stood, taking me in, gaping at me. "Tuvy, how did you do that?" She rolled her shoulders back and inhaled, and looked at Mama, saying, "I'm over you and your whole crazy family."

"What did she do?" Mama asked, staring daggers at Shelby.

"She...she...took... I don't know, but...Tuvy made all the pain and heartache go away. It's as if she drained me of it," Shelby said before sidestepping out of the room, leaving me alone with my newly found magic and my mother scowling at me.

Never had I wished more to cry tears of lava as I took in Mother's devilish grin as she spoke softly to herself.

"We have been waiting decades for this ability to rise again."

PART II

CHAPTER
TWO

Tulya

"**D**onovan Malachite can't stop looking at you," Prim whispered in my ear.

"Little Drummer Boy"—but make it a modern, snappy version, complete with a lead foot in the fills—echoed in the background, yet I heard my friend loud and clear.

Swatting her away with my hand as if she were a pesky fly, I spoke softly. "Please, I don't even want to hear it. You know this—I'm not into him, or anyone. I can't be. Also, I think it's pretty clear I don't get involved with men who carry all that swagger. I mean, look at him. He's the epitome of bad boy. And, well, I'm nothing like that."

"He is staring right at you, my gorgeous, redheaded vixen, and he looks hot as… And so do you."

Lord help me, but when Prim got on one, she stayed there.

"Stop. Maybe he's dreaming of you, my stunning, tiny brunette." I tossed a version of her words back at her, raising an eyebrow at my closest friend.

She fluffed her freshly styled beach waves and rolled her eyes. "He's definitely not thinking about me, and I'm most certainly not pining for him. You know that." The last part was a primal growl, and I knew it only too well.

If there was a single thing I'd grown to accept, it was Prim having had one crush all her life, despite it being the bane of my existence.

"He's not the one," I persisted to try and convince her.

"Shhh," she protested. "Let's concentrate on you."

"I'm not here for love," I stated emphatically before taking a long pull of champagne.

Leaning in again and bringing her lips close to my ear, Prim whispered, "What about sex? Are you here for that?"

She couldn't see me turning my eyes in my head, but she must have known—she pinched my forearm before moving a step or two backward, never taking one eye off the other side of the room.

"Seriously, Tuvy, a woman cannot live on friendship alone. You should allow yourself a little romp in the sheets." She emphasized the *romp in the sheets* with a shoulder shimmy.

We were leaning against the bar in my family's cavernous dining room, surveying the scene, and suddenly I regretted agreeing to do so because Donovan chose this moment to look up and gaze directly at me. And wink.

My friend couldn't help herself. "Did you see that?" Prim had been boy crazy since we were twelve; a little more than a decade later and nothing had changed.

"Primrose, quit it..." was all I could come up with.

"Oh, the full name is coming out," she taunted with a soft giggle.

It was my family's annual Christmas party, and if I wasn't expected to attend, I'd have stayed in my cottage toward the back of their land, reading by the fire, ignoring the world around me. Alas, there was no denying Mama what she wanted, so I was present and accounted for when it came to the festivities.

My family had been hosting the party for decades, long before I was born, and it was my duty to continue the tradition in the future. That didn't stop me from trying to pawn the responsibility off on my younger sister, Caro. She was only thirteen months my junior, and quite the social butterfly—unlike me—

but Mama wouldn't consider it. The party was typically handed down to the first-born sibling, meaning it would have been Bruno and his spouse's burden, except for what happened that miserable year...the one where the party was co-opted for an engagement celebration. Except the nuptials never took place, and my mother had gone into overdrive when it came to the festivities every year after.

Thinking about my brother and how he got off easy when it came to party duty had me giving the room a quick survey, finding him in the opposite corner clutching a lowball full of bourbon in one hand and some blonde's ass in the other. Mom would never reprimand him after he dumped Shelby for her; it was what she always wanted him to do. As the sister of the Minister, the most powerful decision-maker in all of Rubia, my mother saw herself as the second-in-command. No doubt she was hungry for the position herself. There was no way she would allow our gene pool to be watered down, except now a future generation wasn't guaranteed.

Then again, Bruno had complete amnesty when it came to mostly anything. Apparently, even getting married.

"Hellllooo, Tuvy, you there?" Prim shook my arm, her dark eyes searching my face.

"Yeah, sorry. I was checking on Bruno, making sure he was still standing upright." I didn't know why I said it. Clearly I was in some sort of brain fog, discussing Bruno with Prim.

Of course, my best friend refused to turn and look because she'd been harboring an unrequited crush on my big brother, fifteen years our senior, for as long as I could remember. She pretended not to—but I'd seen all the signs. Every now and again she breathed a note of it my way.

Like now, with a satiny coral dress hanging off one shoulder, showcasing her smooth ebony skin, she swallowed and ran her own hand over her shoulder, trying to take a peek without anyone noticing.

"It's always a hard time for him," she said, making his case and furthering my theory that she was saving herself for him when he was finally *better*.

Not in the mood for any more Bruno talk, I nodded, pretending she was right. The last thing my brother had was a hard time; his difficulty was deciding who to take home to his bed.

Trying to end the subject I'd stupidly brought up, I said, "I know... Maybe I should find Caro and we can talk him into leaving."

"It's not your or your sister's job. You and everyone else knows that ever since Shelby he hasn't been right. Eventually, he will heal." Prim didn't give up her endless defending of Bruno.

Of course, I knew what had occurred. I'd been privy to the entire event when I should've been playing with dolls or out in the snow. My fingers tingled at the thought of it: the night I discovered my power.

In our small world, we all had at least one source of magic, sometimes two, and we could be granted additional ones as we served the country. As luck would have it, mine was more in demand than most, and sadly, created a dynamic with my mother I hadn't wished for—ever.

My capacity hadn't been seen for two generations—the ability to mend a broken heart—and at the age of six, I'd sucked all of Shelby's pain and suffering out with the mere touch of my palm, sending my mother into a frenzy I'd never seen, and that said a lot. Mom hadn't wanted to tell anyone until I honed the skill to perfection, but Shelby blabbed the story all over Rubia, and good old Ezza began using me without any regard for my age.

We might be a smallish sliver off the coast of New Jersey, cold in the winter and stifling hot in the summer, but our homeland was a fully functioning island, with a population close to that of Aruba, hovering around one hundred thousand.

Right about now, the supposed sun and warmth of the Caribbean seemed appealing...

The powers that be in North America knew we existed on maps, and indigenous people inhabited the islet but pretended we didn't. Of course, we came and went as we pleased in our own airplanes, and they looked the other way. We held numerous business holdings in New York, Chicago, Hawaii, and Los Angeles, to name a few, and visited theme parks in Orlando, but we didn't mingle. That was both the spoken and unspoken rule. In Europe, where we might have more dealings than the US, the same boundary held true—no attachments. It didn't stop us from curating style and luxury items from Paris.

"Here he comes" was all the warning Prim spewed before Bruno was long forgotten and Donovan Malachite was standing in front of me, snapping me out of my reverie and dreams of a new Chanel bag.

"Happy Christmas, Tulya," he greeted me, using my formal name and not taking his gaze from me.

I couldn't help but run my shaky hand down the front of my skintight dress. "Same to you, Donovan," I responded, meeting his emerald eyes.

"Prim." He greeted my friend, using her shortened name.

Instead of saying a word, she nodded, slung back her champagne, and casually mentioned, "I'm going to check on Bruno. Someone has to…I think you're right." Typical, she would nominate herself to do it, which was not what I'd suggested. But without another word she scampered off, leaving me with Donovan.

"It's a beautiful party," he said, replacing Prim in leaning against the bar next to me.

"My mom still plans it. That's why…it's her specialty." I tried to make my tone less sardonic, but this night always brought out the worst in me. I took a calming breath. "Mostly everyone knows I could do without this whole spectacle."

On that, I finished my bubbly and watched as Caro floated across the room, her best friend Jules on one arm, and Maximillian, her boyfriend at the moment, on the other. She stopped to say hello and greet everyone in her wake, the perfect sibling.

Taking a risk, I snatched a peek at Donovan, who was watching Caro too.

"The good daughter," I mumbled under my breath.

"I thought that was you. Rumor has it you're under your mother's thumb morning, noon, and night."

I rolled my eyes. "I pull my weight around here, like the rest of us. We have the magic for a reason—and my family is steeped in the lore."

He laughed, interrupting my diatribe. "Is that what they told you? Is it your responsibility to make everyone as pain-free as possible? Is that part of the mission of the powerful House of Vegga? Making sure everyone is happy and in love?"

I swallowed hard. "You don't have to taunt me."

Winking at me, he spoke in a hushed tone. "And miss that sexy, small pout making an appearance? Never."

"There's nothing wrong with soothing a fellow Rubian." I didn't know why I continued to banter with him. He was pressing my buttons, and for some reason, I liked it.

"Oh, she's a romantic."

I couldn't help it; I felt the blush creep up my cheeks. Not openly, but in the privacy of my own quarters, I'd fantasized about love for most of my life. But that's what it was, a fantasy.

"Can I replenish that for you?" Donovan looked at me with soft eyes, pretending not to have noticed me drift off—I told myself it was the booze in his tumbler.

"I can," I stated and turned around, eyed the bartender, and waved my empty flute in the air.

"Hope your mom doesn't see that." His voice rumbled next to me, making a silent path from my ear to parts I didn't want to mention in conjunction with Donovan. "If there's any night you're expected to act like a lady, it's tonight," he continued.

The bartender handed me my freshened beverage, and I said, "Thank you" before turning and looking at the man next to me. "You know, you always got on my nerves, even in grade school, when I was nothing but a kid who looked up to you."

"A kid? Younger than me? By three grades?" he teased.

Donovan was exactly three years older than me. I knew because we shared a birthday in February. "Maybe that's part of your powers, dominating those younger than you?" I couldn't help the small chuckle escaping me.

"And now, tell me—do I still get under your skin at the old age of twenty-four?" Donovan chose to ignore the reference to his skill set—igniting discomfort in the form of physical pain—probably because it was the opposite of mine.

"I didn't say under my skin, Don. We all know what you can do when you get inside someone."

"Do we now?"

He raised an eyebrow, and I let out a small chuff. Leave it to Donovan to turn my mentioning his evil magic into a sexual joke. We'd known each other practically all our lives, but when I found my ability to take pain away and Donovan discovered he could dole it out, we became unlikely friends.

As for my shortening his name, I wasn't sure why. I preferred to keep a formal boundary between us.

His palm ran over my exposed forearm. The dress revealed about as much skin as Mama would tolerate. Never one for sleeveless or strapless, she expected a short sleeve at a minimum. This year I went with one three-quarter sleeve and one bared arm in an off the shoulder sheath she'd turned her nose up at. Although she couldn't say much since I came running every time she needed my magic, including the two times I'd been sworn to secrecy—when my father found himself in bed with another woman. I'd erased his lover's ache while my mom doled out a tongue lashing to my father.

"I like the feel of your skin," Donovan whispered out of nowhere.

"I didn't say you could touch me" was my response despite the goose bumps breaking out along my flesh. He might have annoyed me for most of my life, but I wasn't immune to his handsome face and brutish body. Not to mention his gruff voice sending ripples through my core.

"You're right. My apologies. Maybe I wanted you to see my hands can be as gentle as they want." He finally pulled his fingers away, and I regretted my rapid response.

When he wasn't looking directly at me, I caught him throwing a quick glance at the other corner of the room...the one opposite Bruno. Looking closer, I saw he'd been clocking his brother, Magnum, tossing back a drink and chatting with several people.

"Where's Cinder?" I couldn't help but ask about Magnum's fiancée, who was always hanging on his arm. Cinder was sweet, and under other circumstances we might have been friends. But she was engaged to the son of Mama's closest friend, Ceci, and I tried to keep my family and friends separate. It made for less involvement, on my mother's part, in my life. For the record, I enjoyed my solitude.

"I don't know. I was wondering the same." His voice was deep and grumbly, and tickled over my nerves in a good...no, pleasant, extremely soothing way.

"Maybe she's off somewhere with her mom, looking at some new jewels in my mother's wardrobe." It was a likely scenario, especially knowing all of them the way I did.

"Hmmm, maybe." He gave me a glance, the side of his mouth curving up.

Then he pushed off the bar an inch or two, and I already missed him even though he didn't leave yet. I bit my tongue, punishing myself for thinking it. Love, relationships—none of that feeling stuff was for me.

Raising his glass, Donovan said, "Merry Christmas, Tulya."

"Why don't you call me Tuvy?" It came blurting out of my mouth and I wasn't sure why, other than I was trying to delay his departure. Tilting my head, I allowed my red waves to mask the blush creeping up my cheeks.

He leaned to the side, narrowing the already slim gap between us, and the shivers appeared again. I'd been corralling my magic long enough to know that heartache brought heat to my spine, and happiness carried the opposite sensation.

His profile a breath away from mine, he spoke. "Because Tuvy is for friends and girl talk. To me, you are a full-fledged woman and you deserve to be addressed as such—Tulya."

My toes tingled and I shivered as if ice had been dripped down my back, even though the fire was roaring in the corner and the room was filled with warm bodies. I'd never been told I was a woman. Mostly I'd been used for my capabilities, my own feelings often disregarded.

"Oh…" I didn't have any other smart quips. "Happy holidays, Don," was all I could come up with.

"See you in the new year," he said as he lifted fully away from the bar and walked off, leaving me to wonder why I'd asked about my nickname.

It wasn't like me to care, or at least admit it mattered. Mama would never allow me to pick who I might love; my magic was too powerful to share with a partner she didn't choose. It was the reason she had me sequestered in a cottage on the property. And ultimately, why she let Bruno do what he wanted. His only resource was fire starting, and she'd hoped he'd marry a woman with deep powers. But now he was Rubia's resident playboy.

Thinking about my brother had me looking up and catching him with his right arm around Prim and his left around the blonde. I tried to catch Prim's eye, but she purposefully avoided me. I'd made it clear over the years that I wouldn't help her if she fell for Bruno—something she never paid any mind to.

Deep in thought, I didn't notice my mother saunter up on the other side of me.

"He's shameful," she said, and I didn't have to pull my head up a second time to know who she meant.

"This night, it's never a happy one for him," I reminded Mama, mimicking Prim.

"Meet my eye, Tuvy," she responded.

I turned to the side and met her gaze. Since I'd turned sixteen, Mama had this hang-up about meeting someone dead-on when talking with them. It yielded a different kind of influence, to let them know you were in charge. She was well practiced at the task.

I met Mama's gaze and spoke again. "It's this night," I repeated. "You and I know better than anyone it's not a happy one." It had been—I counted in my head—fifteen years, and Bruno still hated the Christmas party. Then there was poor Mama, who lived in a betwixt-and-between place of being pleased over my coming into my potential, and staying mad at Shelby for ruining Bruno.

"This night has remained joyful ever since then. No one would dare ruin my holiday party ever again." She ran a hand over her smooth auburn hair, straightened and silky. For her late fifties, she didn't look it in her cobalt blue gown, accentuating every fit curve. Some said it was her daily running with the animals, others believed it was surgery.

"No one would. That's true." Maybe that was the one small reason why I enjoyed this night every year; I was guaranteed not to be called upon.

"I don't like your friend hanging on him," Mama said sternly about Prim.

"I can't control her, and neither can you." If there was one thing my mother despised, it was being reminded that her ability to control and change minds only reached as far as animals. Although she had been honing her most recently gifted power, and quite frankly it was something I never wanted to experience. I could only imagine if she'd had the magic ball capability when Shelby had hitched herself to my brother.

Lord knew she'd tried to influence Shelby long before the failed engagement.

"I expect you to have a word with her" was Mama's only response before walking away.

After a long breath, I turned and ordered one final glass of bubbly before retreating to my cottage, alone.

CHAPTER
THREE

Tulya

My smallish house on the outskirts of my family's property was my refuge. On sunny days, I took solace in staring at the magnificently appointed stones lining the façade. On cold nights, I relished in my claw-foot tub.

I'd only left the party ninety minutes ago, so when the frantic knocking came as I slid into my bath filled with hot water and bubbles, disappointment blanketed my heart. *Bam, bam, bam* rang steadily from the large wooden door at the front of my house, followed by, "Tuvy!"

Closing my eyes, I took a deep breath and gently stepped out of the tub, my hair in a messy bun on top of my head and suds dripping from my legs. Not bothering to towel off when the third set of *bams* came, I dragged on my heavy robe and padded to the door. Sometimes I wished I could find sanctuary off my family's property.

Not bothering to ask who it was—I'd heard my mother chanting my name—I swung it open.

Mama, Ceci, Cinder, and Donovan rushed in from the snow, not bothering to be welcomed inside and ignoring my being in a robe, still half wet. Their comfort was more important than mine.

"Tuvy, we need your help," Ceci said, grabbing my hand. "Aaack, you're cold. Donovan, build a fire, will you?"

"It's not necessary." Confused by her sudden worrying about me, I tried to argue but the man was already down on his knees, stacking wood in the hearth. I granted myself a second to take in his back pulling on his suit, imagining the broad muscles under the fabric.

"Tuvyyyy," Cinder cried, and I finally noted she was wearing a heavy jacket and there was makeup smeared across her face.

"What's wrong, Cin?" I asked the question already knowing: as soon as I'd turned toward her, the sweat began to bead at my neck.

She needed my help.

"I'm sorry" was all I said when Cinder didn't respond. Narrowing the gap between us, I began to lift my fingers toward her jacket. She'd have to take it off and let me touch her bare skin. Over the years, I'd found my force worked better skin-to-skin.

A fire roared to life in my living area, and Donovan stood and stated, "Don't be sorry. Be vengeful, Tulya." He stared at me with the same green eyes that had enchanted me earlier. "I need to ask you a question."

My hand was still hovering near Cinder when Mama spoke. "Don't touch her yet, Tulya."

"What is going on?" I brought my fingers to the lapels of my robe, pulling it tighter, the hot and cold warring within me.

"Esmeralda, tell her," Ceci said softly.

"We have been wondering for some time if you can transfer these types of feelings, Tulya?" Mama raised an eyebrow, waiting for me to understand and likely already knowing the answer.

Feeling Donovan behind me, his energy cooling rather than heating my back as a chill ran through me—although not the pleasing kind like earlier—I worried about my future. This was a giant ask, one my mother had never made of me, and I wasn't sure if I'd ever seen it coming. For a quick second I was just a girl and Donovan was only a guy, and I wished my body was normal and felt heat when someone stoked my personal fire rather than ice, ignoring the situation around me.

I forced myself back into the moment. "You mean, take the heartache out of someone and give it to another person? But why would I make someone else suffer?"

I heard Donovan clear his throat as Mama opened her mouth. "Because they deserve it," he answered for her.

I knew Mama had zero softness or empathy, but I couldn't believe this was really Donovan. Turning around, I met his face, and it was lit with anger.

"My brother has made a fool of us." He spoke quietly but forcefully. "He went to Miami to do some business by the beach, and he caught feelings for a regular human."

I held back my surprise. It was bound to happen.

"Now he's babbling on about bringing her back here and marrying her. Procreating with a nobody—it's unheard of. A human, no less."

"Absolutely, I won't allow it. I chose Cinder for him, and I've chosen for you," Ceci said, sliding her gaze to Donovan.

I hadn't realized she'd matched Magnum and Cinder, nor that she had handpicked someone for Donovan. That was on me, trying to keep out of anything directly to do with my mother and her hen crew.

"This isn't about me," Donovan said, his voice ripe with anger.

"It surely is, my dear son. If your brother shames us, it will affect my plans for you."

"Not. Now. Mother. After. Christmas." He punctuated each word, leaving no room for discussion but large windows wide open for me to wonder.

"The Minister would never allow the marriage, let alone a baby," Mama interrupted, consoling her friend.

In Rubia, there was no such thing as separation of church and state, let alone repentance. All actions were deemed allowable or not by the Minister, and forgiveness was rarely offered for transgressions.

Donovan ran a hand through his dark brown hair and the sensual kind of goose bumps started to pinprick at my skin like earlier in the evening. I tried to stave off the shiver but I couldn't, despite learning about his own mother finding him a partner.

He noticed. "You're cold," he had the mind to whisper, before gathering me in his arms without asking.

I didn't argue. It wasn't a touch fueled by need, rather giving, a side of Donovan I'd never seen. "What do you want me to do?" I whispered, looking at Don's chest, wondering what it felt like under the Armani dress shirt. It was a little-known fact that Donovan visited New York often. To shop and, I assumed, do other sordid things.

"Well, can you? Can you take the suffering Cinder is feeling and give it to this human?" he rumbled against me, deep and baritone. Coldness ran all the way to my toes, and he grasped me closer.

"What?" I found the strength to step back and felt my mouth fall open. And I imagined how I appeared, standing there in a robe, hair likely a mess, my face resembling a clown's. "Why? How? No, I've never done that before. Cinder, you can't possibly want this?" I turned to face my contemporary in the room.

She lifted her head, her black waves falling over her eyes, then nodded. "We have to try to keep her away."

"Ceci could go and create a weather pattern she won't survive," I said, not believing the cruelty coming out of my mouth. "Or why not send Donovan to do the dirty work? He can inflict some pain that will send this woman hurtling away." Swinging in his direction, I murmured under my breath, "Didn't you make fun of me for following my mother's orders?"

He narrowed his eyes and mouthed, *Touché.*

Cinder said, "No." She kept shaking her head. "It won't work. Your mother said—"

I heard Mama's boots clop close to me. It was clear these three women had quickly huddled before coming to me.

Mama began to speak, her voice reeking of finality. "You will do this, Tulya. I will put in a good word with the Minister while you are in Miami, with Donovan as your chaperone, of course. He will recognize you when you return. Cinder will join you after you locate and corral the ghastly human who did this, and you will do what we ask. Period. Understood?" Her eyes darkening to the shade of coal, she narrowed her gaze on me. "I said, are we understood?" she repeated. "Your father is aware of my asking and is in full support," she added as if that made a difference or I had a choice.

I nodded, afraid to speak. I knew that when it came to the Minister, Mama never backed down from a plan. She had her reasons and didn't care that I had my own worries.

Causing someone pain was never in my plan; I'd been happy with my skills, allowing others to feel better. This was something different. Taking Cinder's suffering away was one thing but giving it to someone else made me feel sick to my stomach.

"Donovan will be back in the morning to escort you. Get packed."

I continued to nod to my mother, who clearly didn't show up at my house on the evening of her glorious party to ask me if I minded the task at hand. This was a demand, and I was expected to jump for her and Ceci.

"What about Christmas? I'll miss it. It's next week." It had always been my favorite time of year: the food, the songs, the wonderment.

"You will have Christmas next year." Mama delivered that with a straight face as if her party wasn't the focal point of her calendar.

"Sorry we disturbed you" was how Donovan left it. He turned back to stoke the fire, adding a log without even a glance my way.

"Thank you, Tuvy," Ceci said, approaching and yanking me in for a hug, also without permission.

Cinder joined in the thanks, minus the touching. Mother gave me nothing, neither gratitude nor an embrace. In fact, she started walking toward the door, the other women in tow, Donovan rounding up the rear without even a good-bye.

"See you in the morning. Eight sharp" were his final words.

The door closed behind them, and the only bright spot was it would be warm in Miami. I could hide in the heat of the sun. Otherwise, I worried how many cold flashes I would have in my chaperone's presence. My spoken-for supervisor. Funny, he didn't mention it earlier when he said he liked my skin…

Maybe it was a new way of inducing pain?

CHAPTER
FOUR

Donovan

The door to my home office flung open, a dark and stormy Magnum prowling toward me like a lion after its prey. I was in no mood after working all day, attending the party, and now an unplanned trip to the States fast approaching. Thankfully, I wasn't one bit afraid of my baby brother; at twelve months apart, we were almost twins.

"What the hell do you think you're doing, Don? Dragging Tuvy to the States to go after V—"

That was how he referred to his American fling, Valerie. V.

He glared at me with identical green eyes, the same ones our father's family was known for, and I ignored him.

"Donovan, fuck off," he came back with, slamming his fist into my desk. "Mom let me in on your plan. What I can't seem to figure out is if you want to ruin my life or avoid yours. You know, the one Mom is crafting for you?"

This got me to look up at my brother; after all, he knew how to push my buttons. "I wouldn't talk about crafting to me. You couldn't stand how much Mom adored Cinder, so you went and fucked around and got feelings, and now you want to rain hell down on us. I'm not going to allow you to tarnish our family name."

He leaned on the desk, both palms flattened on the mahogany wood, and shot looks of venom at me. "You don't know a damn thing what I did."

If looks could kill, his would have taken me out in one glance.

He carried on. "Don't you dare sit there at Dad's desk and act like my father, ruling over me. Dad is gone and you're hardly a year older than me, so shut it, Don."

Our dad had passed away close to seven years ago, leaving me in charge of the family business. And my brother still wasn't over it. Magnum was furious that he wasn't named my equal in running our family's real estate portfolio. It had always been the plan, me in first and Magnum as second-in-command. Dad had readied us in his own way; the Malachites had carved the path for decades in investing and property management, helping others maintain Rubian wealth.

Magnum kept at it. "I mean, you still live at home like a damn child."

It was the truth. I resided in the north wing of the house, and despite it having a separate entrance and a good deal of privacy, I stayed with our mother.

"And you ran away like the petulant son," I tossed back. I raised an eyebrow while waiting for a response.

"At least I'm independent and go after what I want. V and I are in love, and if you do this, I'll never forgive you. Who is to say Tuvy will either?"

"Enough! You need to cut her loose," I roared, standing up and approaching Magnum. "Get out," I continued through gritted teeth. "I am going to the States, and I will do what I need to do in order to protect this family and Rubia. It's been a long-standing order from the Minister, no cohabitation with humans."

"I am human," Magnum protested, his fists clenched like a child about to have a tantrum.

"You are *humanlike*," I corrected. "Our powers make us unique, despite looking like a regular person. You know as well as I do that our DNA is different. And mixing human chromosomes with ours will water down the powers, bringing shame on our family."

"You're such a kiss-ass," Magnum said while hitting the desk again, before turning and walking out, using his mind to slam the door on his way out.

Foolishly, I sent a zing of shock up his spine. He didn't have any right to address me like he had. I was the only one with the family's interests in mind, not to mention a stronger power. Magnum could only move objects using his mental will. It always bothered Mother that his ability was so mundane.

Blowing out a long breath, I listened to hear if he went to argue with the woman in question, and sure enough he did. I wasn't worried; my mother could handle herself with the best of them. Tulya's mother, Esmeralda, had been a notable friend in that way—teaching her the art of coercion and getting what one wanted by design. Which was likely why Ceci was so hell-bent on this match; Cinder's family came from extreme powers. If anything, it was an arrangement to deepen our family's capabilities.

Deciding that work had escaped me after Magnum's tantrum, combined with it being late and Saturday fast approaching, I flicked off the light in my office. Stepping into the corridor, I pulled the door shut and turned left toward my personal quarters, the hallway lit by only the faint floor lights. My eyes grew heavy.

After my dad passed, I turned his private chambers into my residence, leaving behind the small apartment I'd kept from my university days and moving back home into the care of my mother's housekeepers. When he was alive, my father used the massive bedroom to rest in the middle of the night or day, while he worked excruciating hours. One time, an ex-girlfriend of mine from high school had suggested he took lovers. I ended that relationship immediately. There were many constructive criticisms of Donovan Malachite Senior, and adulterer was not one of them. His temper and tenacity in business relations and deals were seated in his need to love, care, and provide for his wife and family.

Opening up the door to my bedroom, I turned the light on, sliding the switch down to dim the chandelier. I wanted to lie down on the mahogany sleigh bed I'd purchased as soon as I moved in and spend a few days in the sheets, avoiding what was to come. But I had to pack.

Traveling to the States, chaperoning Tulya, was not on my wish list. Yet when I opened my armoire, I pulled out sweaters and shirts I was certain would make her look at me. While spending the next few days, weeks, or whatever it took to seek out Valerie while being near Tulya was less than desirable, it was also my greatest fantasy.

The redheaded, fair-skinned, angelic beauty had my eye since we were in middle school, maybe before that. She'd handled everyone with such grace, always smiling and sending warm and caring looks. She'd speak softly, thanking the teachers, trying to go unnoticed. Back then I didn't know what the feeling was in my gut, and later in my groin, when I'd spot her in the hallway or class. But in high school, when she was still in eighth grade and I was a junior, I became educated in the biology of it all.

It was only then that Tulya began to understand the depth of what she could do when every brokenhearted high schooler asked her to take their pain away. While I was on an opposite path. At first, I couldn't harness my ability to cause agony, and Tulya obliged almost every request to remove it. We were two ships passing at night for lack of a better description.

Sadly, ingesting all the suffering began to take a toll on Tuvy's own heart and energy. There was simply too much breaking up and making up and then ending things all over again among teenagers. The roller coaster of it all made her go weak, and she spent a few weeks at home rehabilitating her strength.

It was during this time that I learned my mother would never permit my feelings for Tulya. Ezza was her closest friend, and she understood the magnitude of her daughter's power. Ezza would never allow Tulya and her skills out of her grasp; she'd wield them for all they were worth, milking them for additional abilities lying in wait, among other concerns my mother refused to get into.

I began to resent the women's friendship and the inside knowledge my mom seemed to know. But there wasn't much I could do. Ezza was a dominant force, and my own mother was desperate to be marked as Rubian royalty. I didn't buy into any of it other than my father's making me promise to see to my mother's happiness.

One thing for sure, I'd never be fool enough to shower Ezza with my brand of magic. So when it came to the two older women, I learned to play by the rules. Which was how I came to be assigned the task ahead of me, shuttling Tulya to an assignment she didn't want, in a place she'd only been once or twice. Ezza always had an eye for the Minister's role. She wanted to be the first woman to hold the office, and her daughter was her ticket. My mother was the lemming, who thought she was a part of it all.

Deep in thought, I finally realized I'd laid out enough clothes for a month, including a swimsuit, dreaming of Tulya on the beach.

Blowing out a breath, I scolded myself, tossing everything into a suitcase, thinking I'd buy incidentals in Miami, before yanking off my shirt and pants, letting them fall to the floor, and lying down in my briefs. Morning was moments away, and I'd need as much energy as possible to deal with the actual mission, let alone keeping my feelings for Tulya corralled. Earlier, my talking to her, touching her arm and spending time close to her, had been a momentary lapse in judgment.

I had to try harder.

My fist met her door with a severity even I was ashamed by, but I had to resist the pull to be a comfort to the woman; this was family business. "Tuvy," I hollered, my voice echoing around me, using her nickname, trying to maintain boundaries. I'd already complimented her full name, saying it was for a woman, and now I was her chaperone.

The door flung open and there stood my worst nightmare and my life-sized fantasy.

With her scarlet hair down and flying all around her delicately made-up face, I forced myself to shut my mouth in record time. Under other circumstances and with anyone else, I would have said something like *Morning, gorgeous*, but wrong place, person, and time.

"I need two minutes," she said, leaving the door wide open and pivoting the other direction.

"The car's running," I whispered to no one.

"Help yourself to coffee," she yelled back before heading down the hallway.

Destined to wait, I walked back to my sports car and turned off the engine, clicking the locks despite no one being around for a mile.

Slipping inside the house, I rubbed my hands together to warm them up, and took a beat, looking around. The only other time I'd been in Tulya's cottage was last night, and I'd been so agitated on multiple fronts that I hadn't noticed anything other than the fire I built. It now sat extinguished, heat pumping from the vents instead.

It was a simple interior, inviting gray hues and a million throw blankets and pillows, without any words printed on them yet all beckoning someone to get comfy. The open kitchen was a combination of stainless and white, a contradiction to the rustic exterior.

A small desk sat by the window, an expensive computer set up on top of it and a bookshelf to the right. For a moment, I'd forgotten Tulya was a writer. She wrote thrillers and sold them under a pen name. I couldn't think of what it was—I'd never read one but heard they were dark and full of depth.

Made sense, that since her mother kept her in this little house like a caged bird, she would create her own imaginary worlds.

"Ready?"

I turned and found Tulya standing there, black vegan leather pants hugging her curves, a V-neck white sweater, and her hair tied back and secured, keeping her safe from my running a hand through it.

I nodded, unable to get the words out, and started moving toward the door, clocking her luggage and grabbing it forcefully—not that I would be so bold with my own feelings, considering the task in front of us. The thought had me internally laughing; I was as brash as they came but I knew our mothers' position on us.

"Coffee to go?" Tulya called from behind me, kicking my thoughts back into place. I shook my head and went through the alcove, walking toward the car and trying to gather myself while lugging her shit.

Moments later, she came floating out, now wearing a leather jacket and tenderly carrying a thermal coffee mug. I couldn't help but think of her touching me with such gentleness—or not.

As I turned the car out of her narrow driveway, making tracks in the fresh snow on the way to the main drive, she spoke softly, almost for herself.

"I hope I don't see this stuff for a few days."

"You won't. I gather you brought sunglasses?" I asked, grateful for the road to keep my eyes on.

"And a swimsuit… I don't plan to be all work and no play, if I'm missing the holiday."

That was exactly the opposite of what I planned to be. We needed to find Valerie, send for Cinder, and do the deed as quickly as possible. But when it came to Tulya, my resolve was becoming nonexistent.

Out of the corner of my eye, I watched Tuvy take a long sip of coffee as her brow furrowed.

"Euro for your thoughts?" I couldn't help myself.

"We're going to the States. Even I know they use dollars," she flung back.

We typically dealt in euros in Rubia since we didn't have our own currency. No exact reason as to why, but they always had been preferred. Plus, we enjoyed the exchange rate.

"I know exactly what they use in the States. I was offering you a euro, which is worth more than a dollar, in exchange for what you were thinking so hard about."

I passed Tulya's family's castle of a house, complete with the turrets on top, a true contrast to the Spanish stucco-type homes lining the streets of Rubia. When I made a turn onto our main highway leading to the small airfield, I noted Tulya seemed to breathe a sigh of relief.

Thankfully, only private planes flew in and out of Rubia, making it easy to schedule a flight wherever, whenever one wanted.

"If I can't do what *they* want, I'll be punished. I'm not even sure I can do it, and yet here I am, being sent on this wild mission for a sole purpose. One that will test every boundary or limit I have ever had. And I'm not like you. I don't want to hurt people." She spoke softly, pulling on my absent heartstrings.

Squeezing the steering wheel, I fought back the desire to send an electric shock to Ezza. "I don't want to necessarily hurt people either." I tossed Tulya's words back to her. "I didn't ask for this to be a part of my abilities, just the same as you didn't beg for your magic."

"Well, I use mine for good."

"You mean, your more noble power is wielded at the bidding of your mother." I couldn't help but send a zinger. I never liked when I was pigeonholed as evil for the abilities I'd been assigned at birth.

"I don't see Ceci asking you to use yours on this mistress of Magnum's. You're nothing more than a glorified chaperone on this trip."

I felt my foot press on the gas pedal and pulled it back. Fury began to furl in my belly. "My mother doesn't tell me when to use my magic. Ever." My temper was beginning to flare, not because Tulya was wrong. She was right. In our little Rubian empire, my family used me for my leadership but didn't boast of my capabilities. I'd been given a "forceful power," and it was perceived negatively. I had to prove my value other ways.

"I see your mind ticking away." Tulya continued to challenge me, and I secretly loved it.

"Go on, shrink me. Is that another one of your do-gooder skills? Maybe your mom has you going around using that too?"

She glared at the window in front of her, the anger running through her veins palpable. "So? It's not like you're here on your own. Ceci demanded you follow through on this problem."

"I'm not denying we are shackled to the wishes of our respective mothers, but you seem to be caught up in the wholesomeness of what you can do—at the expense of anything decent for yourself."

"What do you know?" She swiveled sideways, her gaze meeting my profile.

I couldn't tell if I loved or despised her silver-gray eyes drilling into me. Did she see through my ultra-thick façade?

"It's easy to grasp—you sidestep any happiness for yourself," I said through gritted teeth, knowing I should've kept my mouth shut.

"You don't know anything about me," was her weak rebuttal before crossing her arms over her chest, abandoning her coffee in the cup holder and staring straight out of the windshield until we arrived at the airstrip.

It occurred to me that nothing upset me more than Tulya being hurt.

CHAPTER
FIVE

Tulya

The delicious Florida heat licked at my exposed midriff as I relished a glass of red wine, all by my lonesome on my balcony. We were staying in one of the hotels Donovan's family invested in, and while I was annoyed to be sharing a suite with him, I did have my own bedroom complete with a small wet bar. I'd be taking full advantage of that feature—avoiding the one in the main sitting room as much as possible.

When we'd arrived this morning, there was a car waiting for Donovan to whisk us away…except he wanted to head straight to Valerie's house or some of her hangouts and look for the woman causing all the ruckus. He assumed Magnum had warned Valerie, which in and of itself was a violation—telling a human about our powers and how we planned to use them. I too assumed Magnum had shared this private information, and if I guessed correctly, he did the deed long ago.

Our ultimate advantage was our human likeness. Outing our capabilities and the existence of Rubia was frowned upon. Actually, it was forbidden by the Minister and all previous generations. We blended among "regular people," and we allowed those around us to assume we were the same, unless we were on our own island.

The thought of it caused my heart to pound. It wasn't often that we used our magic on humans. Mostly, the magic was reserved for Rubians. I'd be lying if I didn't say I was scared to death over this assignment. Everything about it—spending time with Donovan, hurting a human woman I'd never met, and failing Mama. Especially the latter. As much as my mother annoyed me, pleasing her was the only way to have peace in our home, and while many Rubians moved out and on from their "Houses," in ours it was only by excommunication. It happened by literally burning someone's belongings to the ground, and I didn't want to be the black sheep in that way.

My phone buzzed and I knew better than to ignore it. After all, it could be Mama.

Checking the screen, I noted it was Caro and blew out a sigh of relief. While we'd had our differences, I knew she loved me. She'd come to say good-bye to me late last night as I packed. I might have always been jealous of her ability to please Mama, but we were close.

I picked up. "Car—"

"Turn your phone off," she warned. "Let it go right to voicemail as soon as we hang up."

I didn't have to ask why. Ezza was not only the Minister's sister, but she was next in line should anything happen to him or if he decided to retire (which was unlikely).

My mother had spent her life trying to live up to her father's legacy of being the biggest, baddest, boldest Rubian there ever was. Under him, Rubia prospered, procreated, and glowed in its glory era. I believed my mother both feared and revered the Minister position. She would be the first woman to hold it if she ever did, and therefore, she'd spent her life living and breathing Rubian policy. She was going to follow every rule, and make sure everyone else did too.

Gathering myself, I asked Caro, "He reported back, didn't he? *Gawd*, Donovan. Am I not allowed a few moments of peace and solitude in the warm weather?"

I took in the ocean not too far off in the distance, lapping at the shoreline, and inhaled the sea breeze. All I'd asked for was one afternoon of this…and Donovan had acquiesced without my having to beg or bat my eyelashes at him, so I didn't think he'd rat me out. But of course he did.

"He mentioned to his mom that you didn't go looking for her—*the evil seductress* as they call her—right away. Mama is on a war path, and there is only so much I can do. She was on a call with the Minister, and you're probably next. I tried to spread some gentleness on her edges, I promise."

Caro's magic allowed her to bestow tranquility on someone. At times, she'd calmed someone so much they'd fallen asleep, but her capabilities didn't go far with Mama. Our mother was able to shield certain people out, and Caro was one of them. Maybe that was why Caro was the favorite child; she could only be a pawn in my mother's game.

"She's going to chew you out." My sister stated what I already knew. But Caro didn't always do Mama's bidding; occasionally, she stood up for me.

"All I wanted was some time to enjoy this moment. The weather, blue sky, a few seconds of freedom. We don't know how it will end. I've never done this before."

"I know," she whispered. Then, "Believe in yourself, and turn off your phone" was all she said before disconnecting the call.

Doing as she demanded, I'd followed up with a whopping swig of vino when a knock sounded behind me.

"Dinner?" Donovan stood in the doorjamb in jeans and a polo shirt, the single word coming out as a question.

I lifted my wine to my lips and took a sip.

"Or are you having a liquid diet?"

It was clear he didn't like my silence, but I was having a quick second to take in the man in front of me. I might be furious with him, but he continued to be equal parts forbidden and enticing.

"Tulya? Hello? Do you want to eat?" His voice was all grumbly and irritated.

It should have pricked at my nerves, but it only ratcheted my pulse in a good way. I liked being able to affect the great Donovan. With my free hand, I ran my hand under my now wavy hair. It felt glorious to let it down, allowing the saltiness in the air to mingle with the fine strands.

"It's not even sunset" was my answer.

He took a step closer and seemed to inhale me before barking, "We have an early morning."

It was clear I was working on borrowed time. "Apparently they already know our every step, or misstep, back home."

"I'm not here on vacation," he grumbled.

"Neither am I."

"Are you hungry?"

We were in a standstill, staring one another down, and I didn't want to be the first to break…but I couldn't help myself. If there was anyone who could get me to do their bidding, it was this hot asshole.

"Dinner," I simply stated before gulping back a little more Cabernet.

"Let's go," was all he offered up, turning toward the living room of our suite.

"Here? Or somewhere else?" I inquired from behind him.

He pivoted, taking me in. "You don't need a real shirt if that's what you're asking."

Hmmm, he noticed my half shirt… "Okey-dokey." I played along with his coy attitude.

Snatching a blazer off the chair, I tossed back the remainder of my wine and hit the main room.

"Let's go!" I shouted, the liquor coursing through my frazzled veins.

Donovan held the door open, waiting for me to exit, and we walked toward the elevators, his hand coming to rest on my lower back, navigating me. And chilling me to the bone.

"You okay?" he asked, stopping short.

"Yes, fine. Why?" I didn't dare look at him, keeping my gaze ahead.

"Because you just shivered."

"It's fine."

"Tulya, a cracker is fine. A salt and vinegar potato chip is fabulous. There is a lot of distance between the two. What is wrong? Are you nervous?"

He used his hand to nudge me to face him, quickly dropping his fingers from my shoulder. I didn't know how he did it—went from laissez-faire to bossy to caring in milliseconds.

"I'm seriously great. We need to eat and get to sleep so we can get on with it." I plastered a smile on my face, hoping Donovan refrained from any more small touches, preventing me from having to explain what he did to me...

We walked through the lobby, and I took in all the couples in love and vacationers here for a good time and wished my mission was different.

"Want to walk?" Donovan asked me when we stepped outside. "I thought we would go for sushi, and it's not far."

I felt myself nodding, thinking I loved sushi and Florida, and maybe even small parts of today.

We strode side by side on the sidewalk for two blocks in quiet, a fusion of both good and bad tension tethering us.

"Here." Donovan finally spoke when we stood in front of a neighboring hotel. "The rooftop is spectacular, and I know you wanted to have a respite. For one day," he said, holding the door open. He uttered the thoughtful words quietly and only for me, and I wanted to grovel for him to put his hand back on my lower spine.

We rode up the elevator, and as soon as the doors opened, my mouth fell.

"It's gorgeous," I muttered, taking in my surroundings. Wooden canopies draped in flowers and leaves covered the entire rooftop, petite booths and tables with gauzy tablecloths filling in the space below them. I could see tiny tea lights spread throughout the space, twinkling despite the sun still being in the sky.

"I thought you might like it." Donovan guided me with his palm on my back toward the hostess, and I willed the chills to stay away.

Soft holiday music filled the area even though there wasn't any snow to be found on South Beach.

"Malachite for two." Don spoke authoritatively, and the young brunette hostess nodded.

She found our name and said, "Right this way."

Sadly, my back was suffering the loss of Donovan's hand.

The hostess went to pull out my seat, but Donovan beat her to it and sent her away with a hushed, "Thank you."

"This is really...I don't know, splendid? Is that the right word?" I said, looking around in wonderment.

"It's a small piece of heaven," Donovan agreed.

My head whipped around and my gaze found his. "You're a softie, Mr. Malachite? A lover of paradise?"

He opened his mouth to reply but the server appeared, stealing our moment and asking us if we wanted still or sparkling water.

Donovan looked at me, and I said, "Sparkling."

"Anything else to drink?" The server turned to me first.

"Cabernet?"

"We have that," he answered my one word.

"Espolon, neat," Donovan stated.

"Right away," our server replied and was off.

"I shouldn't say this," Donovan started, all grumbly, staring at me.

All of a sudden I felt self-conscious and wanted to yank my half shirt down, wishing it to grow on its own.

"Stop," he interrupted himself. "You look perfect."

I wondered if he could read minds...

"No, I can't, but your face is an open book at the moment."

I redirected him back to his thought. "What shouldn't you say?"

The server had been pouring our sparkling water while we discussed this, and Donovan took his time, enjoying a sip. "I like paradise as much as the next person, but I think I may be a lover of making you happy. I've tried not to indulge in the idea, but it keeps coming to the forefront of my mind."

A wineglass slid in front of me and I was grateful for a gulp of liquid courage, unable to peel my eyes off Donovan. His green eyes were sparkling, his hair forming small waves in the humidity. "Why shouldn't you say that?"

He put his hand on the table, a gold Rolex shimmering between us. "Because it's an occupational hazard."

I swallowed back any pleasant thoughts or words. I was only a job to Donovan, no matter what he said otherwise. "Then we should eat and get after what we came to do."

I didn't know what I was thinking, dredging up silly schoolgirl crushes on Donovan, or even wishing for one or two grown-up days with him. The task at hand had to be done or my mother would be out for my neck, even though I wasn't sure how my body would take the exchange of feelings. But let's be honest, no one really cared. And certainly Donovan didn't mean he loved making me happy.

No one was concerned with my joy. It was my job to make sure others didn't feel pain. Period.

CHAPTER
SIX

Donovan

"Thank you and good night," Tulya said without looking at me, stomping off to her room.

After I'd gone and mentioned her being an occupational hazard, she'd barely looked at me, let alone said anything more than the tuna roll was delicious and asking to try my salmon sashimi.

After I paid the check and she finished her wine, we walked back to our hotel in the same silence we'd shared earlier.

It wasn't until she closed the door to her bedroom that I told myself the rift was for the best. I needed to get this done and over with, and back to Rubia. My mother had her own relationship visions for me, and I had a plan to stop it. *Eyes on the prize*, I told myself.

Padding back to my quarters, I opened my laptop and checked my email, smiling when I saw the signed contracts. I hadn't been worried, but wanted my vision tied up tight.

Our family had long been invested in housing and hotels in the States as silent partners. Our real estate portfolio was expansive when it came to outright owning apartment buildings, mostly because we hired a manager or two. My father believed hotels needed more onsite supervision from the owner.

Originally, I disagreed. And then I changed my mind, seeing it as my out. Which was why I was in the middle of buying my first hotel and moving where it was located. My mother could never argue with my deceased father's ideals, could she?

I was close to being off to Hawaii...far away from Rubia, where the expectations and rules to perform or obey were squelching. I loved the place, and it had all the amenities I needed, but it had grown old in the way the citizens thought. Business was better when it was bigger where I was concerned. I wanted a more gigantic existence.

Of course, I didn't plan to fall in love with a human or marry one or bring anyone back to Rubia like Magnum—I'd forever be mostly a rule follower—but I did intend to avoid the marriage my mom was arranging for me. If I was away most of the time, no one would want me.

Falling for a woman, creating a family, and living happily ever after wasn't high on my to-do list.

As I slid in between the covers, I tried to hush the Tulya rush both my mind and body were experiencing. My palm slid down my thigh and over to my heaviness on a path it had traveled many times before, but I had to stop myself. It was disrespectful to Tulya. And more so, torturing to me. I'd never wanted anyone the way I wanted Tulya, and we just couldn't ever—

My phone buzzed on the nightstand, dragging me from my illicit thoughts.

Knowing it was either my mother or Magnum, I snagged it off the table and hit answer call without looking. "Hello?"

"Asleep already?" Magnum asked, a hint of something sinister in his tone.

"Yeah, I'm heading to bed...before I take care of your problems."

"I'm asking you not to do this, as my brother, Don," Magnum pleaded. "I love her, man. She makes me stronger."

A long breath escaped me. My brother was under some serious delusions.

But all I said was, "You know I have to, Mag. She will eventually weaken you, or us," before disconnecting the call.

It wasn't because I was afraid of our mother and the havoc she'd bring if I didn't. It was the Rubian legacy on the line. Our family, namely. The House of Malachite was in the balance. Tulya's family might hold the direct line to power, but ours captured the economy.

We couldn't commingle with humans, or the auras and powers would cease to exist, and then it wouldn't matter how much damn money we had. We'd be dead in the eyes of the Minister.

My unique ability wasn't one I enjoyed or cared to pass on, which was why I didn't plan to procreate—unless I honed something better. As we acted and served in the best interest of Rubia, we acquired enhanced skills.

Slamming my eyes shut, I willed sleep to take me before my thoughts went too dark and sinister, my own morals failing me when it came to the redhead across the common room.

"Rise and shine." I spoke over the brim of my cappuccino as Tulya made her way out of her room, her robe cinched too tightly around her waist. I worried she was cutting off her air supply.

She looked my way and stared right through me.

"I ordered some food and coffee," I said as a peace offering.

Tulya nodded, making her way to the cart. Her hair was tied back in a bun at the nape of her neck, face devoid of any makeup. She'd never looked more beautiful. In another world, I would wake up next to her every day.

Now, I watched each of her actions like a Peeping Tom, as her lithe fingers lifted the silver coffee carafe—I was both amused and titillated. I scolded my brain and urged my heart to get a hold of itself.

She poured a hefty mug full before taking the pitcher of oat milk and adding a touch of it to the steaming hot liquid. Without another word, she turned on her heel, mug in hand, and walked back toward her bedroom, her ass swaying underneath the plush robe. My hands tingled, wanting to touch and do things they were not permitted to do.

Taking a slug of hot liquid, I told myself to hurry up and find Valerie and extract myself from this situation.

Already in my suit, as if I was here to do official business, I plodded to the cart and snagged a piece of turkey bacon, wondering how I could summon my partner in crime to start our mission. I strolled to the large floor-to-ceiling window and caught the sun in the sky, the ocean in the background, and wondered what the fuck was wrong with me. I could be on a run or sitting by the pool—why did I always have to be so stringent when it came to my mother?

"Ready. Let's go," interrupted my thoughts.

Despite her tone being terse and sarcastic, I was thrilled at the reprieve from my own brain.

"I think you're going to be hot" was all I got from her as we walked toward the elevator.

"Well, if I could wear a skirt like you, I'd do that, but my legs never look quite right in a dress."

She rolled her eyes. "Please, no reason to act like a jerk. I was simply saying a suit isn't necessary."

I didn't get into how this was my armor against my rapidly beating heart and pulsing emotions. A pair of chinos and a golf shirt would have made this feel like a date, and this way, I was dressed for a business appointment.

"Thank you for the worry," I came back with, not wanting to insult Tulya any further.

"Not concerned, just stating a fact."

"It's December, not July," I grumbled and she ignored me.

With that, the elevator opened and we rode down in silence, Tulya sliding a pair of sunglasses on as we exited.

Outside, we waited for the valet to bring the car around. We slid into our respective seats, and I connected my phone with the GPS and put the car in drive.

"Do you have a plan? Or are we going to aimlessly cruise around?" She didn't turn to look at me but kept her shaded eyes looking ahead.

"Listen, Tulya, I'm sorry you have to be here. I don't want to be doing this either, but we both know the wishes of our mothers come before anything else." I felt the lie all the way to my gut. I did want to be here; I needed to right my brother's wrong and I didn't mind the time with Tulya. These were stolen moments.

"You're not the one whose power is going to be compromised, and we all know you don't have to do what your mother wants. *I do.* Your mother isn't related to the Minister."

I felt myself nodding, but not able to agree verbally. "My family's name is on the line. I can't stand around and watch Mag destroy everything my dad built. And you and I both know if he goes through with this love affair with Valerie, the Minister will darken our name. He's your uncle, not mine."

Her lips pursed together; she had no rebuttal because I was right.

Darkening was a real thing in Rubia. If the Minister felt you disobeyed him or the rules, he'd cast a spell on your family, turning all your wealth and happiness into nothing.

We continued on in silence, Tulya cracking a window and allowing the air to flow over her face. The GPS guided me to what I thought should be our first stop.

"Is this where she lives?" Tulya asked as I slowed the car in front of a small bungalow in Fort Lauderdale. The white house sat on a small parcel of land a few blocks from the beach, and I knew for certain Valerie couldn't afford to live here on her own.

I nodded and explained, "This is where she grew up and still lives with her mom. Her dad apparently passed a year or two ago."

Tulya shrugged. "I still live with my mother…"

Fuck, I can't catch a break when it comes to this woman.

"Hardly. You live on your own. You support yourself." It was the first time I'd mentioned her career to her.

"You know about me?"

Putting the BMW in park, I turned toward her. "It's not a secret, is it? You should be proud."

She shook her head. "No. No, it's not a secret, but Mother would prefer I not do it. Mostly, I'm proud I make my money."

"Well, looks like I'm not the only one who doesn't have to do what their mom wants."

Without responding, she opened her door and stepped out into the sunshine. I took a beat and wondered why her mom didn't care for her writing. I'd never heard anything about it.

I watched Tulya stride in front of the car, the light fracturing off her sleek hair, I got out myself.

Maybe her inner secrets and mysteries were best kept from me.

"Brothers or sisters?" she asked as we walked up the pebbled path.

"One. Brother."

"Do you expect to find her here? Just waiting to be reprimanded by you?"

"No. I suspect worse," was all I gave her. I hadn't shared with Tulya that my brother likely told her about our plan, the powers involved, and to run.

Pulling her shoulders back, giving the appearance she had no such fears, Tulya rang the bell.

In the background, I heard a woman say, "Let me get it, Blake."

I knew the brother was Van—rolling my eyes at them both having names starting with V—so I had no idea who we would find named Blake until the door swung open, and staring at me was a small girl, maybe five or six years old, with the same fucking green eyes as myself...and my brother.

Feeling like the air had been squeezed from my lungs, I breathed in and out as Tulya's hand came to my shoulder, trying to steady me as best she could.

"Hi," the small child said to us as a woman in her late fifties rushed up behind her.

"Blake, go wait in the kitchen," the older woman stated, her tone part authority, the other half love and adoration.

I felt my mouth still hanging open. And for someone who considered themselves unflappable, it was a strange sensation.

"Hi, I'm Tuvy and this is Donovan. We're looking for Valerie." Tulya took over, a slight smile on her face, her eyes directly on Valerie's mother...and the grandmother of my brother's baby?

"She is not here. I'll let her know she had some visitors..."

With a frown on her face, she went to close the door. All of a sudden, I was less worried about Valerie and more concerned over the child. I needed access right now.

CHAPTER
SEVEN

Tulya

The woman started to close the door in our faces. My heart pounded in my chest and the back of my neck burned from the pain rolling off this woman, yet I couldn't let her shut us out. Don's face had gone pale, and I could almost hear the venom pulsing in his neck.

"Can we wait? Will she be back soon?" I set my palm on the door, stopping it, and caught Don side-eyeing me. He raised an eyebrow, perhaps unsure of my aggressive stance.

The woman, who hadn't told us her name, shook her head.

"We don't mean any harm," I lied, but catching sight of the little girl changed everything. Much more was on the line—Magnum presumably had a half-human child.

"I don't believe you. Valerie is away for a while, and you're not welcome to visit."

If my feet were not keeping me planted in place, I would have swayed from the force of her words. They were equal to a slap in the face.

Next to me, Donovan cleared his throat. "I understand Valerie may have run and left those instructions, and if I hadn't laid eyes on the little one, I might have turned tail and come back another time…" He paused and set his palm on the door next to me, pushing it the rest of the way open. "But, since apparently the child is my brother's, therefore being my blood relative, I'm coming in." He began walking over the threshold.

"You can't do that," the unknown lady protested.

"I can and I am." He started to strut forward with the confidence of a man who hadn't just foreseen the demise of his family's name…

"She's not your blood."

Don stopped in his tracks at the woman's baseless words and opened his eyes wide. "Two words. Malachite green."

He pushed on, taking my hand and dragging me with him.

As soon as we wormed our way to the back of the house we hadn't been invited into, Don looked at me and spoke quietly. "I need you to talk to her."

I nodded despite our touch and go in the car; this clearly wasn't the time to hold a grudge when it came to Donovan.

Blake, as the woman had called the girl, sat at the table coloring, her brown curls falling around her face. When we appeared, she looked up.

"Hi, I'm Tuvy," I said, slipping into the chair across from her.

I could hear the grandmother yapping on the phone in the other room, chanting, "I tried." She must've been explaining the predicament to Valerie. Perhaps she would have been better off monitoring us, but this woman had proven to not be the smartest, allowing a child to answer the door.

"And this is Donovan," I added, sliding out the chair next to me.

"Hi, I'm Blake. You look like my daddy." She stared straight at Don, and the tension hung heavy in the room.

"He's my brother," Don stated, matter-of-factly.

"What's your grandma's name?" I asked Blake, thinking I should request this woman to be present. No matter how I felt about Valerie or what Magnum had done, this child should have some sort of advocate.

"That's Mimi Marley," Blake said. "She's watching me because Mommy went to visit a friend, before we leave to go live with Daddy."

"Blake!" Marley entered the room and yelled the girl's name. "Remember, Mommy said don't tell anyone." She tried to temper her tone, but it didn't help much.

The girl nodded, then added, "But this is my daddy's brother. Daddy told me Uncle Donovan lives near him, and look, now he's here to see me."

This situation was worsening by the minute.

"I'm sorry, but these nice people have to leave. I just spoke to Mommy, and she will talk with you when she gets home." She meant chat with Blake, not us. Marley didn't even spare us a glance.

There was an invisible connection between Donovan and me, and if I didn't know better, I'd think he was funneling his feelings into me. He wanted to roar and bang on the table while yelling at Marley. I knew none of that was the way to win over his niece or keep himself in her good graces—I wasn't even sure if he wanted to remain there, but she was a kid. There was nothing won by upsetting a child.

I brought my hand to his forearm and gave a small squeeze. He turned and looked at me, and I shook my head. Watching him close his eyes, I heard him exhale.

"We don't have to go, Blake. In fact, let me call your daddy and we can plan for you to get to know us. Your family." His eyes softened in a way I wasn't sure they ever could.

Yanking his cell from his suit pocket, he hit some buttons.

"He didn't want that. This, or whatever you're planning," Marley whispered, finally getting her tone under control.

"Can I talk to Daddy?" Blake was staring at Donovan with wide, hopeful eyes.

Of course Donovan didn't see because he was looking at the table when he barked, "Magnum, we have to talk," into the phone.

I could hear the deep rumble of Mag's voice on the other end but couldn't make out what he was saying.

Don, stood, his six-foot, three-ish stature dominating the room.

"Is there a reason you never mentioned having a child?" He had enough decency to turn away from Blake as he spoke.

Marley was now seated next to Blake, running her hand through the girl's hair, pushing it behind her ear and kissing her cheek. Despite her gruff demeanor, she had to know there wasn't going to be anything pleasant to come out of this meeting.

"Magnum, this is not good for…" Donovan paused.

My thought was he was trying to avoid mentioning Rubia, our powers, and our real mission in being here—although I suspected Valerie and her mother knew some of the more intimate details.

"…our legacy. Our family…but she may… She needs to come be with us."

He gave a quick turn and looked at his niece and she gave an almost unnoticeable twitch of her nose. I watched as he rubbed his forehead and now stared more intently at Blake while raising his eyebrow. She'd done something. I had no idea what, but it didn't matter. She'd exhibited a power, heightening the stakes.

"No, not her. But your daughter, yes." He said the last part while moving into the other room.

I stole a glance at Marley, and she'd picked up what Donovan was meaning.

I decided a diversion was needed when it came to Blake, and myself. "What are you coloring?" It was likely that Donovan was going to stop at nothing when it came to this child, and my mother and Ceci would not be happy until I did what we came here to do.

"A dragon," Blake answered.

I took a closer look. "A pink dragon."

"Yes, a girlie dragon. Mommy says we are girlies, and we have to stick together."

If her mom had been smarter, she would have taken Blake with her, knowing we were coming.

Donovan re-entered the room, holding his phone out. "Blake, your daddy wants to say hi."

She jumped off her chair and catapulted herself into her uncle's arms, throwing her hands around his neck. For the second time today I was shocked by Donovan. He had no clue what to do with the tiny person looped around him, but he put his palm underneath her weight and held her in place as she took the phone.

"Hi, Daddy," she said. There were a series of *Mmm* and *Hmmm* before she said, "Mommy went away for a few weeks. I'm not scared." There were a few more *Okay*s and then, "I crunched my nose and Uncle Donovan felt it."

"Say bye," Don interrupted. "So we can visit," he added, and the call was over.

Marley said, "I think the visit has been long enough. I'll have Valerie let Magnum know when she is back, and he can tell you." The grandmother stood, signaling she'd had enough.

I also got out of my chair, fearing Donovan might be stuck, and deciding it was time to get him out of there.

"We will see you soon," I said to Blake, unsure if it was true.

"This is for you," she said, holding out the pink dragon drawing. "You're a girlie too." She ran back to Donovan and held on to his leg. "I don't have a blue one for you, but I will make one next time.'"

Everything about this mission just became a million times more complicated, and I wasn't sure whose mother would be more mad.

CHAPTER
EIGHT

Tulya

It had been ten minutes since we'd walked out of Valerie's house—without seeing her, but learning about the existence of Blake.

Donovan was busy white-knuckling the BMW's steering wheel and focusing his venom on the road, while I wondered if I should say something, comfort the man in some way, or sit silently.

Unable to take the tension anymore, I had to ask. "Do you want to talk about it?"

I watched his hands grip the leather harder. "No," he said through gritted teeth. "Actually, I do, but not to you," he added.

Grateful he didn't take his gaze off the road, I felt my cheeks burn with embarrassment. I knew Donovan was hurting, and it pained me that it wasn't the kind of hurt I could take away. My powers were limited to affairs of the heart.

Before I could give it too much consideration, I caught the man in question slapping his hand on the dash, hitting the call button. And in a matter of seconds Magnum's voice echoed in the car.

"Donovan, WHAT did you do? You're playing with fire," he roared.

"ME?" Don's own anger radiated around me. "Magnum, you had a kid—"

He paused and looked like he was going to spit, from what I could tell. "Years ago. You. Never. Told. Anyone." He punctuated each word. "How could you do that? How dare you?"

"Dad was already dying, and he'd sent me to the States to take a class. I was young. She was naïve. We liked each other and fooled around. Dad would never want me to desert my daughter."

It was the most heartfelt I'd ever heard Magnum.

"I'm not even going to say there were ways, things to do, ways to take care of this, because I just met *your daughter* and she has fucking powers. And now... now, Magnum, not only do I need to take care of your human woman, but I need to take the kid. I'm pretty sure that's called kidnapping, but you know Mom will never let her go with what she is capable of—"

"What? What are you doing, asshole? Abort this whole mission of yours. You're not taking my daughter. That's fucking kidnapping. And no way is fucking Tuvy getting her hands on V."

"Abort? No goddamn way. It just got a million times more intricate, and you know it."

My head hurt from Magnum mentioning me in such an awful way, but there wasn't a bone in my body that believed my mom or Ceci would give up now. And clearly, Donovan planned to still go through with the pain transfer and figure out a means to get custody of Blake.

"You can't just *get a kid*, Don. She is with her mother, and they should both come be with me."

"Listen here, Magnum, I'm taking the kid. She is a Rubian. With one twitch of her nose, I knew it. And there is no way she is staying in the States, away from us, with that type of power. If I were you, I'd be ready to prep Mom about all this and figure out what you're going to do with Blake when she gets to Rubia. And let Valerie know she is not welcome there—ever."

I heard the gasp escape my chest.

"You can't," I whispered to no one.

Except Donovan heard me, and before I knew what was happening, he'd jerked the car to the side of the road. We were in some bougie neighborhood, lined with cafés and coffee shops, but I didn't have time to study it.

At some point he'd disconnected the call on his final marching orders, and I now sat surrounded in silence, Donovan breathing fire at me.

"Tulya," he said.

"Yes?"

"You do not get to judge me." He looked at me, his green eyes penetrating my soul, waiting for me to respond. "You do not. I must do what my brother can't."

"I'm not," I finally said. "But she's just a kid. Her mother is all she's ever known." I couldn't help but think of my broken childhood, thanks to my capabilities. And now Donovan wanted to take Blake from her mother. I didn't dare spill all that... Not now, likely never.

"A KID who showed the emotions running through her soul with a twitch of her nose. With the second twitch, she showed me mine. Bright red anger and lavender confusion. A fucking child with that ability. Don't pretend it doesn't have to be protected, Tulya. She's half human. We don't know if this works on the other kids at school. And she cannot be running around the United fucking States of America doing that."

Sadness washed over me at the sight of the man in front of me and the possibilities running through his brain. He had a poor way of showing it, but somewhere in there, Donovan was scared for Blake.

My brain told me not to, but my hand moved to cover his and I spoke calmly, trying to bring down the burning inferno radiating off him. "Don, listen, this is a mess."

"You can say that again, a mess... That's what you come up with," he gritted through his teeth, staring at my fingers covering his.

"It's more than a mess, but I don't know what to call it. Your mom is going to lose it. My mom is going to run to the Minister, and we know they are both going to come down on me hard." He side-eyed me. "I know, this isn't about me, but those two are going to want action. And Cinder... Oh God, Cinder is going to be hit with such a harsh reality. A kid. One with magnificent powers, and our tiny country will go to war for her."

"Tell me something I don't know, Tulya. I have maybe three days to wrap this adventure up. You will be home for your precious Christmas." Despite his harsh rebuttal, he wound our fingers together.

"This doesn't have to all fall on you, Donovan. You don't have to be your brother's puppeteer. I will do what my mom has asked of me. I will transfer the pain, but Magnum should come and deal with Valerie and his daughter."

"No. He will never accomplish what needs to be done. He's gone for them. The most I can hope for is he's telling our mother now about the reality we've discovered and doing that dirty work."

"I don't know if I agree with any of this, but I'm going to go along for you, Donovan. Because you deserve it. You're a good man."

I said it; I meant it. Not once had I needed to take pain away from someone Donovan hurt. I was beginning to see that even if he had capability to cause pain, he didn't wield it unnecessarily when it came to the heart. If his brother was the devil, he was the white knight—just not mine. I was in the middle of reminding myself Ceci had an arrangement for Donovan when I felt his palm slide up my cheek and his lips met mine. At first gentle, but applying pressure within moments of us connecting, we sat making out in a car in South Florida. I heard Donovan rustling and pivoting to meet me better, his other hand leaving mine and cupping my cheek. With his palms holding my face to his, he ravaged my mouth. I met his tongue stroke for stroke, leaning in, wanting more, whatever that was...

And then he pulled away.

"I know, I didn't ask. I'm sorry, but you do this to me, Tulya. Something no one has ever done. You bring up feelings and desires I shouldn't have."

"You didn't have to ask. I reciprocated," I breathed out, forbidding myself to beg for more.

"Now isn't the time for us to get involved," he responded and started the car. "Another time, years ago, maybe. But my sights are focused on my next steps, and now there is an extra one. Cleaning up Magnum's mess."

He pulled away from the curb without giving me a chance to respond, which was quite okay because I didn't have one. Instead, I sat there, my pointer finger touching my lips where he'd kissed me and wondering why they felt so ice-cold.

"Mom, I know." Donovan answered his phone as we walked back into the suite after remaining silent for the rest of the car ride.

In the elevator, he'd avoided eye contact, and it was only when his palm found the small of my lower back as we made our way down the hallway that I realized his shying away from the kiss was self-preservation.

"I didn't know. What the fuck?"

I watched him nodding his head, unsure if I should go to my bedroom and let him be, or stay. It was only a matter of time before my phone rang.

"Yes, I'll watch the swearing, but how would I know about your granddaughter? Magnum acted as if this all happened recently, post-engagement. Obviously, not."

I rolled my eyes at that as I bent down and helped my tired feet out of the strappy sandals I'd been wearing.

Padding barefoot to the bar, I checked the time. Almost one in the afternoon, which was well past my not-before-noon rule, signaling a vino was a-okay, according to me. I poured myself a glass of Cabernet and headed toward the balcony.

Donovan was in the middle of giving the same spiel he'd given me—the nose twitch, the emotions, his brother needing to man up—when my phone buzzed. There was no delaying the call, so I hit answer and slid the balcony door open, balancing the stem of my wineglass in my fingers and the phone in the crook of my neck.

"Tulya, are you there? I don't have time for games."

"I'm here," I told my mom, gulping some vino. Closing my eyes, I allowed the sunlight to wash over me.

My mother was in a state. "Ceci told me. She's making me go see the Minister with her. Thinks since I'm his sister, he will soften his words. Doubtful. It's imperative you do the pain transfer now. We need Magnum here with Cinder, raising that girl. As theirs. I heard what she can do."

I took a long inhale. I should've known those two would have a plan within moments.

"We didn't find Valerie, Blake's mom," I said, knowing these real people with names were nothing more than pawns to my mother.

"You will. Donovan will see to it."

I didn't bother trying to explain how I wasn't sure I could even do what they were asking.

"Okay," was my response, deep in my own thoughts.

"We plan to do as much damage control as we can. Magnum's daughter will live among us. Eventually she won't remember life before Rubia."

Swigging back wine, I wondered what realm my mother existed in. It wasn't reality. "I don't know about that. Her grandmother seems pretty formidable," I mentioned in some sort of desperate attempt to soften her.

"It doesn't matter. Magnum made a catastrophic mistake, and we will fix it. Do what you need to do, Tulya."

She disconnected the call, and I knew it was the end of our talk.

My needs, worries, or concerns didn't matter.

CHAPTER
NINE

Donovan

I found Tulya sitting on the chaise outside on the balcony, a bottle of wine and an empty glass resting on the table, her head tilted back, eyes closed.

I'd wanted to talk or maybe be close to her. She was equal parts soothing and forbidden; I had no idea what to do when it came to this woman.

"Sorry," I mumbled, not wanting to disturb her peace.

Opening her eyes, she spoke, her voice raspy. "It's fine. I was just thinking. Come, sit," she beckoned, pointing at the chair next to her. "You doing, okay?" she asked me while running a hand over her cheek, before leaning forward and snatching her glass and pouring a little more wine in. "I'm not, which is why I'm hiding out here with this." She waved the bottle in front of me.

I felt myself nod. "I spoke with Magnum. He is going to arrange for us to meet with Valerie."

She raised an eyebrow, and I watched a small piece of her red hair fall in front of her eye. More than anything, I wanted to brush it away, to touch her with my finger…to kiss her again. And again.

"I don't know if I believe that," she said softly.

I couldn't help but smile. I secretly adored how she didn't mind challenging me.

"He isn't the type to roll over like that," she went on.

"I know, that's reserved for me. I'm the family pushover," I replied.

"Hardly, but you know that you're not. You do what is expected, when you know it's the right choice."

"Or the only one…"

"Tomato, tomahto," she quipped. "I'm under strict orders to transfer the pain. My mom expects you to bring Blake back and I'm guessing your mom has made it known Magnum and Cinder will raise her."

I nodded. That was the plan our mothers had concocted. "It's my best guess that Magnum thought he'd bring Valerie and Blake back to Rubia, and with their daughter there, no one could say a word to him. But we certainly blew that by coming here and discovering his secret."

Leaning forward, Tulya touched my knee. I was sitting in the straight-backed chair kitty-corner to her, and this slight touch wasn't enough. I wanted more, to move closer and run away all at the same time.

"Is this all right?" Of course she asked if her gesture was okay, because she was Tulya, and she did mostly everything right.

I gave another nod.

"I'm worried for that little girl. I don't want them looking into her power or capabilities too much, pressuring her, or anything that will take away her spirit. She's going to have enough change coming to Rubia, you know?"

Swallowing all the emotions lumped in my throat, I searched for the correct response. Only Tulya would consider the child's feelings. I suspected hers were typically overlooked, like they were being now.

"You will be there," I said.

"We don't know. I've never done this type of transfer…and to a human."

"Why? It's not like our powers don't work on regular people. They do. We know but choose not to use them…often."

She just stared at me as if this was information to her; she truly believed we never tried our magic on humans.

"I don't know. I'm worried. That's all."

I'd wanted to mention the kiss in the car, but now we'd gone to this dark place, and I wasn't sure what to say—

"I'm hungry," Tulya rescued me by stating. She stood up from the lounge and nabbed the bottle and glass to take inside.

Like a lost puppy, I followed behind.

Inside, I found her leafing through a room service menu.

"Do you want to go out?" I didn't know why I asked. Last night ended horribly, and this afternoon was even worse.

"Don, what do you want? We're here to do a job for our mothers, that's all. Eating is for survival." She smoothed her hair back into a low ponytail while keeping her gaze on me.

Every ounce of intelligence I had fled my body as my feet took me closer to the woman questioning me.

"I'm sorry. *Again.* I know I'm upsetting you. A lot." My words came out stilted and unsure, which was unlike me. But then again, this woman unraveled me. "I don't want to upset you. In fact, I want to do the opposite. I want to make you happy and…feel good…more than good. But we are here on a task, and I don't want it to get all muddled. You, me. Your aversion to suffering, my ability to dole it out—we are a strange combination."

I left it at that; I wasn't sure how much Tulya understood about commingling our skills.

Except in this moment I was standing directly in front of the woman, and while we were no longer at the holiday party, alcohol running through our veins (well, she'd had her wine), want and need pulsed through me.

"I want to make you happy," I repeated. My hand rested on her shoulder, and she didn't shove me off. "It doesn't seem right in this instance, but it feels more than right," I continued.

"You confuse me. One moment, you're shamelessly flirting and the next pulling back and bossing me around. Another minute, you're kissing me, and then…"

I didn't wait to hear what she said next. My mouth found hers and I grumbled, "May I?"

She nodded against my forehead as our lips mashed together with a feverish need.

I wasn't sure whose tongue entered first, but now they tangled together, the tannins of her wine making me heady.

The room service menu flitted to the floor as my hand roamed up her back and her palms slid down my sides, coming to rest on my hips as we made our way backward to the wall.

"Tulya," I moaned.

"You feel so good," she mumbled back. Her palms ran the length of my back, and I could feel her letting go of any reservations she had.

In this moment, I hoped Magnum took a while to show up with Cinder. There was nothing I wanted more than these borrowed seconds, minutes, hours, maybe days with Tulya.

CHAPTER

TEN

Tulya

With my back plastered against the wall and Donovan's hard body pressing into mine, our lips ravaging one another, I wanted to stay like this forever.

"You feel so good," I boldly said, certain I'd never spoken those words to anyone.

I'd had three or four boyfriends since high school, all of them Rubian, none of them remarkable, probably since they were all Ezza-approved.

Donovan's hand gripped my waist, snapping me back to the present, squeezing ever so gently, holding me in place and sending sparks throughout my body. A low growl emanated from Don's chest, and he continued to devour my mouth before pulling away abruptly.

I felt my mouth hanging open in shock, something my mother would have been disgusted by.

"You are hungry," Donovan stated matter-of-factly. "Let's get something to eat…and then pick up where we left off." He followed this all with a wink.

"Maybe we should talk?" I stood up straight, smoothing my dress, wondering if this had been a smart idea.

"Eat and talk," he said, walking toward the room service menu lying on the carpet. "Do you still want to stay in?"

"If we can eat on the balcony, I do."

He nodded and picked up the phone.

"Are you going to ask me what I want?" The whole dating thing was a bit unknown to me, but I was pretty sure I could decide what I felt like eating.

"Hi, room service?" Donovan kept going with the call. "We would like one of each entrée, and one of every dessert."

I raised an eyebrow when he looked up.

Holding his hand over the receiver, he said, "This way we don't waste time looking at the menu."

I decided a glass of water was in order and poured myself a Pellegrino.

Now, Donovan padded toward me, phone call over, and he wrapped an arm around my waist from behind. "I shouldn't want you as much as I do, but here we are," he whispered in my ear.

"Don't hurt me," I whispered back, which was easier said while not looking at him. Somewhere deep inside, I knew the pain would be inevitable. My mind was screaming *his mom has an arrangement for him*, while the heart beating in my chest simply didn't care.

He didn't say *never*, or *I won't*. He replied, "I don't ever want to hurt you, Tulya."

I craved him so badly, this was enough for me.

It was sometime in the middle of the afternoon, Donovan sat on the floor, still wearing his suit pants, dress shirt untucked, feet under the coffee table, with a half-eaten spread in front of him.

I'd stood up to get myself some more water but couldn't help sneaking a glance at the man in front of me.

We'd laughed over the enormous amount of food he'd ordered and then devoured a bite of everything. It had been more fun than expected.

"I've never had a room service party before," I admitted, showing another card I probably shouldn't have. Messing around with Donovan was a game of high-stakes poker, and the house always won.

"Room service picnic," he corrected.

"I like it." I spoke freely, smiling. It was the first time I'd felt genuine happiness in a long while.

"This is really good," Donovan said, pulling me into the present, helping himself to some more chicken paillard.

We were only eating, a basic function. I needed to stop getting ahead of myself. "It was, but I have to say I'm partial to that burger," I joked while slipping next to him, our thighs touching on the floor.

"Have a bite." He pointed to the plate with the ginormous cheeseburger and onion rings.

"I'm saving myself for that chocolate cake."

"Are you now?" Donovan raised an eyebrow and reached for the plate with the molten lava cake, or whatever they called it.

"I love the way the center melts…"

He put a spoon in the middle of the confection and opened up the pastry, allowing the gooey sauce to run over the plate. Scooping up equal parts cake and chocolate lava, he brought the spoon to my mouth. Like a well-trained dog, I opened my mouth and bit down on the offering, a moan of unparalleled proportions coming from the back of my throat.

With watchful eyes, Donovan spoke. "That's torture. Plain torture, watching you do that."

He scooped a second bite and teased my lips with the spoon. My body obeyed, my tongue coming out to taste the goodness.

"You try," I kind of mumbled.

"Are you sure?" he teased, one side of his mouth turning up in a smile.

I nodded, grabbing the spoon, filling it with chocolate lava and lifting it to his mouth. He took the bite with fervor.

It didn't take him long to snatch the spoon back and set it on the coffee table, before yanking me close and taking me in a long kiss.

He slid us together to the carpet until we were lying side by side, our lips in a well-choreographed tango. His palms held on to my cheeks and his forehead lightly grazed mine.

"A chocolate kiss," he grumbled into my mouth and my hips scooched closer to him.

We stayed like that for a while, kissing, grinding like two young fools, as if we didn't have more pressing matters to attend to. Our breathing in sync, Donovan was the only oxygen I needed in this moment.

When he broke free, his lips ghosted my forehead, then my cheek, before he spoke. "You're so beautiful, Tulya."

All my barriers tumbled down with these couple of words. To think, a few days ago, that I was resistant to any come-ons from this man. "Back at you, Donovan," I said, smoothing my hand down his face, taking him in… "What are we doing?" The question popped out of my mouth without my directing it to, and I wanted to take it back. I didn't care what we were doing; I wanted to do it.

"We're doing what we want. That's what," was all Donovan said.

Sadly, we were interrupted by his phone ringing.

"It's Magnum," he said, and I knew the magical moment was behind us.

Maybe it was for the best.

I didn't wait around for much after overhearing that Magnum had spoken to Valerie and she was back in Miami. I knew what task was staring me in the face—the hardest job I'd ever been asked to do. Without saying anything to Donovan, I retreated to my room and filled the bathtub.

Enveloped in vanilla-scented bubbles, I closed my eyes and dreamed of a life where I wasn't in servitude to Rubia. One where I didn't have to make sure everyone else was pain-free, except me.

My phone rang, pulling me from any delusions of love I might have been having. Drying my hand, I picked it up and set it on the side of the tub on speakerphone.

"Caro?" My sister's name bumbled out of my mouth like a question, likely because we didn't speak daily at home. We loved one another, but Caro was an extrovert, and I was the resident introvert.

"Tuvy, are you okay? Mom just told me everything. She's back from the Minister's."

He might be our uncle, but we never called him by his name—Elon—only *the Minister*.

"I'm fine. I haven't really had to do much yet... I guess I'm waiting on Cinder, and then it will all start..." I sank a little deeper into the bubbly warmth.

"That's why I'm calling. Apparently Cinder is refusing to come now. She's very upset about—" I heard her take a breath. "The kid," she finished, her voice almost nonexistent.

"What?" I'd never expected that. My mind was always on Cinder getting what, or who, she wanted. "She's keeping Magnum," I stated, thinking she was getting exactly what she'd begged for and then some. "Isn't that all she wants? Her man?" I spoke quietly, wondering if maybe Cinder would give up and move on, and I wouldn't have to do the transfer.

"Yes, but she said since he had a child with someone else, apparently that takes something away from her. Makes it less special. At least that's what I heard through my channels."

This gave me a little laugh. My sister had channels, and I craved peace and solitude. "The Minister won't allow her not to raise Blake as her own. You heard Blake can do some complicated emotional telling or showing already, in kinder?" There was no reason to lie to Caro; she'd hear it eventually if not already.

"Mom told me as much, and said to keep it quiet. But she is now telling Cinder she has no choice but to come and follow through. Mom is spitting mad, and annoyed she has to do the Minister's dirty work while holding Ceci together. By the way, Ceci is crying nonstop and I haven't seen Magnum."

I blew out a long exhale.

"Are you okay?" my sister thought to ask me. "Is Donovan being nice?"

I slopped my free hand out of the water and dried it on the towel over the edge of the tub. With it, I attempted to smooth my hair back, feeling fidgety over the Donovan conversation. "I'm fine, mostly spending time in my room outside of doing what is needed."

"At the Christmas party, I saw you two talking. I wondered if maybe there was more."

There was no way I was giving in to my sister's prying or theorizing. "No, he was ordering a drink and I was at the bar."

"Hmm," she responded.

I knew Caro, and she was a dog with a bone when it came to gossip. But we were not flirting, at least not for long. Donovan was apparently betrothed, and I was forbidden to be happy for some unknown reason. For a quick beat, I wondered who Ceci had picked for him, and I couldn't help but be curious why it was under such wraps.

Caro finally relented and changed the conversation. "I thought maybe you would make it back for Christmas, but I think Cinder is really digging her heels in. I'm sorry, I'll miss you."

"Yes, it looks like I'll be having dinner in the hotel and taking a hot bath for the holiday."

"Sounds sort of nice, yeah?" My sister didn't enjoy the confines of routine and the holiday the way I did. Caro was to excitement and living loud like I was to solitude and quiet.

"You know what? It kind of does," I admitted, letting Caro off the hook.

"Listen, call me if you need to talk," she said in a rare moment of sisterly love.

"Will do." I hit end call and laid my head back and closed my eyes.

This was apparently my new normal.

CHAPTER
ELEVEN

Donovan

The following morning, Tulya met me in the common area and we headed down to the car without a word spoken. It was devoid of any pomp or circumstance too—the tether binding us the afternoon before long broken.

She'd stood by the bar and listened when Magnum called; he'd been yelling up a storm, saying Valerie was furious with him. She was losing her shit over us meeting Blake. I'd not-so-politely told him that Valerie should've thought about that before running away, and like the fool Magnum could be, my brother admitted she was back at home with her daughter. Tulya overheard this and her face fell. I understood her sadness. She knew her task was upon her. Almost immediately, Tulya had retreated to her room, and I didn't see her again until she appeared for her coffee an hour ago. I'd told her we had to go see Valerie, and the only response I received was a short nod.

It wasn't exactly how I'd wanted or expected the previous night to go, but such was my life, steeped in family responsibility and doing what was right for Rubia.

Tulya didn't seem to understand we couldn't be together indefinitely or forever, whatever kind of whimsical ideas she had, so it was for the greater good.

Except when my lips were on hers, I didn't get it either.

"Are you sure we should go? What if we scare off Valerie before Magnum and Cinder get here? It could be a while." Tulya spoke softly in the car, her voice full of trepidation.

"You heard?" I asked, and she confirmed.

"My sister told me Cinder is giving your brother a hard time. She didn't mean it as gossip," Tulya quickly added the last part.

"I know."

We drove along, and I took a quick glance at Tulya's profile. Today, she wore her hair back in a sleek ponytail. With the sunlight hitting it through the window, it sparkled like a ripe cherry. Her creamy skin complemented the brightness in just the right way, whatever it was, and I wanted to run my tongue all along it. I ached to be with this woman in ways that didn't make sense.

"I'm hoping he gets her to change her mind quickly, while I'm hoping to get Valerie used to the idea of Blake coming with us..."

"You may have a better chance at getting pigs to fly."

I couldn't help the laugh rumbling out of me.

"Seriously," Tulya added. "No mother is just going to say bye-bye to their baby, and 'Have a good life, I'm never going to see you again.'" She stared out the passenger window, presumably fuming.

"I'm sorry this is so upsetting to you, but there is no other way."

"There is." She whipped her face toward me, her mouth in a tight line. "Blake could have visits with Valerie. Valerie could come to Rubia. She clearly knows all about us, so who cares? Her daughter will be living there. She's not going to risk anyone getting hurt or discovered."

I turned the car onto the street with the small bungalow we'd visited yesterday, and a rock began to form in my stomach. In my heart, I knew all of this was wrong, but what could I do? "How about this—you ask the Minister."

"Fine, I will." She had the door open before I even shifted the car into park and was trekking the sidewalk to the front door.

I jogged to catch up with her and we rang the doorbell.

The door swung open and a short brunette in a pair of jean cutoffs and a skimpy red tank stepped out, barefoot. "No! Go away. I didn't invite you here," she said, giving me a death stare. "Especially you." She turned her focus to Tulya and then she spat, the spittle landing on the ground, making it clear my brother had shared more than we even considered.

I watched the rude gesture hit equal to a slap in the face, as Tulya turned her head abruptly to the side as if she'd been smacked.

"Valerie," I said in as soothing of a voice as I could.

"Nope, don't *Valerie* me," she mocked, mimicking my tone. "I don't know what kind of voodoo you want to practice on me, but not today, not now, or ever," she said, stumbling over her words, jamming her finger in Tulya's face.

I started to think Tulya had been right—this was a mistake.

"And as for you, Donovan." She said my name as if we'd been introduced. "Your brother let me know your plan, and my answer is a firm no. Blake will stay right the fuck here with me, and so will your brother if he wants to see his daughter."

I caught a look of shock on Tulya's face at Valerie's using such a vile swear word. Only a few days with Tulya, and I knew that wasn't her style.

Clearing my throat, I considered telling Valerie to calm down, but I wasn't foolish enough to think it would work. She would come at me for mansplaining and I wasn't up for the lecture. Instead, I asked, "Can we go inside?" I didn't think she would oblige, but this wasn't the type of conversation I wanted to have outside.

Valerie crossed her arms over her chest, the tops of her breasts popping out of the tank, and I knew in an instant how she'd bewitched my brother. And it wasn't only her booming body. Magnum liked an attitude, an edge, and this woman had enough for the entire neighborhood, maybe all of Florida.

"Blake isn't here," she said defiantly.

"Valerie, listen," Tulya interrupted, taking a risk I wouldn't have. Yet she was Tulya, her tone gentle despite being verbally attacked earlier. "We don't have to see Blake…today…but we do need to talk with you. Could we do that?"

"Talk," Valerie demanded, her painted red lips forming a pout.

"It would be best to do it without all your neighbors listening in and watching," Tulya added.

"We will be quick," I bargained. Honestly, I wasn't even sure what I hoped to accomplish. Clearly, this woman was not going to enter into any agreement with us, and I didn't even know if my brother was entirely on board with… anything, quite frankly.

"Five minutes," she said to me, refusing to look in Tulya's direction.

She turned and walked through the same door we'd entered yesterday; I held it for Tulya, my free hand grazing her lower back as she entered.

As soon as we were inside, Valerie turned and shrieked, "You had no right to come here."

Recognizing we weren't making it into the kitchen again, I spoke in the small foyer. "You might have been right if Blake didn't exist, but now we know she does. And we have every right to be here."

"Whatever you want to say, say it."

Tulya started to respond. "We don't want to overstep, but—"

Valerie turned to Tulya and cut her off. "Not from you. I know you're here to assert some sort of dominance or voodoo on me, and you won't be doing any of that."

"She is not here to do any voodoo, as you call it." I defended Tulya, thinking it wasn't a lie in the actual moment. "Valerie, Blake is part of our community." I treaded carefully, not knowing how much she knew.

"Oh, I know all about your world, Donovan. If you couldn't put two and two together, I've been with Mag for a long time. We have a freaking baby, a kid now, and he wants me to come with him to your Rubian paradise. I know all about what you can do to others and what she can do, and it is not going down," she said, glaring at Tulya. "I'll tell you this—I'm well aware of what my daughter can do. And you must be naïve if you think I would risk anything happening to her."

"She belongs in Rubia, and you don't." I couldn't help myself. I felt my fists and teeth clench.

"Get out," Valerie said while stomping to the door.

Tulya tried to smooth things over. "What he means is…we've never had a human in Rubia, not even to visit."

"Go, and don't come back. Magnum is the only one I will speak to about his daughter."

"I hate to break this to you, but Magnum is my younger brother, and it's thanks to our family's business that he can afford to come back and forth to see you. So I will be back with him."

I thought I'd gotten in the last word, but the woman my brother had fallen for bested me when she added, "Then I would chat with your mother and make sure she knows Magnum is with me and not the woman she picked."

The door slammed behind us as soon as we stepped out, and I practically ran to the car. Inside the vehicle, I slammed my hand into the wheel before pulling out of the spot. About two minutes into my ride, I turned to tell Tulya she was right, we shouldn't have gone, and realized she wasn't there.

Fuck, I left without her.

Stopping in my tracks, I did a quick U-turn and drove back to find a very agitated woman standing on the sidewalk, arms crossed, toe tapping.

I didn't care that I jammed the car into park and jumped out; it was a rental.

"I'm sorry, there's no excuse. I'm an ass," I rambled.

"I'm only happy you didn't run me over."

"Fudge." I almost swore again, this time to Tulya. "I'm an ass, like I said. I was so mad." I put my arm around her and guided her to the passenger side. "Here you go," I said, opening the car. She slid into the seat, and I gently closed the door.

I ran around the front and jumped in. I didn't shift into drive, rather turned and looked at the woman next to me. She was sitting there giggling.

"What? You thought this was funny?"

She attempted to get each word out through laughter. "You…said…fudge."

"I'm trying to be polite in front of you, turning over a new leaf and all that."

She rolled her eyes. "I'm not a delicate flower. But I'm sorry I'm such an afterthought." She mumbled the last part. "I tried to help in there."

"Tulya, you are not an afterthought. Never. I was so livid, and then I went to tell you that you were right. We shouldn't have gone there—I don't think this is going to end well for Magnum. He is convinced he is stronger with Valerie by his side, and now I know why. She is formidable and a real lifeforce, and he has a kid with her!"

She shook her head. "You cannot take that girl away from her mom. But we all know my mother, Ceci, my uncle, and whoever else is involved is going to force the issue. That's my burden, and yours." I watched a tear spring to the corner of her eye, and I gathered her hand in mine.

"We'll figure it out, okay?" I said it, but knew she was right. We weren't here to figure anything out; we were here to do something Tulya didn't want to do.

She gave my fingers a squeeze and said, "Let's get out of here."

All I could do was grip her fingers back. Why? Because upsetting the kindest person I knew wasn't high on my agenda, yet I'd lied to her. There was zero chance of figuring anything out.

CHAPTER
TWELVE

Tulya

Leaning my head back into the lounge chair, I closed my eyes and soaked up the warmth. Christmas music filled the air around me as the salty smell overtook my senses. It was December twenty-fourth, so I was definitely missing the holiday at home. Originally, I thought I'd have a pity party for myself, but then I caught a glimpse of Donovan working in the room, pounding away on a laptop, rage rolling off him.

The anger wasn't directed at me, but I'd kept my distance nonetheless.

It had been three days since our visit with Valerie, and Magnum still had not appeared. According to Caro, Cinder was on one and was refusing to speak with him.

My mother had called me this morning to check on both my physical and emotional state, and to see if I was keeping myself healthy and even by eating right and resting. She wasn't concerned about me, but more herself. My powers seemingly worked better when I was feeling my best. Sadly, I'd come to accept the selfish side of my mother if it meant she paid attention to me.

I assured her I was one hundred percent fine, more for Donovan's sake than anyone else. If I let on that either one of us was upset, my mom would put more pressure on the situation, and I didn't think Don needed that. Not sure why I cared so deeply about Donovan's state, but I did.

We retreated to our respective rooms after the interaction-gone-wrong with Valerie, and Don's subsequent deserting me at the scene. I'd ordered a sandwich from room service that evening, eating alone with my Kindle on the balcony.

Yesterday, Donovan worked, and I split my time writing and sitting in this same lounge chair at the pool. We'd danced around going to dinner, thought about sushi again, and then Magnum called and spoiled the mood. I'd forgone dinner for a glass of red and a Biscoff cookie or twenty.

Now, "Walking in a Winter Wonderland" played softly in the eighty-degree heat as I tried to enjoy the holiday as much as I could. This was the one day of the year I enjoyed being with my family, home in Rubia, eating, laughing, opening gifts. My mother always seemed more relaxed, and my dad played the role of doting husband and father.

A server approached, interrupting my memories when he asked, "Can I bring you anything?"

"Happy holidays," I wished him.

"Same to you."

"I'll have a club soda, splash of cran for color. Why? Because it's Christmas, and I want at least some holiday joy. Maybe a cherry or two."

He nodded at me and said, "My pleasure."

Reaching into my bag, I tugged out my Kindle and decided to read. I was in the middle of a small-town second-chance romance during the holiday season, my guilty pleasure during this time of the year. It was the final scene, when the hero decided he couldn't live without the heroine, and he'd asked the pilot of his private plane to turn around and go back to the small town he'd sworn he hated.

It was such catnip—a man changing his entire life plan for the girl…

A shadow over the chair darkened the sky around me and I went to look up and thank the server only to discover it was Donovan delivering my beverage.

"I believe this is yours," he said, handing me the cold glass with an umbrella floating in it.

"Thank you," I replied, raising an eyebrow.

"I decided to join the land of the living," he said, lying out on the chaise next to me.

"Or you can't get any work done because everyone cut out early for the holiday," I quipped, taking a sip of my club soda.

"That too."

I nodded at his admitting defeat. "Can't drown yourself in work. It won't get Magnum to comply any sooner."

Donovan cleared his throat, about to reply when the server popped back over.

"Anything for you?" he asked Donovan, keeping his eyes trained on the man in question.

"Tequila, blanco, neat."

The waiter nodded and scurried, picking up on Donovan's mood.

"That bad?" I didn't have to say who I was asking about.

"He's coming. The day after tomorrow. Cinder agreed to visit his daughter for the holiday and meet her."

"Do you believe him?"

"She told me herself. My mom cornered Cinder and let her know this was how things would go, and she's falling in line. If she wants to marry Magnum, she will raise Blake as her own."

I knew my mother and Ceci would eventually structure a solution to the entire fiasco, and it appeared they had.

The waiter appeared with Donovan's tequila, and I promptly said, "Well, then cheers to the last few days of peace."

"Merry Christmas, Tulya," the man beside me responded, clinking his plastic glass to mine.

"I never imagined I'd be spending the holiday with you." It slipped out, but Donovan had a reply.

"Can't be that bad. Is it?" He ran a hand through his hair, which had become wavier the longer we stayed in the humidity.

"It's perfect," I said, not lying. I was mostly content by the pool, not eager to do what I'd been sent for. And when he wanted to be, Donovan Malachite was extremely charming.

"Now, there's no need to go overboard, but I will agree that spending the holiday in sunshine rather than snow is perfect."

"Amen," I responded.

"I was hoping you could help me with something." Donovan looked toward me, holding his phone.

"I guess it depends."

Despite the heat radiating around us, a tiny chill ran through my veins. I'd come to know the sensation as the Donovan effect. I'd never admit it to him, but he made my body do things it never did for anyone.

"I have a few items in my cart here, for delivery from Neiman's, so you don't have to leave the pool, but I was hoping you could..." His words came out as a long run-on and all mixed up; he was nervous. "Well, I was hoping to get a few gifts for Blake, and if you could advise which ones are best, I'd be grateful. They're going to deliver them here this afternoon and then we can take them when we go with Magnum."

I'd give it to the guy: he liked the little girl. Not in a weird, abnormal way, but as in she was his niece and he wanted her to be happy. We had smaller boutiques on Rubia, where we stocked unique items, but I could tell Donovan thought *more* and *bigger* were both better when he handed me the phone. I scrolled through the items, including a faux fur coat, a dollhouse, and a pair of rhinestone-covered boots.

"The coat is for Rubia," Don explained without my asking.

I gave a curt nod, figuring as much. Jumping in on the fun, I perused the site with a smile on my face. I bought most of my clothes at Pinky's in Rubia, but I was beginning to think I would have to visit Neiman's myself.

"I love this pink warm-up suit and the doll with the matching outfit," I added, thinking it would make Blake happy. She seemed like such a loving and affectionate child. I placed the phone back in his hands and said, "I removed the camo jacket and the Star Wars Lego set. I do think she would like some Legos, but I don't think she's watched that movie yet."

He fiddled with the phone and asked, "Maybe just a cute Lego neighborhood?"

"Perfect."

He hit a few buttons and I heard the whoosh of something sending, and it was done. "I also was hoping to have dinner. Here, in the lobby? Tonight?"

"Are you asking me?"

"I don't think either of us wants to be alone..."

"I'm in," I said, letting him out of his misery but also sort of excited. I was starting to think this might be my most memorable Christmas yet, Rubia long forgotten. Donovan could be so vulnerable when he let his ego take a rest, and in this moment, he was building a special shelf in my heart for himself.

It was a bad idea on my part and a risk on his. Our moms had different plans, and taking note of the turn of events with Cinder, those two women got what they wanted.

CHAPTER
THIRTEEN

Donovan

"Happy Christmas." Later that same day, I greeted Tulya as she made her way out of her room in a red dress, fitted on top and a bit flowy on the bottom. I didn't know what it was called other than perfect. This woman had been tantalizing me in a new and bold way since the holiday party.

"Merry Christmas to you." As she spoke, her eyes practically sparkled with lightness.

For a hurried moment, I worried about what was to come, but then I shut it down because we had now. I hoped. Pausing, I took a sip of my bourbon, silencing the rush of anxiety, need, and want coursing through me at the quick flash of her strappy silver stilettos.

"Cheers," she said, taking note of my beverage.

"I ordered a bottle of red," I said, waving my palm toward the bar.

"Thank you." I watched her walk toward the counter with glasses and the vino, and the need to touch her hit me like a thunderbolt in the chest, not that I knew what it felt like other than seeing it in the movies. Lord, I was a heap of hormones and errant thoughts when it came to Tulya.

"We can have a glass here or...take it downstairs with us?" I finally gathered myself and asked. My tone came out like a question—I wanted her to know this night was about her.

"I'd love to have a glass on the balcony." She turned to look at me. "Is that okay? Will we still be on time for dinner?"

"We can eat at any time. They're holding our table."

She tilted the already opened bottle and poured into the wide-mouthed glass. Taking a sniff, she swallowed a taste. I watched, like the voyeur I'd become.

"Come on," she said, strolling by me, taking my hand in hers and leading the way to the sliding glass door.

My feet obeyed. A smitten soldier I was.

"One thing Rubia doesn't have...a warm Christmas," Tulya rambled, her voice tender.

"You look beautiful," I whispered, walking to her side, my free hand coming to rest on her hip.

We stood there staring at one another.

"I bought this in the store downstairs. I was holding out hope of being home for the holiday when packing." A small laugh escaped her as she admitted this, and I wished she giggled more. Tulya tended to be serious, but I imagined that growing up with her mother, there was no other way to be.

"It's made for you. The dress." I stumbled over my words.

"I guess somewhere deep inside I knew we would still be here, and the holiday with my family wasn't happening. Anyway, a good excuse to shop." Despite her laughing off the circumstances, I felt her sadness at being away.

A small wisp of her hair came free from the tight bun she wore at the nape of her neck, and my hand didn't wait for direction—my fingers reached out of their own volition and brushed it away from her face.

"I'm sorry you're not home either," I whispered, but it was a lie.

"Thank you for making it special. Dinner, the wine, time by the pool."

"Tulya." Her name came out on a breath. "You are the one making it special because you're you. Please don't forget that, no matter what happens."

A sudden sense of doom ran through me. It could be because of how much I wanted this woman. And there was no scenario where that worked long term. Or it might be what lay ahead of us. Or both.

"I don't want to disappoint you…or my mom…or your mom." With each person she didn't want to let down, her voice became softer.

"You won't," I said before my hand left her hip and gathered her close by the nape of her neck and gathered her in for a kiss. My mouth melded to hers and she kissed me back as fervently as my lips were savoring her.

We stayed like that for a while, our mouths leading the way, hopefully setting an example for other parts, until a brisk wind pushed by us. I felt a chill run through Tulya and pulled back from her body, placing my forehead on hers. "You're cold," I stated.

She leaned into me in rebuttal, stealing my body heat without any words.

"May be my happiest Christmas ever," I admitted. I didn't give a shit anymore. I wanted Tulya in my bed—even if it was for only one night. I knew that made me some kind of selfish prick, but she wasn't immune to me, and she also knew the standards set by our mothers.

Again, my brain was a jumbled mess, thinking like a teenager on a dead-end path. *Why do I fear my mother?*

"Dinner?" Tulya put me out of misery after taking the final swig of her wine.

I nodded and this time I took her hand in mine and led the way.

"Wait!" She stopped in her tracks inside the room and tugged me to the mirror. Swiping her hand over my mouth, she removed the smear of lipstick taking up residence there. "One quick second. Let me fix mine," she said before disappearing into her room.

If she only knew how much I missed her already.

"Well, right now my mother is likely sipping a brandy, while Dad is carving the roast. I have to say this shrimp cocktail suits me better," Tulya said at dinner.

I nodded. "I think all of this suits you better."

"We always have a hulking roast and potatoes au gratin on Christmas Eve. It's the one time of year Ezza allows herself to be a glutton."

"Ezza," I laughed while saying.

"There's only so much I can say. *My mother this* and *my mother that*... She's certainly overpowering even when speaking about her."

"True, I'm sorry to agree. Tell me more," I requested. Something about Tulya rambling set me at peace; it squashed all the anxiety coursing through my veins. I plucked a shrimp and dipped it in the cocktail sauce and waited for my date to speak.

"After we stuff ourselves silly on red meat, we go to sleep heavy and full before waking on Christmas Day, when we start all over again with a huge brunch."

"Brunch may be the most underrated meal. It can be anything you want—breakfast food, dinner stuff, cocktails or coffee."

Tulya smiled. "Well, now I know the way to get you to bend. A mimosa, a bagel, and perhaps some roast beef?"

I'd fallen for the easy way we joked with one another. It was simple and natural, how relationships were intended to be—not forced. "I'm a sucker for a mimosa," I admitted with a wink.

"Our brunch is mostly breakfast foods. We always have a French toast casserole and eggs with a side of turkey bacon. There is always an offering of muffins and rolls, sweet and savory. And of course, mimosas. Then, it somewhat turns into an all-day thing, where we nibble on all the leftovers from the night before and the morning throughout the day. We don't do a formal dinner, only graze until bedtime."

"Sounds fun," I said, taking a sip of sparkling water, thinking what it would be like to celebrate with Tulya and her family.

"It's also the only day Ezza is easygoing. We don't expect company, and her brother goes with his wife, so we are not concerned with the Minister or his kids."

"It makes me understand why you didn't want to miss it. It's the only twenty-four hours of relaxation in your house. But I'm sorry if that was overstepping…"

"No, you're not. It's okay," she said quietly.

"We are from the same mold. Your mom appears to be as controlling and daunting as mine."

"You are not wrong."

The server saved us from going down a potentially dark and serious rabbit hole, delivering salads and replenishing our drinks.

"Gorgeous," Tulya commented at her plate.

"If only I made you smile like a plate of greens," I teased.

She served back the humor. "It's the pomegranate seeds and roasted pears that do it for me."

In another life, I could get used to this banter. Tulya made me want to forget Rubia and the expectations that went along with living there.

"What about you? What is Christmas Day like for the Malachites?"

I ran a hand through my hair, sweat forming at my neck. Between all the want and need for this woman taking up residence in my cells, coupled with the tasks in front of us, I was feeling the heat of it all.

"Honestly, the holidays are not a huge deal. My father never liked them very much and my mother gave in to his every whim. We'd do a small dinner on Christmas Eve, usually a seafood-type pasta, garlic bread, wine, and open a gift. Growing up, Mag and I would usually play all Christmas Day with whatever was under the tree, and later video games when we were teens. That's about it."

"I had no idea." Her words were soft and filled with care.

If I pressed, I bet Tulya would invite me to be with her the following year. The promise of it did things to me I didn't care to admit. "My grandmother passed away on Christmas when my dad was young, and he never got over it. My mom did her best, but her loyalty always went to my father," I tried to explain.

Tulya's hand reached across the table and took mine in hers. I looked up at her, our gazes meeting. A fission of energy toggled us to one another in a way neither of us fully understood.

"I'm glad we're having our own little tradition, even if it's only for one year," she added, squeezing my fingers. "This is setting a new bar. I may not want to do the roast and brunch next year."

I swallowed every emotion lodged in my throat. How I wished this could be a forever tradition. I was liking this too much—Tulya, Florida, the dress, cocktails, the holiday chatter, every fucking thing.

"Actually, I was somewhat surprised Magnum wanted to come see Blake for the holiday, but it's nice. Maybe he is more invested than I give him credit for. I don't know, but this is all so new. Mag, a daughter, excitement over the holidays, you name it."

She set down her fork; she'd been devouring her salad in a way I wished she reserved for me. She took my hand again, and the current was now electric between us.

"Um, excuse me, you're the one who last-minute ordered and delivered half of Neiman's to Blake's house."

"That's because if I was a kid, I'd want someone to spoil me for the holidays. Speaking of," I said, reaching into my pocket, "I had a small trick up my sleeve when it came to all my ordering and delivering, as you say."

I pulled out a petite pouch and slid it across the table with my free hand, not even daring to remove my fingers tangled with Tulya's.

"What? When? We didn't say we were doing this."

"I know, but I know this wasn't how you hoped to spend the occasion. Or quite frankly, you hadn't wanted to be here at all. So, I tried to do something to cheer you up." It was already more than I liked to admit aloud, but Tulya unnerved me.

"Thank you. I wish you'd said something. I was out shopping and didn't even think to do gifts—"

"Open it," I interrupted, not breathing any more life into her worry over me.

The only negative part was her taking her hand from mine so she could untie the pouch. I watched her slip out the heart-shaped earrings, a myriad of red rubies and pink sapphires, and her mouth opened to a small O.

"Donovan! No one has ever... What? These are too much."

It was the type of reaction I'd wanted but never would admit—even on my deathbed.

"They're... I mean, they're... I don't have the words." She held the earrings and stared at them for a beat.

We'd spent the evening chatting freely, relishing one another's company, and this was dessert for me. If I could make her this happy again and again, I would. "Put them on."

"I feel so awful. I didn't get you anything. I didn't realize we were exchanging, and they're so extravagant."

"Stop feeling awful, I want to see them."

Her hand shook while removing the backing of one. I admired her lithe fingers and pale pink painted nails.

Clearing my throat, I spoke again. "I know this is out of the ordinary, you being here, doing this for my family, and I wanted you to know I care. Period." I was trying to make it seem like a thank-you gift. The words I didn't share were how much I was beginning to care about her as a person.

Rather than go on, I watched as Tulya slid her hand up the nape of her neck and removed the stud she was wearing and placed the heart I'd selected on her ear.

"Perfect," I murmured, and it was.

After arranging the second one on her other lobe, she put her diamond studs in the pouch and slipped it into her purse. "Thank you so much. I don't even know what else to say," she said, staring at me, her eyes beckoning orbs of gray.

They were my personal airstrip—I wanted to land a plane there and never leave.

She brought her wine to her lips as the server made his way back, explaining there was either a buffet or an à la carte option.

"Do you like sea bass?" Tulya quickly asked me, and I nodded.

"The sea bass for two is incredible," our waiter interjected.

"Then we will have that and any sides you think may go well with it." I appreciated the server's attentiveness but didn't want to waste my precious time with Tulya, so I hoped he understood my curtness.

"Some more sparkling water?"

This time I nodded and added, "Thanks," before eyeing the beautiful woman across from me.

He got the message and smiled, only popping by briefly when delivering the aforementioned items.

We filled our bellies on fish, a departure from Tulya's usual holiday fare, and allowed the alcohol to calm our nerves. So by the time we walked toward the elevator, Tulya leaned into my side, fully showing some sort of affection for me.

"What's with the *happy* Christmas and not merry, by the way?" A laugh ran through her words as we waited for the elevator.

"Honestly?"

She looked at me. "Yes."

The answer came out in a breath; it felt as if I was revealing the freaky part of my soul. "Well, in the UK, where I do increasingly more work, Happy Christmas means have a content holiday, and I really like the feeling behind that."

She took my hand in hers and squeezed. I guess she liked it too.

CHAPTER
FOURTEEN

Tulya

No matter how many walls, shields, or emotional boundaries I tried to stick up, I couldn't prevent myself from falling for Donovan Malachite. He was knocking down every obstacle like a bulldozer destroying a building.

"Would you like another drink?" he asked me once we were tucked inside the common area of our suite.

I was going to miss this small cocoon we'd burrowed ourselves in. When our task was successfully checked off, we would go our separate ways. I shook my head. "I don't think so. I'm too full..."

Truth was, I'd had enough alcohol and needed to be able to think clearly when it came to this green-eyed man. My pulse was beating a drum inside my body with uncapitulated need, and I had to get myself under control. It wasn't even because of the earrings, only him.

Donovan's bed was mere footsteps away from mine, and the greater amount of time I spent with the man of my dreams, the more I wanted to find myself tucked in there—in his arms, next to his strong chest and six-pack. Tangled in the sheets for hours, sweaty and spent.

Luckily, he poured two waters, handing me one before walking back toward the bar and taking his own glass of clarity.

"I hope it was a content start to Christmas." He spoke gruffly, picking up on our discussion while waiting for the elevator.

"It was." My voice came out breathless. "It was the best Christmas Eve ever." My finger came to touch an earring, sending chills up and back down my spine. These hearts would always transport me back to this moment. "It wasn't the expensive gift that made this the greatest day, but rather the thought you put into it," I blurted out.

He smiled and nodded, not acknowledging my confession. Maybe thought was my language of love? I thought back to my research for writing several lovers in my books, and the theory came to mind. I missed writing at my desk. The quiet and solitude enveloping me, yet I felt my feet taking me toward Donovan, my hand placing my water on the end table.

"I can't stop thinking about Blake. Mostly, I hope Cinder likes Blake. That she is kind to her, welcoming to her, or whatever everyone back in Rubia is expecting. She's just a kid. Poor Blake has no idea what she is mixed up in." I rambled on, searching for something to fill the silence.

"I don't want to talk about them now," Donovan said, pure authority dripping in his tone.

I looked up at him, our gazes crashing.

"Don't mistake me. I care about Blake, and I know she's only a child," he said, "but it's not a subject for now. Once all that shit starts, the spell will be broken. All hell will break loose."

This man had a way with words. He was right, there was something magical happening at the moment and I knew it would be over all too soon.

"I want to kiss you," he said, his palm coming to rest on my cheek.

I felt myself nod.

His lips hovered near mine. "If I'm honest, I want to do more, much more, Tulya." He spoke at a level only for me, even though I was the only one in the room.

Again, my head nodded on its own.

Our mouths crashed into one another. His hand traveled up my back, coming to settle gently at the base of my neck, keeping me in place—as if I would move.

I breathed out a sigh and his tongue found entrance into my mouth. To think it had been a week since we flirted innocently at my mother's party. I couldn't believe this was happening.

Yet my own tongue danced with his as my hand found purchase on his hip.

He dug his length into me, and it was a delicious friction. One I suspected I could never tire of.

"Tulya," he moaned. "I'm pretty sure I've wanted you all my life. There are decades of pent-up desire running through my veins." He didn't wait for me to respond, only swooped me into his arms and carried me toward his bedroom. "Is this okay?"

Struck speechless for the third time, I signaled with a nod, yet again. Nodding was becoming my official language.

Once inside, he set me on the bed and hovered over me. He began the kiss all over again. This time he held his weight up on his elbow, but my hips kept reaching for more pressure, all of Donovan. I wanted to supersize this—my guilty pleasure.

His other hand roamed my side, lifting my dress with it, allowing his palm to singe my skin.

A low moan funneled out from my mouth, filling the air around me.

"Tulya," he said again. As far as I was concerned, he could say it a million times and I wouldn't tire of hearing it. "All of this is against our better judgment, but I can't stop."

He was right, but I didn't want him to pull the plug… "Don't," I replied.

Except he pulled away, and I felt barren.

"Sit up," he demanded, and I acquiesced.

Thankfully, this was all a dance for him to yank my dress over my head, revealing my evergreen silk bra and panties.

Donovan stopped and stared, a low hum emanating from him. "Christmas colors, I see," he said and winked for the second time this evening. Something else he could do a bazillion times and I wouldn't complain.

"I couldn't resist. Do you like?"

"Taunting me?"

There was something about the way we spoke honestly and it all flowed so easily from serious to joking that set this man apart for me.

Now, he gently encouraged me to lie back, and he didn't take his eyes off me as he stood and ripped off his shirt and pants, leaving him in a pair of black boxer briefs. He'd lost his blazer and shoes somewhere in the living area.

Still wearing my heels, I kicked them off at the edge of the bed and slid up toward the pillows. Donovan prowled after me, the hunger rippling off him.

Finally, his mouth hit my nipple in a whoosh of hot air, and it pebbled underneath the now damp silky fabric.

"It's a very happy Christmas for me," he teased.

I found a boldness I didn't know my soul embodied and guided his lips back to mine with my pointer finger under his chin. He obliged, kissing me into oblivion.

We stayed like that a long while, our lower halves moving, seeking friction until Don murmured, "I need you."

I responded with, "I want you." I'd never been so daring, but Donovan brought out the raw woman in me.

He rolled onto his back and shrugged off his underwear, immediately coming back and sealing his mouth over my other nipple, leaving my bra on before traversing down south, shoving my panties to the side and making me squeal with his tongue. My entire pelvis rocked. It was shameful, but he had me in such a state of need.

I should've felt embarrassment at how I let go, but I couldn't bring myself to do so because Don kept whispering, "That's it, let go."

"Oh...I can't, I can't take, I'm going to..." I rambled on right before I exploded, my world in three-dimensional color at the moment.

I think he said "Beautiful" and then found his way to the nightstand for a condom. Clearly, I'd been a sure thing—also couldn't bring myself to care.

He slipped it on, and I watched with what I only assumed were hungry eyes.

In a matter of moments, he was back on top of me, his weight on his elbow once again, but this time his free hand helped to guide himself inside me.

"Fucking decadent," he whispered as he slid deep, and I couldn't have agreed more.

We moved slowly at first, picking up pace until we were both on the precipice, lips and tongues and teeth biting, nipping, licking anywhere we could find a spot. And then we went over the edge, riding out the cascade until all the moans and shivers subsided, collapsing in a heap.

Which is exactly how we woke up on Christmas Day, twenty-four hours from Magnum arriving, and no clue what we had just started...or ended.

"Good morning" rang in the room before I'd opened my eyes.

Finally doing so, I took in my surroundings. I was still in Donovan's bed, the sheets a twisted mess, and he stood before me in a hotel robe, holding what appeared to be a latte.

"Merry Christmas to me," I said, sitting up and taking the mug from his hand.

He turned around, and I worried for a hot minute before he returned holding his own mug.

Sitting down next to me, he clinked his cup with mine. "I don't have any more gifts," he declared before taking a gulp of his java.

"I didn't have any...at all."

Leaning forward, he gently pressed a kiss to my forehead, careful so that neither of us spilled.

I'd never imagined this tender side of Donovan, yet here it was on full display. For the first time since I'd been here, I thought about calling Prim. Except I didn't really want to share this half of Donovan. The one I'd been fortunate to spend one night with.

"Last night was a gift," he said, his declaration hitting me like a bullet in the chest.

It was a one-time thing, I feared. In reality, I knew that the moment we started. I didn't know why I was hurt. This was why I'd shut him down at the party over a week ago.

Prim would say I was a goner. She'd look me square in the face, her lips pursed, eyebrows raised, and wait for me to admit how far into Donovan I was… So I decided not to call her after all.

"Do you want breakfast?" he asked while gazing straight at me, his gorgeous green eyes a myriad of emotions—lust, want, sadness, and potentially something close to like or adoration.

I was hungry. Sadly, I didn't think what I wanted was on the room service menu.

CHAPTER
FIFTEEN

Donovan

Tulya tied her robe and followed me out to the living room, eyes widening at the scene in front of her. I'd woken early and had an idea—it was born less out of selflessness and more out of selfishness. I wanted as much Tulya as I could get in a small period of time…and minutes I could grab with her were a bonus since I didn't think we would ever be a possibility other than a fling.

Spread out in front of Tulya's eyes was a huge Christmas brunch spread. There was French toast, muffins, sesame seed rolls, eggs with and without cheese, turkey bacon, fruit, Christmas cookies and, of course, a pitcher of orange juice for mimosas.

With the blinds open, the sunshine poured in, illuminating Tulya's face and warming the room.

"Oh. My. Donovan. This is. I don't know." She punctuated each word, strolling around the elongated table, her pointer finger lingering a beat by each item. "You recreated our holiday brunch," she said, practically out of breath.

"I want you to be happy." It was all I could admit.

From the side-looks this morning, we both knew this relationship had a shelf life, similar to the food in front of us. I hadn't intended to mention anything more about our expiration date; it wasn't worth spoiling this glorious moment.

But while seated on the balcony, sipping on mimosas, empty plates set in front of us and happy families celebrating below us at the pool, Tulya asked, "What about when we finish this task? What's your plan?"

I didn't know if she meant when it came to her and me, or what exactly she was getting at. Running a palm over my forehead, I wasn't quite sure how to answer.

"Your mom seems to have plans for you," she added, sensing my hesitation, clarifying her question.

I guessed she was more of a "get the elephant out of the middle of the room" woman.

Blowing out a long breath, I said, "She always does."

The warm breeze ruffled Tulya's hair, which was sufficiently mussed from our night in the sheets. I had no idea why she brought this subject up, but my dumbass feelings wouldn't allow me to bend the truth. I wanted to keep her for whatever time I could, but also forbid myself from lying to Tulya anymore. "I'm leaving Rubia," I blurted out without thinking. That was the thing with Tulya: she made me reckless.

"What?" She leaned forward and stared at me. "*Leaving* leaving? How? For a vacation? For work?"

There was no skirting the issue now. I mimicked her expression. "*Leaving* leaving."

She raised an eyebrow but didn't say a word.

"I'm working on a deal. A hotel deal, the kind my dad never wanted to do, but I've been eager to do since I took over. I'm going to Hawaii. For good."

She stood and moved toward the railing, and I gave her the moment.

"Do you have an American lover, like your brother?" she asked, her brow furrowed.

"Come on," I responded, "don't do that. We may not be a thing, but I would never do something like that… Two women at once. That's not me."

This earned me another eyebrow raise.

Shaking my head, I said, "No, I *do not* have an American lover, but I'm also not getting involved in an arrangement like my brother and Cinder. I do enough of my mother's bidding. Romance will not be another assignment."

She came toward me and put her palm on my cheek. I did not expect this type of reaction from her. "So, you've decided to forgo your own happiness while everyone else has theirs? You're here in Miami, resolving things for your brother, making your mom happy, and getting to know Blake. And then what? You'll say adios and go to Hawaii, banishing yourself? Sounds similar to what you may have accused me of—"

My hand came to her waist. "Yes, I'm sorry, it does. But we know this is how this has to be."

"No, it doesn't." I caught a quick glimpse of the pleading in her eyes before she schooled her expression, let go of me, and turned around.

Standing, I gathered her from behind, pulling her back to my front. "It can't be with us…my sweet and kind and beautifully stunning Tulya. We could have had some fun at home, but now I'm expected to get serious with someone, make a life, produce bold and brazen Rubians."

She swiveled around so fast we both almost lost our footing. "Look, I know we are doomed, never meant to be. But maybe…we could have fun now? Or I don't know, talk to our mothers?" She yanked away and buried her forehead in her palms. "Lordy, I cannot believe I'm begging like this, carrying on like a jilted woman. We had one night." Her long hair tangled in her face, and she swept it back with a rough hand.

I approached, smoothing a few stray strands away from her eyes. "Believe me, I want way more than this one night. I'd like to hoard them all, but it's not in the stars for us."

Inside my head, I screamed at myself for ever flirting with Tulya, let alone last night.

"Why?" It came out quiet and scared, unlike the brave Tulya I had come to know.

I didn't know if she meant why not us or why did I care about whoever my mom picked for me. But I asked, "Do you know why it can't be us?"

Her lips pursed before she responded. "I'm not daft," she said, still tucked in my grasp. "Our mothers would never allow it. They're too good of friends or whatever. We've said this a million times. They wouldn't let us get in the middle of them."

"This is the best part of you, Tulya. You hold such great power, yet you are so innocent. You look beyond all the inner workings of Rubia, ignoring the underground of shit swirling in the air. It's so thick, you can almost grab it by the handful."

"I don't think I'm looking beyond, as you say. They are comrades in everything, those two."

If I wasn't thinking about Ezza and Ceci, I'd be hard. Thankfully, they were like a giant bucket of limp dick. I had a full-blown thing for strongheaded, naïve Tulya. "Not because of some silly reason, sweet Tulya."

"Please stop with the sweet, it's too much."

I didn't respond to that request, rather moved my hands to her upper arms, gently forcing our bodies to allow our eyes to meet. "Because we cancel one another out. I'm a knife and you are a salve." She looked at me, her brow furrowed as she solved my riddle. "You take pain away. And when I want or need to, I dole it out, sometimes mercilessly. Our powers are complete opposites."

"So? It's not like you're out there, sending everyone into painful fits. I don't understand." She stopped and then started again. "Or maybe you *are* causing irreparable harm?"

Brushing my lips across her cheek like a starved lover, I wanted to give her only comfort, never pain—always. "No, I'm not making anyone suffer who didn't earn it," I said into her ear. "I didn't ask for this capability."

Her forehead came to meet my chest. "I'm sorry. I didn't mean to say you did. I didn't either, but I don't understand."

I needed a long breath while taking a moment. Then I spoke. "There is the chance we could make one another powerless. Or our children, if we got that far, would be born without abilities… Our mothers won't permit either of those scenarios to happen. That's why they're busy looking for matches. To alter abilities and trying to build stronger ones."

She stepped back and stared at me. "My mother is tampering with future potential power? No! The Minister is against that sort of thing…"

"It's true" was all I answered. She kept walking away from me as I moved toward her, reaching out. I took her arm in my palm and she steadied. I didn't want to control her; my only thought was protection.

"How do I not know? What is she planning for? A new Rubian way?" Her feet brought her to me and she burrowed in my chest. "I live on her property. She uses my power all the time to her benefit…yet you and I have the tingle when we are near one another. There is some connection. You zig and I zag, but as if it's meant to be. Why didn't they tell me about this?"

Tulya rambled into my pectoral, but I heard every one of her concerns, especially the unspoken tether between us. "That's why I'm going to Hawaii. Now it's even more crucial."

"Because of me?" Tulya looked up, her eyes damp.

"I was going either way, but we can't be. And truthfully, after I untangle my brother from his mess, I don't want to be a part of any more Rubian nonsense."

"Maybe I will come to Hawaii?"

I smiled and tipped her chin with my pointer finger so she could look at my eyes. "Your mom wouldn't ever allow it, and neither would mine."

Walking away, she said over her shoulder, "Well, I may only be a pawn in my mother's game, but I have today. I'm going to the pool and enjoying my holiday without my spoiled, manipulative family."

She disappeared into her room, emerging in a swimsuit and jean shorts, a tote tossed over her shoulder. Long gone was chatter over the buffet or the holiday.

All Tulya said was, "Be back up later," and left the room.

Since I was nothing more than a fool, I didn't follow or seek her out later. I figured the mood had been spoiled, and she needed time with the knowledge I'd dumped on her.

I made sure to tell myself this wasn't about my own self-preservation.

CHAPTER
SIXTEEN

Donovan

I'm downstairs

Magnum texted one word when he arrived. I slipped my suit jacket on and texted back.

Coming.

Tulya wasn't in the common area yet, and knowing how nervous she had been when we first came to Miami, I didn't want to rush her. Not to mention we'd had dinner mostly in silence on the balcony before retreating to our respective bedrooms last night—too much to say and not enough time to ever make it through it all.

Honestly, I didn't even know if Cinder had shown up. Part of me would be relieved if she hadn't. Tuvy and I needed extra time in our bubble; I wanted to go back to Christmas Eve when she was in my bed and underneath me.

So I needed to prolong her having to do something she didn't want to do—the transfer—and show her how much fun life could be free from our mothers. A small sliver of my heart started to think she could come to Hawaii with me. The other seventy-five percent wanted to get this shit done. I had to put up a boundary with Tulya and get back to the life I was building without her and all of Rubia.

Not to mention, my mother was not patiently waiting.

With a soft rap on Tulya's door, I spoke through the wood. "They're here. I'm going to meet them. You come down when you're ready."

"Five minutes," she called back without opening the door.

I waited a beat, hoping she would appear with a soft smile or caring embrace. It was a dangerous want, but my entire being trembled at the idea of pulling her into my arms and kissing her one last time. Instead of listening to my outlandish desires, I walked out of the suite and toward the elevators.

As soon as the doors opened downstairs, I saw Magnum and Cinder sitting in the lobby. She was drinking a coffee, and he was tapping his leg up and down. My brother was nervous—the problem was I didn't know over what. Cinder liking Blake? Blake liking Cinder? Alienating Valerie?

"Mag," I greeted him, and he stood and shook my hand.

Apparently he'd compartmentalized this into official business.

"Happy Christmas," I said, then decided to test the waters, turning my attention to my brother's fiancée. "Cin, you look lovely." She sat there in a denim miniskirt and sequined T-shirt. She looked more like she was going to a pop concert and not to meet her almost-husband's daughter from another woman. A child she'd only just learned about— and a mistress who was trying to steal her fiancé.

"Where's Tuvy? It's time for her to do her magic and get me out of here. Period. End of sentence."

Well, I wouldn't even call her mood lukewarm—it was frigid or cold at best.

I nodded. "On her way."

"We brought gifts." Magnum changed the subject, pointing behind him to a bunch of gift bags. "In addition to what you ordered," he quickly added, a nod to all that I had done. "I picked up some art supplies and candies," he explained.

It was clear Magnum knew his daughter and cared about her, which I assume was why he'd kept her a secret. He had to know it would come to something like this. If he didn't think the Minister and our mother would step in, he was only being naïve.

"I had everything else delivered to the house," I told my brother, trying my best to ignore Cinder's attitude raining off her.

"Valerie's, you mean?" Cinder took the moment to speak with a sinister look on her face. Nothing about this meet-up made me feel good, including when my brother's fiancée added, "Here she is, the answer to my prayers."

She knew better than to use Tulya like she was some disposable commodity, yet that was how she was treating her. Then again, Tulya's own mother acted that way to a certain extent. All of it made my blood boil.

"Magnum, Cinder, good to see you," Tulya said, coming to my side, the roller coaster we'd experienced the last two nights set aside for the business at hand.

Tulya and I kept a respectful distance, which felt equal parts horrible and awkward, but it wasn't necessary to give away our secret. Especially since it ended now.

"Let's get to work." Cinder stood and tipped back her coffee before setting the empty cup down.

"Are you ready?" I quietly asked Tulya.

"She is," Cinder responded before Tulya could even nod.

"Come on, Cin," my brother said, running his hand down Cinder's back. "You said you were going to try," he tried to whisper to his fiancée.

If Hollywood were making this movie, the critics would call it not believable. We, as Rubians, looked like humans, had powers similar to witches and warlocks, walked about the earth with no one knowing our secret. Earning money and living our posh lives, until *boom*, my brother has a torrid affair, fathers a child and falls for the woman, while being engaged to a fellow Rubian. Leaving us now, here in the States, trying to transfer feelings between one of us and a human, and basically steal the child, all the while hoping the fiancée likes the kid. And praying we didn't endanger Tulya—at least I was doing the last item.

"I am, I am," Cinder said, leaning into Magnum. "Especially once Tuvy takes this pain from me."

I made quick work of stealing a glance at Tulya. She held her shoulders high despite the weight bearing down on her.

Again, an insatiable need tugged at me to comfort her but now wasn't the time. Actually, *never* was.

I handed the valet my ticket and he ran for the car while Magnum came up behind me carrying the gift bags, Cinder's body language anything but saying she was going to try.

Marley answered the door with a sour look on her face.

"I wouldn't have allowed this," she mumbled but was stopped short by Blake scurrying to her side. "But here we are."

"Daddy!" Blake squealed before launching into Magnum's arms.

It was a well-practiced move and it was clear they had done it many times before. As startling as this knowledge was to me, I glanced at Cinder who looked like she'd seen a ghost. She was pale white, almost translucent. I was worried she was going to faint. We'd never imagined a child being involved when this whole idea materialized—I couldn't help but ponder whether it would have changed the course of action.

Surprisingly, Magnum took notice of Cinder and put one hand on her elbow, holding his daughter with the other arm.

"Hey, Bumblebeeeee," he said, kissing Blake's forehead.

Desperately, I wanted to check in with Tulya, but I couldn't take my gaze off my brother—the family man—and his slowly fading fiancée off to the side. My God, what a mess he'd made.

"Hi, Daddy. Merry Christmas." The small girl curled into his shoulder in another well-rehearsed move.

"Shall we go inside?" I suggested, thinking Cinder should sit and we should take our spectacle somewhere private.

Marley moved without a word, allowing us entry. Magnum headed in first, still holding Blake. Cinder stayed by her man's side, giving a quick glance toward Tulya with a pleading look. I grabbed the gift bags Magnum had set down and waited for Tulya to enter, my hand taking a quick moment to touch her lower back.

She didn't respond but I knew she felt it. There was some sort of zing that happened when we touched one another. I'd felt it get stronger the more intimate we'd been, and I knew it wasn't my imagination. Sadly, it was likely our polar opposite powers clashing, trying to make order out of the madness.

"Mom!" Blake jumped out of Magnum's arms and ran toward the kitchen where we first visited a few days ago. "Mom, Daddy's here, come on." I heard Blake from afar.

Taking in the room, I recalled seeing the tree the other day. Fresh, if my nose served me right, decorated in all white, a star at the top. Underneath sat several presents, I assumed the ones I sent.

Magnum was clearly familiar with the space and stood next to Cinder as she took it in herself. On the mantel sat a framed photograph of Magnum holding a tiny infant-sized version of Blake in his hands. A piece of my heart shattered seeing how much of my brother's life I hadn't known about; I couldn't imagine what Cinder was feeling but I was starting to think it didn't matter.

Turning my attention across the room, watching Tulya squirm by the tree, I knew she could feel Cinder's pain heightening.

"Come on." Blake's voice carried through the room as she ran toward the kitchen, reappearing, dragging Valerie by the hand. "Can we open the gifts now that Daddy is here?"

Valerie leaned down and talked at eye level with Blake. "We can, sweetie, but remember, let's be calm, and don't forget to say thank you."

It was clear Valerie was ignoring everyone else in the room, and I was fine with that until Tulya came close and whispered, "Break the ice."

I made a quick note that Marley had long disappeared before nodding toward Tulya, knowing she was right.

Of course she still went on, making her point. "For Blake." Her words were meant just for me, but I saw Magnum take notice of us.

"Hi, Valerie," I said, approaching the woman, palm extended. Blake rushed under my arm toward the tree but looked back and her mother had no choice other than to shake hands with me. "Thank you for having us," I added.

"Blake has never seen her father on Christmas. I would never deny her that experience."

"This is from Tuvy and Uncle Don! That's what the card says," Blake shouted.

She was an advanced reader apparently—no surprise. Blake tore through the paper and found a Lego set I'd picked out.

"Oh, wow! I love it!" She jumped up and down before grabbing another present.

"This is from Daddy and Cinder." She said the second name quietly, looking up at her mom.

"I hope you love it, Bumble. Both Cin and I do." Magnum walked over toward his daughter, guiding Cinder, who was holding his hand.

Blake looked up from her unwrapping, taking in the woman clinging to her father.

Magnum spoke quietly. "This is Cinder. She's very special to me."

I had no idea where he came up with the shitty expression—*very special to me*. He was marrying her, for fuck's sake, but for once, Cinder kept quiet. So I followed suit. My heart and head were scissoring in half, torn between what my mother required of me and what might be best for my niece.

This entire situation was happening backward—the meet-and-greets, introductions, and important messaging after tearing open the gifts. The sitting around together like one big gathering before any decisions were made; it was bound not to last. If this was a business deal, it was going wrong, but even

I knew this whole shebang was personal and way out of my league. Not to mention, none of us could wield our powers but Tulya. This wasn't the place for Rubian ways.

Fuck, when it comes to any kid, let alone my human niece, I have no clue what to do or how to act.

"It's so nice to meet you, Blake," Cinder said, dropping to her knees. "Let's see what's in there." She pointed to the gift.

"Oh, an American Girl doll! I wanted one!" Blake danced around holding the present Tulya had picked out for my brother and Cin to take credit.

I flashed her a quick look and she winked. If I could steal a million of these moments with her, I would. But I'd sealed my fate yesterday with all my honest talk.

"What is this?" Cinder asked, pulling something else out of the package, trying to get involved when she was nothing more than an interloper.

It was in this moment that I felt sad for Cinder. It was becoming clear where my brother's heart remained, and it was not with her.

"A matching outfit for me," Blake declared, jumping up and down. "Look, Mommy, an American Girl! And we are twins."

For a quick second, the tension in the room disappeared and the different parties with varied interests all cast their smiles on the innocent child dancing with joy. We were an alliance formed only by concern for Blake.

That is, until Valerie said, "So nice of your dad."

"And Cinder," Magnum added, trying to get back to the moment of unity.

"I don't know her, and she is no one to my daughter," Valerie tossed back, heightening the room into an emotional crescendo.

Unsure of what to do, Blake retreated to the tree, while Cinder wiped a tear from her eye. I caught Tulya running a hand under her hair and over her neck. Clearly, Cinder was sending distress signals Tulya couldn't ignore, her body answering the call.

Blake broke the tension. "Oh, another one from Uncle Don."

Tearing through the paper, she found the box holding the coat. "Silly, we don't get snow in Florida." Blake ran up to me, wearing the furry puffball of a jacket, still hugging my leg despite the confusion over the present.

Valerie cleared her throat, not leaving anything to chance, seemingly knowing what the warm coat was for. "It was very nice of you all to be so thoughtful and think of Blake. But she has so much, so I think that's enough for now. Like I said, she never gets to see her dad on the holiday, so why don't we allow them some time?" She waved toward the front door rather than the kitchen, basically asking all of us to leave.

I felt my eyebrows rise and heard myself saying, "We are her family too." This little tyke had captured my heart, and whether it was because she was blood, plain cute, or both, didn't matter. A wild urge to protect her took over when it came to Blake, yet I looked to Tulya for guidance.

Blake might have stolen my adoration, but Tulya had become my guiding star, which was the opposite of what I meant to happen when it came to the latter female.

CHAPTER
SEVENTEEN

Tulya

"Let Magnum have a few minutes with Blake," I said, noting Donovan's gaze directed at me.

I began walking toward the door without a response from him. Truthfully, I needed a moment. My body was radiating so much heat, I decided this was what menopause must feel like…and I was a long way off from that juncture. It didn't help that Cinder was a gigantic ball of stress and feelings. She was strung out more than anyone I'd ever helped, and the longer I waited, the more my own symptoms ratcheted. Except my stupid body had no idea what it was actually about to attempt; it only itched to take the suffering away from Cinder.

"Okay," Donovan agreed, and his palm met my lower back. I reminded myself he was stepping outside and relished in the slight relief I felt on his touch, a cold chill taking over my sauna-like status.

Of course, I kept these thoughts to myself and remained moving.

Once outside, Cinder nearly collapsed onto the walkway, sitting down and burying her face in her hands. I had to shift my eyes from her as it was all too much for my internal system.

"If that's how you feel, *Cindy*, what about me? Magnum is the father of my child." Valerie opened her mouth—stupidly—saying Cinder's name wrong.

I was in the middle of deciding whether it was purposeful or not when Cinder shouted, "Don't talk to me, and my fucking name is Cinder."

Donovan said, "Cinder, Valerie, enough." He spoke both their names firmly.

"What?" The two women spoke in unison for what would probably be the only time.

"You need to calm down. Both of you." That was all he said, and Cinder promptly dropped her head back in her hands.

During all this I'd lost the tiny bit of touch with Donovan, and my temperature was spiking. Cinder was nowhere near calming, and if I was honest, this wasn't great for me.

"Valerie," Donovan shifted his attention, "we need to talk." He spoke quietly, moving his body close to hers so no one could eavesdrop. "You know Blake is special. And she's certainly captured my love in a few days. She's sweet and kind...and like us." He stumbled through his emotions and explaining. "She's not going to be able to stay here. She belongs in Rubia," he finally spit out.

The bright sun beat off Donovan's hair, casting a glow on him, and I could see a small sheen of perspiration forming along his brow. Despite his words being cool as a cucumber, or however that expression went, he was not relaxed.

"That's why we were going there. To Rubia," Valerie said as if that were still possible, or ever going to happen. I'd give her this, she was one stubborn lady.

"Listen, I know you're not daft, so you have to know by now that's not happening. It's forbidden."

"I don't listen to you. Your brother makes his own rules."

I turned to see if Cinder was watching the verbal sparring, and she was, her head rapidly ping-ponging between the two.

"My brother doesn't make his own rules. Neither do I. We answer to the Minister, and this is not permitted. Over and out. I wish there was an explanation that would get through to you, but I can't find it."

Valerie stomped close and waved her finger in his face. "I don't abide by your rules, and neither does Blake—"

"She will. The Minister will be sure of it, and the sooner you get that, the faster this can be resolved."

"Lucky for Blake I don't answer to the Minister."

The pair continued to spar, likely drawing the attention of a few neighbors.

"She's Rubian," Donovan said, whispering the second word. "And my brother has already broken the law by telling you about us. There will be no saving grace here. Blake will need to be taken to where she is like others—"

I felt myself nodding, which was a stupid move, but he spoke the truth.

Valerie turned her attention toward me. "What the hell do you know? You're the witch who was sent here to make things worse for me."

"Hey." Donovan's tone turned sinister. "I'd watch your mouth, Valerie. She's the Minister's niece," he followed up with, protecting me.

It wasn't needed, but it didn't go unnoticed. "Let's all calm down," I started to say.

"No," Cinder stood abruptly, interrupting me. "Let's not calm down, Tuvy. This woman," she said, poking her finger at Valerie, "this woman doesn't fit with us here, nor in Rubia. Magnum went against the rules and higher law, and she, sadly, has to pay the price for his mistakes. I'm sorry for you," she said while turning to face her arch nemesis. "But you can't be mad at me or Tuvy. Get angry with Magnum. It's an age-old story, be careful who you fall for... He didn't heed it, and neither did you. But here's the thing—Magnum is Rubian, and he knew better. You didn't, I'll give you that, but your daughter is also Rubian. Magnum and Blake belong in Rubia. And, well, his indiscretion and the resulting child is my battle to deal with when it comes to *my future husband.*"

Cinder's voice was rising, my own body temperature along with it, and Magnum was gripping his forehead while Valerie clenched her fists. Everything was unraveling, and I wasn't sure where to center my focus.

"Valerie, you don't have a choice. I'm glad you're allowing Magnum some time now. I'm hoping he's preparing Blake for a change," Donovan said, simply stating the facts as he believed them.

Squeezing my eyes shut, I could feel Valerie raging. Donovan had just made everything ninety million times worse, tossing gasoline onto a burning wildfire. Except when I opened my eyes, I didn't expect Valerie to charge Donovan, fists in the air, pummeling his chest and screaming for the whole world to hear.

"You will not take my daughter!"

Donovan's own hands came to wrap around Valerie's wrists, gently guiding her from his body. "Valerie, please don't touch me," he spoke calmly. "Let's go inside, maybe to the kitchen?" He continued to be calm, despite beads of sweat now lining his forehead.

"I'm getting Magnum," Cinder declared, storming toward the door.

"Cin—come here," I pleaded. It was clear no one knew what a young and impressionable commodity Blake was. My only understanding of her age and the current predicament was when I came into my power close to her age. Everyone around me sought a piece of my soul, and I didn't want that for Blake. She deserved to just be a kid.

"No. Do what you came here for, Tuvy, and shut up. Just be quiet and do it!"

Out of the corner of my eye, I caught Donovan shaking his head. I wasn't sure if it was because he knew I was scared to death of the transfer or if he truly thought it wasn't the correct time.

There wasn't an opportunity to ponder it because Valerie took off after Cinder, and Donovan turned toward me. "I'm going to kill my brother. Of course, after I get Blake safely back to Rubia. She cannot be trusted here—"

His words were hurried and slightly frantic, yet I argued, "That's not your call."

"I'm the head of my family, and it is my fucking call, Tulya. You know this. The House of Malachite is mine to guide into the future. Your family has their way, and we have ours. We don't operate like they do here in the States. Whether we agree or not, it doesn't matter. We have long-standing rules and customs," Donovan spit out at me.

Hurt could have taken over, but I knew he wasn't wrong. Mostly, my heart bled for Blake. "You can't just take her," I argued back.

"Don't you think I know that? That's why I'm trying to have Magnum handle it, but Valerie is a...a nightmare—"

"Whoa," I interrupted him. "She's a woman afraid of losing her child. You can't really believe that about her."

"Okay, you're right. I'm sure she's a lovely woman and a great mom. But let's be honest, Magnum is gone for her, and I don't think he will push her hard." His green eyes looked venomous as the vein pulsed in his neck. "I'm doing the best I can," he said, his palm coming around my wrist softly. "I don't want to hurt you, or Blake, or anyone. But I have my mom and your mom and likely the Minister breathing down my back. It's more pressure than the business deals I'm working on."

"I wish it wasn't like this."

My words were quiet as was his "Me too." Then, "Come on," he said before he weaved his fingers through mine as shouting emanated from the house. He added, "We're not doing the transfer today." It was as if he'd read my mind. "We have to calm them all down, and then Mag is going to have to make sure Valerie stays put with Blake."

"Can't wait to see that," I murmured as we walked inside the house and a glass came hurling through the air.

"You're nothing to me," Valerie screamed at Cinder.

I couldn't help but notice the confidence Cinder marched inside with; she wasn't the least bit spooked by the crystal pitcher that had been aimed at her head but hit the wall instead.

Magnum at least had the idea to hold Blake close to his body, her back against his thigh. Poor thing, her head whipped between all the anger-spewing adults in the room.

This was deteriorating, and I wondered if I should go look for Marley...

until Magnum dropped down to his knees and turned his daughter to face him.

"Bumble, I'm sorry," he said, pulling her into his arms.

I wasn't sure when Magnum had become Dad of the Year, but taking a quick look around at Donovan and Cinder, neither did they. The only one who appeared unsurprised was Valerie; she'd seen this side of him before.

"This isn't about you." He brushed a stray hair off his daughter's face. "I love you, but I made some mistakes. You know where Daddy is from?"

Blake nodded and said softly, "Somewhere far away, not like here, but I know I'm not supposed to tell."

I didn't think any six-year-old would understand or get what any of that talk meant, but I suspected having powers like she did heightened Blake's awareness.

"Well, where I live, everyone can do...*special things*...like you." We all watched in wonderment as Magnum worked his way through explaining what the hell was happening to a little girl.

Blake nodded. "Are you mad at me because I showed Uncle Don what I can do?"

"No, no, sweetie." He spoke softly, rubbing his hand down Blake's cheek, swiping a tear. "We are very proud of you." Magnum looked toward his brother for the first time, silently asking him to agree.

"We are," Donovan whispered before walking close and also getting down on his knees.

My body, specifically my ovaries, went into overdrive, but Valerie's approach toward Don was like a cold shower.

"Get up," she said to Donovan, and this time Magnum intervened.

"V, that's Blake's uncle. He is not going to harm her."

Hurt spread across her face, but she did as he suggested and backed off.

"I am proud of you, Blake. I swear." Donovan touched his forehead to hers, and it was a silent promise to never use his power on her. This man in front of me would never inflict pain on a child. Hormones pinged and ponged inside my body.

"We are worried about the other kids you will meet," Magnum said. "They won't understand—"

Blake interrupted her dad. "I won't show them."

"I know, Bumble."

It was a sight—two grown men, arms around a small bite of a kid, comforting her, knowing they would hurt her by taking her away from her mother—as Cinder, Valerie, and I watched from above. Three totally different women with opposite wants, needs, and wishes. Yet here we stood, frozen in time, unable to move from the scene in front of us.

"We will talk later because today is our turn to celebrate Christmas, and we want to share the holiday. But we want you to come see Rubia, where we live, and there are other kids like you."

Blake nodded. "And Mom? She's coming too?"

Magnum shot Valerie a look, and she pursed her mouth.

"Of course," Magnum lied, or said full of wishful thinking... I wasn't sure because he hadn't mentioned Valerie coming back to Rubia again.

"That's forbidden," Cinder whispered, and Magnum shook his head. She quieted too.

Silently, I wondered how Magnum was such a force over all these women, but I didn't have time to dwell.

"How about we let Magnum have the rest of the day with Blake?" Donovan stood and declared, taking my hand and nodding his chin toward Cinder.

"What about—"

Donovan cut Cinder off. "We'll all come back tomorrow."

Magnum leaned in and whispered something to Donovan, who was now standing and holding Blake's hand.

"Thank you," I said to Valerie, thinking it was the polite offering. She dismissed me with a wave. Not wanting another fight to break out, I started toward the door. "Come on, Cin." She side-eyed me and then started moving, a sinister look on her face. Cinder wasn't going to forget this when it came to Donovan, and she wasn't going to wait long for the transfer.

"I will see you tomorrow," Donovan told Valerie and followed us out.

"What the fuck, Don?" Cinder stomped toward him as he neared the car.

"Get in, Cin. I'm doing what I can. If you want any hope of taking Blake with us and doing the transfer—since both go hand in hand—we have to calm Valerie and keep her here."

"You should have done it now, but you're being all soft with Tuvy and a hard-ass to me."

He ignored her.

We all got inside the sports car and Donovan flicked on the engine.

"It's not me who messed up. It was your brother. *Is* your brother," Cinder continued to rant.

I watched Donovan's profile, and he was gritting his jaw. As he put the car in drive, he spoke. "You're not going to like what I have to say so I'm going to lead with it. Magnum is spending the night there with Blake."

"What?" Cinder screeched from the back seat.

I now understood why Donovan had waited until he was driving to speak. If she could, she'd run back inside the house and drag Magnum out. I could sense every one of her painful emotions in my nerve endings. I was so hot, it felt as though I'd spiked a fever.

Donovan took a quick moment to run a hand through his hair. My own fingers itched to comfort him in some way. I didn't know when this change inside me happened, but it had. Another habit, or feeling, or I didn't know what to call it, that I had to squash. Quickly.

"We are going to stay with you, and then tomorrow, return and do the transfer. Then, we need to speak to the Minister about Blake and bringing her back."

"Fuck off, Don. Just take the kid. I will raise her. She's clearly adorable and smart and has stolen the hearts of everyone. She loves Mag and she will love me. Ceci will be sure of it."

"It's not that simple," I'd started to say when Donovan interrupted.

"This is a child, and while she's clearly way more attached to my brother than I ever understood, we can't just take her."

I risked a quick glance at Cinder, who was sitting with her arms across her chest like a forlorn child, and I reminded myself she didn't deserve any of this either. She hadn't known that the man she loved was having a torrid affair in the States and had a child he was deeply invested in. All this being said, she didn't get to just rip the aforementioned child from her mother's arms.

"I'm in charge," Donovan said authoritatively but not forcefully. "This is the plan. Dinner, go to bed, transfer, call the Minister, and proceed."

It bruised me somewhere deep that Donovan wasn't advocating to skip the transfer, yet I sat in the car, wondering if the *go to bed* part in his list included us together… I wanted that more than I cared to admit. Although, my wishing for a forever with Donovan was something I would never own up to.

CHAPTER
EIGHTEEN

Donovan

Hitting mute on the phone, I let a growl escape my chest. My mom was on a bender, and it wasn't a particularly good one. Were they ever positive? It didn't matter in this moment, because dear Mommy wanted all of this done yesterday and wasn't particularly pleased about Magnum staying at Valerie's. She'd heard about the arrangement from Cinder, who had quickly locked herself in her hotel room, saying she'd be out in the morning, and called her soon-to-be mother-in-law.

Which led to now, and my being stuck on the phone with an extremely angry and hostile Ceci.

Still on mute, I roared again, silently reminding myself about my Hawaii plan. It couldn't come soon enough. The second I restored order to my family where Rubia was concerned, I'd be on my way to Hawaii. I needed to put distance between myself and the entire lot of Rubians and their rules.

Except it might be nice to harbor one to keep me warm, sleep by my side, challenge me…but it wasn't possible.

Back to reality, my mother was still yakking away on the phone—Blake would come to Rubia, Valerie would stay in Florida, Magnum must obey, and Tuvy would damn well perform. It was a long list of *woulds and musts*, not a *could* or *maybe think about* muttered. My mom and Ezza operated in a world of what everyone was expected to do, and there was no consideration for anyone else's feelings.

As I was about to hit unmute and let my mother know I was handling it all, there was a soft knock on the door.

Swinging my door open, Tulya stood in front of me, a tumbler of scotch in one hand and a tender smile on her face. *You okay?* She mouthed the question, not knowing the call was on mute.

I nodded and waved her to come in, although I had better ideas for when it came to my bedroom and Tulya.

She handed me the tumbler, and I said, "God bless you, mute," pointing to the phone. With a wink and a slug of the scotch, I hit a button and went back to my call. "Mom, listen, I got this. It's all going to be resolved. I know Cinder is mad, but in order to make this all happen, I had to make sure both Valerie and Blake stay put. Valerie is slippery, and the only way to keep her nearby is Magnum."

My mom continued to drone on. "Why wouldn't you just do it all today?"

Grateful the phone wasn't on speaker, since Tulya had lain back on the chaise, my mind went to a better place—Tulya and myself, no clothes, sheets.

Despite the phone being near my ear, I hit the lower volume button; no need for Tulya to hear my mother talk down to me. I swallowed my pride and answered my mother.

"Because—because Blake is just a kid, Mom. And she's unique and special, and we need to take our time when it comes to her." For a quick second, my heart ached over leaving Blake for Hawaii. I shooed away the feeling. It was absurd. I'd only just met her, and beyond her being my brother's daughter, we didn't have a bond.

"Well, get it done tomorrow and hurry back. The sooner we have this situated, the sooner we can deal with your engagement. Again, I can't understand why you allowed your brother to get engaged first, but I bet you're rethinking it now. You're the head of the family and will stay in a prominent position."

"Enough about me."

I had to end this discussion. There was no way I could sit on the phone any longer and discuss Emelee, who my mother wanted me to marry, with Tulya close by. It was the first time I'd thought about her by name since the holiday party. I didn't know why, but now when Emelee entered my mind, I despised her even more than before. Until a week ago, she was nothing more than a hinderance of my mother's. She was only a *she*, not a real person named Emelee. Now, she was a rival of Tulya's…sort of, and I hated that. For Tulya or me, I wasn't sure.

"I'll get this all done. I have it under control," I said before disconnecting the call. Looking up I caught sight of the most beautiful woman I'd ever known, staring at me with raw need in her eyes. It should have made me feel dishonorable, but when it came to Tulya, every rule I knew dissolved.

"I'm sorry it's all come to this," she said from the chaise, her voice gravelly with emotion.

"You have nothing to be sorry for." I ran my hand through my hair, spending a slow beat marveling at the exquisiteness in front of me. "Where is your drink?" I finally asked, sick of all the *sorry*s and *we can't*s and family aggravation. For one more night, I wanted easy—

Who the hell was I kidding? I wanted this each and every evening of my life.

"Oh, I left it out there on the end table," she said, starting to sit up, her hair cascading around her face.

"Sit," I instructed and went to fetch her wineglass, refilling it and refreshing my scotch before returning to sit by her feet on the edge of the chaise. "Cheers." I handed her the wine, and her pointer finger reached out to touch my thumb. It was a tiny gesture, but one meant to say *it's all going to be okay.*

"If it makes you feel any better, I heard from Caro, who wanted to check on me. She was worried because I hadn't even called or messaged during the few days of Christmas, but you know what happened then. Anyway, she said my mom is in a tizzy too that this isn't getting done faster."

I took another gulp of scotch, allowing the burn to hit my belly, and then I reached out, taking Tulya's empty hand. "You're so beautiful," I blurted out, my pulse beating *Fuck the rules*.

"Don," she whispered.

"I love when you shorten my name," I admitted like a teenaged, lovesick fool. She squeezed my fingers. "I'm sorry Caro was worried, but also I'm not. It was the best Christmas of my life," I said with some kind of hazy word vomit.

"Caro covered for me, which is slightly surprising, but she said I texted her to tell everyone Merry Christmas. She also reported that Bruno is misbehaving. Apparently he saw Prim on Christmas Day. *Lordy*, he's going to get me in more hot water."

I noticed her face was clean of any makeup and took in the loose white sweatshirt hanging off her shoulder, clocking the absence of a bra strap. I wanted to start licking her right there at the tip of her clavicle and not stop until I hit home.

"I am tired of all the nonsense," she whispered. "Our families, the drama, and the tasks ahead. I want to forget."

She leaned forward, setting her now empty wineglass next to her, and allowed her lips to hover in front of me. I wanted nothing more than to take her lips—fuck it, her whole body—with mine.

"Time stops when I'm with you," she whispered.

My palm slid around the back of her neck, and I held her gaze steady with mine. "Every minute with you is stolen. I've never wanted to be a criminal more, thieving my way through life if it means more of you, Tulya."

She swallowed and I watched as a montage of emotions flashed across her face. Hurt, caring, fear, adoration—they were all there.

I wanted to pocket each one and hold on to them as a keepsake—the many facets of Tulya.

"I want one more night," I told her. It was selfish and brash, but her eyes told me all I needed to know. Her desire for me was just the same.

"If I can't have all the nights, I will settle for one more." That was all she said before sealing her lips to mine.

I allowed my empty tumbler to hit the soft carpet before scooping Tulya in my arms and carrying her to the bed. My palm found her bare shoulder, then my tongue replaced my hand, my earlier fantasy coming true.

Leisurely taking my time, I explored every single fiber of her body, using all my senses. I watched her breath rise and fall in her chest as my hand grazed small goose bumps pebbling along her skin. I yearned to record the soft moans coming from her so I could listen to them forever. Finally, I inhaled her desire before tasting every ounce of her need. It was a decadent exploration, one I didn't want to end.

After I took my time drawing every last climax from her body, I softly dragged my length from her, and for a short moment I had my fill. We wound ourselves around one another, narrowing all gaps of space—emotional and physical—between us. It was only when we'd exhausted ourselves that we fell asleep in each other's arms for the final time. Never had I ever wanted a night to not end...

CHAPTER
NINETEEN

Tulya

C inder appeared in the common area as I was pouring my coffee. I was still wearing a robe. She was dressed and ready to go.

Luckily, I'd woken early, having to pee, and extracted myself from Donovan's room, so I'd entered from my bedroom. There was no point in starting any rumors back home, and I didn't trust Cinder with any proprietary information. Certainly not in the agitated state she was in, which was becoming more evident by the minute.

"Are you getting ready? We have to go." She stood still, waiting for an answer. Then she began tapping her foot—I was on the clock. Playtime was over where Cinder was concerned.

"I will be" was all I gave her.

I was used to my mother bossing me around, but not a contemporary. I'd meant it last night when I said I was growing tired of the drama and the stress.

"Let's go, Tuvy. My entire life is basically hanging on you getting your shit together."

I nodded, taking my coffee and hurrying back to my bedroom where I guzzled the caffeine and slipped into a quick, hot shower, washing off any evidence of my evening.

With light makeup applied and a green maxi dress draping over my deliciously used body, I slipped into wedge sandals and made my way back out—to my destiny.

Donovan stepped out of his suite wearing a suit, business as usual, his phone tucked into his neck, head nodding and murmuring, "Yes." I assumed it was my mother or his, and pointed toward the door where Cinder was standing, back to tapping her foot. She rolled a finger in the air, signaling she was getting impatient, and Donovan said, "I have to go. It will all get resolved." He disconnected the call. "Let's roll."

I noted he didn't make eye contact with me or Cinder. It hurt, but I understood the predicament he was in. Ultimately, we served the Minister and our families, our needs coming last.

As we rode down in the elevator in silence, heat licked at the nape of my neck so furiously I had to run my palm over it. I suspected it was not only Cinder's unsettledness but strangely, Donovan's suffering.

Maybe it was wishful thinking, but was he aching over not being able to be with me?

Rushing out of the elevator, Cinder spoke the first words any of us had said since leaving the room. "Come on. I checked, and Mag is still there. I looked at his tracking."

I couldn't help but feel sorry for her; she was feeling some sort of way over a guy who clearly didn't share her affection.

"Cinder, when we get to the house, I need you to settle down. First, I have to tackle arrangements for Blake," Donovan said while we waited for the car.

Whining, Cinder sulked and muttered, "Why are my feelings the last anyone is concerned with?"

Turning away and looking back toward the hotel, I had to resist the urge to roll my eyes or smack Cinder. This was a first; I'd never felt so agitated before. Chalking it up to nerves over the transfer, which coincidentally I'd never attempted either, I slid into the car. Donovan holding open the front passenger door for me, allowing Cinder to situate herself in the back seat, was a tiny bit of solace.

Third time was a charm, and Donovan didn't need GPS to head toward Valerie's. I watched his profile focused on the road, his jaw clenched in business mode, and resisted the urge to reach out and touch him. The need to soothe this man was creating a swell in my belly.

Poor Donovan hadn't even shifted into park at Valerie's, and Cinder was out of the car, two feet barely on the ground, on her way to Magnum.

She was still waiting at the door when I walked up behind her, watching it swing open and Blake appearing.

"Hi, Tuvy," the tiny child said, smiling, ignoring Cinder.

"Hi, Blake. Good morning." I greeted her with a warm grin. She was an innocent party in all this.

"Hi…Blake." Cinder copied me, pausing between words, unsure of what to do.

All Blake said was a dull, "Hi," then "Uncle Donny," I heard her shriek next. She leapt into his arms. "I'm sorry I got upset of the coat. Daddy told me about Rubia and how I would visit and stay at the big house where you live."

Despite having an IUD, my ovaries prepared to make a baby at the sight of Donovan smoothing back Blake's soft hair and saying, "That's right," his voice tender with emotion.

I wished I could tell if it was because he was getting his way, or at the idea he wouldn't be at the big house, as Blake called it.

"Come on, let's go inside," Donovan finally suggested, setting Blake down and waiting for all the women to walk in first.

"Don." Magnum rounded the corner and greeted his brother as Blake ran to the back of the house, shouting for her mom.

"You have things handled?" Donovan eyed Magnum, who was wearing the same clothes as yesterday, mug in hand.

"I broached a visit. Let's call it that, okay? Don't make it so severe—"

"Mag," Donovan growled. "She is not coming back here," he whispered with enough sense that Blake might reappear.

"To live. She's not coming back here to live," Magnum countered. "But she can visit back and forth. *It's her mom.* That's all I can negotiate for." Magnum pursed his lips and shook his head, ending the subject as Valerie appeared.

"Hello, again," she grumbled, wearing a silk robe and padding around barefoot.

I was sure this was all for effect, but it was absurd nonetheless. They shared a child; this wasn't some sultry honeymoon. Yet, on cue, I felt Cinder's heartache multiply, my underarms beading with sweat.

"We have agreed to a visit, and that's it," Valerie said. "Don't try to talk me into anything more, Donovan." She held her hand on her hip and stared him down in a way I'd never seen anyone do. He opened his mouth to speak and she interrupted him, dropping a dagger. "She can meet your mother, but I'll go along. No way my daughter is going anywhere without me."

"You can't," was all Donovan responded while Cinder shouted, "No!"

"You can be sure I will not let Blake out of my sight," Valerie screamed back. "And you can shut up," she directed toward Cinder.

Blake went and held on to Magnum's leg, and Donovan's arm came out and went still in front of me, protecting me from I didn't know what as Cinder ran to Magnum's free arm, clinging to him like a monkey. It was sheer chaos, like every other visit to this house—I wasn't sure why I'd expected anything different.

Holding a fresh cup of hot coffee, the steam rising above it, Magnum cleared his throat. I did a quick look around the room, noting Valerie was holding a matching mug. She must have filled them for the pair. It felt so natural and commonplace, but I wasn't about to mention that.

Donovan turned to face his brother, who lifted Blake up in his now free arm, gently shaking Cinder to his side. If one thing was for sure, Magnum's daughter came first. The scene felt as if it was out of a holiday movie, except sweat was now pooling at the base of my neck. Cinder's emotions were climbing through the roof, and personally, I wasn't sure how much longer I could absorb them.

"I want to cut to the chase," Valerie said. "I've already stated that I will be accompanying Blake to meet your family. Magnum agrees, and so it's final."

My gaze went to Cinder, who was balling her fists.

Donovan walked over to his brother and said softly, "Blake, where is your grandma? Why don't you go color with her so the adults can talk?" I didn't know where this softer side of his came from, but it did things to me...

"No!" It was the first time I'd heard Blake object to anything. "I want to go to Rubia. And Mom is coming too, like Daddy promised."

Cinder hissed. Clearly, it had been a big ole kumbaya family situation last night with Valerie, Mag, and Blake. Swallowing all the emotions clogged in my throat, I knew it was time.

"My daughter has spoken, and she wants me," Valerie said while looking at Cinder, who had started to cry while her cheeks were beet red with anger.

Donovan whipped his head in my direction and nodded. This wasn't going to improve; there was only room to decline, and there wasn't far to go...

He mouthed *Now* and my fate was sealed. At some point between arriving here and now, the priority had quietly shifted to getting Blake back to Rubia. Of course, Magnum was still promised to Cinder and mending that was also a main task at hand, but it felt like Donovan had succumbed to Valerie being involved in some way.

It was my moment to help; to attempt the transfer and see if I could alleviate some of the tensions by doing so.

With my feet still planted, Donovan came close, whispering in my ear, "Maybe if she feels something other than lust toward my brother, she will reconsider her stance."

I felt Cinder's gaze on me. *Do it* she now mouthed. With Magnum still holding Blake, Valerie watched us, creeping close to Mag's side. He allowed her to hold on to him, but he knew he couldn't stop what was about to happen. He could only defy his mother so much—

"When you're done, she won't want him, and he will only have eyes for me," Cinder whispered to me while I was still next to her side.

Abstaining from rolling my eyes, I placed my hand on her shoulder, running it up her neck and behind her hair, noting Magnum kissing Valerie on the temple and walking out of the room with Blake. Valerie tried to follow but stopped short with a death glare aimed at Donovan. I suspected he'd sent a shock to stop her in her tracks—a true no-no.

I didn't have time to ponder much more because Cinder's agony was free-flowing into me, and a damp sheen of sweat began to cover my skin, eventually turning to a full-on perspire. I closed my eyes and felt the pain coursing through me. Normally I allowed it to drift right out of me. I'd never done an exchange before, but I'd given it a lot of thought and decided it was better to "store" the emotions in my own body rather than hold on to the two women at the same time, providing a conduit for one to pour into the another. I had my reasons for the plan, and they became clearer the more I took in from Cinder. Wave after wave of anger, deceit, and suffering traveled from Cinder into me. I let it fill every vein, artery, and my heart, willing myself to stay the course. There were more emotions than I'd ever experienced—if I'd opted to share them in some sort of rolling from one body to another situation, I wasn't sure Valerie would have survived. She was only a mom fighting for her daughter. I owed her this much.

I kept on at my task…and while I never wished to do this again, I knew my mother would have me take notes on how it was done for future generations. Deep in my soul, I hoped it wouldn't be my daughter or son who would inherit this ability. Shaking my head for a beat, I almost laughed. My daughter or son with who? I was not destined for falling in love and family life—

Finally, I sensed Cinder's feelings bottoming out and I let go of her neck. As I'd prepared in my mind, I silently told myself to keep everything inside for a few minutes. Typically, I let the anguish dissipate as it went into my body, filling the air around me with warm atoms, but not today. This was a new sensation entirely.

Putting one foot in front of the other, I found Valerie standing stock-still.

"He has me pinned. Every time I even wiggle, he sends a zap," she said to me, looking for pity, and I felt that in my core.

Donovan was using his power on a human; I told myself it was to help me. He wouldn't do this otherwise. I wasn't even sure he wanted to now.

On another day, under different circumstances, I might have given in to her, but not now. My own system was being overloaded. And my mother was waiting.

"I despise you," she said to Donovan. "And you," she spit out toward Cinder. "As for you, it's quadruple whatever the hate I have for them."

I deserved that much; I nodded in agreement at the sentiment. I didn't blame Valerie for her words as I lifted my hand to her forearm. Her bare skin peeked out of the robe, and I touched it with my own clammy hand.

Release, I whispered in my own mind, and the floodgates opened. I pulled the imaginary doors back a little, permitting Cinder's thoughts and feelings to drip one by one into Valerie, and my body began to feel lighter.

Actually, weaker. As the transfer began to pick up speed, my body seemingly couldn't distinguish between in and out, so it took in Donovan's zaps for Valerie as it let out the bad emotions. I began to feel cold. Not the kind of shiver I got from being near Don, but closer to ice filling my bloodstream. Goose bumps broke out everywhere and I felt limp.

The last thing I remembered was seeing Valerie's face contorting in suffering, and I prayed for her bout to be short. Then my world went dark.

CHAPTER
TWENTY

Donovan

"Fuck!" I didn't care that Mag was hot on my heels with his daughter—the scene unfolding before me left me speechless for anything other than profanity.

"Oh, shit," Magnum said, catching a glimpse of what happened before snatching Blake and folding her face into his shoulder and carrying her out of the room.

"Cinder, what the fuck is going on?" I turned and glared at my brother's fiancée, wondering why she was walking around smiling while Tulya was passed out on the floor. "Wipe that slimy grin off your face," I scolded her. "You got what you wanted. Are you happy?"

I couldn't stop the venom from pouring out of me.

"What did you do?" I directed my fury at the two women who'd been in the room—as if they had a clue. One was a full-fledged human and the other a Rubian nightmare.

"We don't know. You were here too. You saw it happen," Valerie stated from the chair she'd slumped into, rubbing her chest above her heart. "I can't help her or anyone now," was all she said, breaking out into tears. "My whole body hurts. All I feel is heartache and vile thoughts." She seemed to be shaking her head to get the thoughts out.

I fell to the floor, unable to be pleased over the transfer working. Why? Because Tulya was out cold. Her chest was still rising and falling but she was completely unconscious. My lips yearned to run over her cheek, but I wasn't that far gone.

"It was too much," I whispered to myself, leaning over Tulya, choosing to caress her cheek with my palm. "Tulya, wake up!" I gave her a small slap on the face.

I was a man with feelings, who couldn't show them, and the object of all my desires was lying there motionless.

"Tulya," I said with more authority, crouched over her limp body.

"Don." I felt a hand on my back. "Come on, let's move her."

Standing, I met Magnum's face, shaking my head. "If I wasn't so concerned, I'd lay into you. But we have one motionless Rubian and another woman sing-songing about getting her man back. Not to mention a human in despair and an innocent *child* with *powers*." I tried to whisper, but the last part came out in a yell; I couldn't care.

"The child is in the other room," my brother said sternly.

"I'll go to the child, my daughter." Valerie stood and said to Magnum, "You can deal with her." She knocked her head toward the floor where Tulya still lay. "She got what she deserved, if you ask me. Not that it was her fault. That one over there pushed for it." This time her gaze cut to Cinder.

"If it was anyone's mistake, it was mine. I went along with this whole plan like the lemming my mother wants me to be." I gritted my teeth at no one, furious at everyone. "Magnum, help me lift Tulya and take her to the car. Cinder, get the door. Hope you are all happy now." I spoke in clipped phrases, each word coming out gruffer than the one before

Magnum bent and slid his hand under Tulya's back. "She's breathing," he commented.

"No shit, asshole. If she wasn't, I would've called 911."

"We can't do that, and you damn well know it."

He had the nerve to question my Rubian knowledge. Him…Magnum, the breaker of every rule. But he wasn't wrong. We didn't see human doctors. For the most part, they wouldn't notice the small synapses that were at the root of our abilities, but we just didn't do it—

"You let your daughter be born and raised right out in the open, tough guy," I slammed back.

He pursed his lips.

We stood there, staring one another down. "Get your hand out from her, I'll lift her myself."

I lowered into a squat and slid an arm under Tulya and grasped her gently into my chest before standing and running my lips across her forehead.

Magnum raised an eyebrow and I shook my head. "Don't go there," was all I said.

"Mom seems to have traded one headache for another," he had further nerve to say.

I walked out of the house, Cinder standing and holding the door, and never looked back at my brother who dared to challenge me when all this was his fault.

"Open the car door too," I called to Cinder, who was flopping around light as a feather. This entire scene gave new meaning to the burden Tulya carried.

I slid the limp woman across the back seat, telling myself that as long as she was breathing, she would be okay. I wasn't sure what to call the state she was in—comalike or maybe a trance?

All I knew was the Minister or fucking Ezza was going to answer to me. Someone had to have known this might happen, and they still forced Tulya to do it.

I drove back to the hotel, one eye on the road and the other on the rearview mirror. In the back, Tulya was…resting? Sleeping? In a coma?

I had no fucking clue.

A few times, Tulya moaned, and it gave me some sort of hope she'd be okay.

Carrying her into the hotel, I ignored all side looks and went straight to the elevator bank. My phone buzzed in my pocket and sweat soaked through my dress shirt—both of which I also disregarded.

It took some careful finessing, but I made it into the room without dropping Tulya, delicately laying her on the sofa.

"Tulya," I managed to whisper.

Nothing—

"Sweet Tulya," I said, trying again to wake her, running my palm along her forehead.

Silence—

My phone started buzzing again as I slid down to the floor, my ass hitting the carpet with a thud.

I answered, seeing who it was. "Ezza." Her name tasted like poison on my tongue and rang venomous through the line.

"I understand the transfer worked."

That was what she led with. My blood boiled over in my veins. "Seriously? You don't want to know about your daughter?" I couldn't help myself. I was sick of Rubian rules and formality.

"I have our medic here. After we finish speaking, he will ask you some questions regarding Tuvy and help you get her settled."

Sweat dampened the collar of my shirt. "After? Settled? Ezza, your daughter is unconscious."

"You know how this works, *dear Donovan.* Serve Rubia first. The Minister is awaiting a full report, including information regarding Cinder returning happily with the child in tow. I can't be worried about the pain left in her wake."

I stood and padded toward the balcony, never more unsure in my life. Should I bitch Ezza out? Or take Tulya for help? Both choices went against what I'd been taught yet were equally warranted.

"What about your daughter?" I repeated my earlier question through gritted teeth, choosing what was behind Door A.

"She will be fine. She's never been pushed to the limit. Basically a cream puff, that one. Spinning her stories, helping me only when I request. Never testing her powers. A lucky lass, the pain has seeped out of her veins up to this point. Now, she asked it to really work for her. Frankly, I should have demanded more from her."

"I hardly think this is the time to diminish Tulya's work or contributions to Rubia." I defended the woman lying listless inside the hotel room. With the ocean lapping in the background, I told myself to get my shit together or my mother and Ezza would get their pitchforks out for me.

"Exactly. Now tell me, do you plan to go back and get your brother and the kid? Now is the time with the birth mother being down and out—"

If I'd exposed any of my feelings for Tulya, Ezza wasn't picking up on it. She was wholly focused on her own mission. "Do I need to? Wouldn't it be best for them to just leave? Valerie can be dramatic, and she was on one about her coming to Rubia with the kid. Whose name is Blake, by the way."

"You need to make sure everything runs smoothly. I've sent the jet."

"Wait, why are you doing all this? Where is my mother?" All of a sudden this was taking a darker turn. I'd been in a haze over Tulya's spell and hadn't thought this through clearly.

"I'm in charge. Your mom is indisposed."

"What?" My voice was rising at an alarming rate. Any minute, I was going to get tossed out of the hotel. "Indisposed?"

Ezza cleared her throat. "Your mom didn't handle your brother spending the night with the woman. Cinder really let her have it, and the Minister and I had to take over. We are making sure this is all resolved, and your mom is resting."

"Serves her right," I mumbled.

"What did you just say?" Ezza took a sinister tone with me, but I wasn't Tulya.

"I said it serves her right. If there is one thing I've learned on this adventure, it's that you—the proverbial you—are way too controlling when it comes to us, all of us adult kids."

"Listen, Donovan, it's not your place to decide how things work in Rubia, so stick to what you're good at. And before that, make sure your brother gets on the jet with *Blake* and Cinder, and not the human woman."

She disconnected the call without asking after Tulya or connecting me with the medic, but at least she called Blake by her name rather than *the kid*. As for Valerie, she would always be *the woman*.

Stealing a glance at Tulya, who was still out, I stepped inside the room and checked that her breathing was still steady. I didn't know what to call this other than a deep slumber. It wasn't a coma or anything natural for the body to do—it was a Rubian reaction to way too much pressure. The latter I was sure of, and I needed the damn medic to tell me what to do.

Snatching my phone out of my pocket, I went back on the balcony and texted Magnum.

Be there in an hour. Taking you, Blake, and Cinder to jet. Be ready.

I didn't have the time or focus to write more. In fact, I stuck him on Do Not Disturb and set about calling the medic myself. We didn't have doctors in Rubia because we couldn't attend medical school, but we had a large supply of medics who'd studied as much as an MD. They ran our small hospital and were responsible for all of the Rubian population.

I assumed Ezza meant the chief medic; she wouldn't associate with anyone else. I just happened to have Abraham's number from when he cared for my father.

Pushing the call button, I waited for him to pick up.

He greeted me as if he'd been briefed on the scenario. "Donovan, how are you? I was expecting to hear from you."

"Cut the formalities, Abraham. Ezza was supposed to put you on a call. I have Tulya here, completely out of it...in some sort of deep slumber. If I'm being blunt, I'm not happy or comfortable with this." It was as honest as I could be in this very moment.

"Her system shut down," he said bluntly.

"So, this happens? You've seen it? Knew it? What the fuck?" The questions bubbled out of me.

Of course Ezza had to know this was a risk too.

"Yes, it's a chance we take when powers are overly tasked, especially when it comes to interacting with humans."

"What the hell?" I paced the patio and peered in the window, and there Tulya still lay, her hair fanned out around her, eyes closed. My heart ached a bit more with every glimpse. "Why would they ask her to do this, then?"

I asked the question without thinking.

"Some answers are above our pay grade," Abraham simply responded. "Also, if I'm not mistaken, she did this for your mother?"

I shook my head. My goddamn mother. I wanted to throttle her—I knew better—but what did she care who Magnum married?

"In short, Tulya's abilities require her body to absorb all the negative emotions of a Rubian. Something inside her acts like a siphon with a sort of vent to push it out of her body. It's why she gets so hot when the feelings start to infiltrate her body. That's my rudimentary explanation."

"But what went wrong?" Not that I didn't care about the process. In fact, I made a note to ask at a later date about my own capabilities. But I needed to know what to do.

"Well, you see, the heat is her body starting to work, pushing the emotions out. I don't know how much she has disclosed but she becomes extremely warm when inheriting the pain. Typically, her system disposes of the emotions, and that acts as a cooling agent. In this case, my guess is she held on to the pain until she could target the human and started to send her the suffering in short bursts, causing her body to overheat. She never cooled off, and she is in some sort of hypersleep."

"This has happened before? You're not even looking at her and know all this."

"Yes."

His one word was curt and final. He'd seen it, Ezza knew it, and he wasn't giving any more. "You need to come and help her. You should be on your way, for God's sake." It was all I had left in me.

"When your brother and his bride-to-be, along with his child, land in Rubia, I will come."

"What? You should be on the jet coming to pick them up." I was feeling twitchy from all of this.

"Minister's orders, especially since your mom had a spell. He is requiring lawfulness be restored."

"And what about his niece? Is he not worried about her?"

"Put a cool compress on her forehead. Apply some ice behind her neck and try to drip some water in her mouth. I'll see you soon. You'd better get your brother packed up." He had the nerve to disconnect.

It had been a day of people leaving me hanging on their orders.

CHAPTER
TWENTY-ONE

Donovan

"I'm not helping you talk your way out of this, brother. You're on your own" was all I said to Magnum as I unloaded the trunk of the car. We were standing side by side on the airstrip, and I couldn't even look at him.

"This is the way it has to be" was all he answered, his lips pursed. "My family is on the plane, and I'm going home."

By family, he meant Valerie and Blake. Not Cinder, who was also on the plane, fuming mad again.

He grabbed his thigh, and I still refused to meet his gaze. "You sent pain my way? Really? Using your powers to do what, get me to change my mind?"

"Tulya is spent, and who knows when she will wake up. Our mother is in some sort of state, so much so that the Minister is intervening. And Ezza is breathing down my neck. No one can help you now."

"When will you stop following every rule? When you realize you feel something for Tuvy and don't want to marry who Mom has set aside for you? Is that when? These Rubian customs are old, and I'm not. Blake cannot be separated from her mother."

I finally turned to face my brother, my eyes tiny slits. "I don't feel a thing for Tulya other than understanding how used up she must feel. I'm in the same position, except I'm not lying anywhere lifeless."

"It's time you took control of your own life, bro, and stop harping on me."

"Whatever. Go and do your damage. I have to go tend to Tulya, possibly indefinitely. Since you're returning with Valerie, the medic may not come."

I'd explained this to him, but he'd refused to bend. He wasn't allowing Blake out of his eyesight, which was the only thing I agreed with him on. Valerie was a wild card, which was why he was a fool to bring her back to Rubia. Cinder had traded her pain for anger, and she was bleeding rage. There was no talking with her. All of this left me helpless in pleasing Ezza and my mother, and securing help for Tulya. But Magnum couldn't care less. He was totally focused on his human love.

My phone buzzed and dinged my whole drive back to the hotel, and I ignored each and every sound.

Stopping at the front desk, I asked for several buckets of ice, sparkling and still water, and a fresh bottle of scotch to be delivered to the room. I cursed myself all the way upstairs for leaving Tulya, but I had no idea who would have stayed with her otherwise.

Rushing through the door, I clocked her lying still on the sofa. I made quick work of checking on her chest, confirming she was breathing. A light sheen of sweat had broken out on her forehead, and I took it as a good sign. Maybe it meant she was fighting back against whatever was attacking her—

Without time to dwell, I got out of my suit and shoved on jogging pants and a T-shirt in time for the doorbell to ring. I snatched the tray from the room service attendant, handing him a fifty and scooting him away.

"Tulya, I'm here," I whispered, taking one of the cloth napkins and filling it with ice, and tying a knot. Bending over, I softly lifted her head up, my hand at the nape of her neck, and placed it underneath.

Jetting off to the bathroom, I ran a washcloth under cool water and returned to spread it over Tulya's forehead. Then I poured myself a scotch, switched my phone off, and sat down on the floor next to the sofa. This was how I spent the night, alternating between refreshing the cold cloth and the ice, running ice cubes over Tulya's perfect lips, and downing scotch while sitting on the carpet.

Surrendering to the exhaustion, I must've dozed off at some time in the middle of the night, and as I drifted back to reality, the sun starting to come up, I heard rustling on the couch. Quickly getting up, I sank back to my knees and stared at Tulya, her eyes half open, staring at me.

"My sweet Tulya," I murmured, my hand finding her clammy cheek. I was stuck in time, unable to move, watching the weak woman in front of me blink her eyes.

She ran her tongue over her lips and I realized she must be thirsty. Jumping up, I poured her a water and brought it back.

"Here, I'll hold it," I said, helping with my free hand to partially sit her up, lifting the glass to her mouth.

She took a tiny sip and then lay back. Waving her hand in front of her face, she shook her head and then motioned with her finger for me to move. I skidded a few paces back when she leaned over the couch and threw up on the carpet. With a tear rolling down her cheek, she squeezed her eyes shut and whispered, "My Lord."

"Shh," I said, coming to her midsection and guiding her to sit. "Let me run a bath?" It came out as a question, while Tulya started to scratch her neck.

"Did it work?" she managed to croak out, her nails doing a number on her soft skin.

I placed my palm over her fingers, stilling them, and nodded. "You seemed to slip into a deep sleep. I'm not really sure what to call it," I explained as best I could.

"But did it work?" she asked again.

I nodded.

"Is Valerie okay?"

I found it interesting she asked about Valerie before Cinder, but judging by the way Cinder was acting, I couldn't blame her. "Yes, she's fine. At first, she felt hurt. But she is all right."

Despite my trying to stop her, she began to scratch herself again, dragging her hand to her arm, her red hair wild around her face. I wondered how I could help—more than I already was.

"I don't feel well" was all she said before lying back down, her hand furiously going at her forearm.

My gaze moved there, and I noticed red hives or welts beginning to litter her skin. A quick check of her neck showed the same red bumps. My hand moved to her forehead, but she showed no sign of a fever. "I think you're having a reaction."

Her eyes moved to her arm where she caught sight of what was happening, and she began to cry in earnest. "What is wrong with me? Did you call my mother?"

I didn't have the heart or the fortitude to share the truth.

"She didn't care, did she?" Her voice, already weak, was barely a murmur. "Call Caro, please. She and I don't always see the same way, but she will get help."

My phone was somewhere on the dining table, but I didn't want to get up. My head was pinging between Tulya and the large piece of mahogany.

"Go, get your phone," she grumbled, picking up what was happening. "Please, call Caro."

I nodded and stood up, noting I'd turned my phone all the way off. As soon as it came to life, it began humming and buzzing with notifications.

My mom, Ezza, Magnum, my mom again. None of them mattered in this moment.

"I don't have her contact info," I said to Tulya, who was now covered in hives anywhere her skin was visible.

She rattled off some numbers—I had no clue how she did this—and then closed her eyes.

Caro picked up the call. "Hello?"

"Caro, this is Donovan Malachite. I'm here with your sister—"

"Oh, thank God, I've been calling her over and over. Is she okay? The jet is back…without you two…and… Never mind. What is going on? Mother is on a bender and your mom is staying in one of our guest rooms, Donovan, and no one will tell me what is happening. We have our differences—Tuvy is quiet and I'm not—but we are still close."

"Caro." I said her name, trying to interrupt her monologue or therapy session or whatever was happening on the other end of the line. "Your sister is here, still in the States. She's not doing well. The transfer of emotions took a physical toll on her, and she is asking to speak with you."

That was all I said before handing the phone to Tulya, who was lying on the sofa, covered in head-to-toe red splotches, eyes damp and missing her usual fiery smile. She took the phone, sliding it to her ear, exposing a welt the size of a grapefruit on her elbow.

"Car—yes, I'm still here. No, I don't know, I passed out or maybe was in some sort of coma, I'm not sure. I don't even know how I got back here." She was talking to her sister but looking at me.

With my thumb, I pointed to myself. She rewarded me with a nod and a smallish smile.

"I've been at the hotel. Donovan didn't leave. What?"

I imagined Caro rapid firing questions and information on the other side of the call, Tulya trying to keep up.

"Magnum is there with Valerie?" This time Tulya sat up, keeping her eyes locked with mine.

It was my turn to nod, but I didn't smile.

"And Cinder? What is going on? Does Mother even care about me? I'm breaking out in some sort of rash. Car, can you get the medic?"

I didn't even want to witness this part of the call, knowing he probably wasn't on his way to see Tulya. Swallowing the many regrets I harbored—after all, I'd witnessed Magnum doing exactly what they told me not to permit—I excused myself to use the bathroom.

Not following their orders? They would make sure I regretted it, I was certain.

CHAPTER
TWENTY-TWO

Tulya

My throat was as dry and barren as the desert, and my skin felt as if bedbugs had lodged in there permanently—I wanted to claw it off. I should drink, but I couldn't stand the thought. My stomach hurt, but I couldn't tell if that was because I had to pee or I was hungry, or it was part of the overall sickness I was experiencing. My dress stuck to my legs, and I rubbed my thighs together, using it to scratch the welts I assumed were there. I was a writhing mess on the couch and not for a good reason.

Clearly, Donovan had stayed to care for me. I wondered at what expense as he made his way out of the room, leaving me on the phone with Caro. He looked like he hadn't showered, shaved, or eaten in a day or two, not to mention he smelled as if he took a deep dive into a bottle of scotch. Judging by the nearly empty bottle on the end table, he had.

"What? The medic won't come?" I couldn't fully grasp what Caro was saying.

"I told you, he was only allowed to come if Donovan fulfilled the task."

"We did the transfer." I argued with my sister as if she had any control. "We did the task. Blake is back in Rubia."

"With the human woman," Caro added.

"That's her daughter… I mean, not every mother is as heartless as ours. I need help," I finally screeched out. I was pretty certain I was going to throw up again, and I focused on the ceiling fan, watching it whir around, willing my stomach to keep it together.

"I know. But you know Ezza, and let's not forget the Minister. They play by the rule book, especially Mom. She so desperately wants to be the Minister."

"Can you talk to the medic? Ask him what to do?"

"He won't. I tried. He says this needs to run its course…as if they knew this was a risk."

"What the heck? Car—they knew? They sent me, thinking this might happen?"

Caro didn't have a chance to answer because I heard my mother in the background. *Is that your sister?* I envisioned her glaring at Caro.

"Mom, she's really not doing well." Caro defended me.

Give me the phone.

"Hello, Tulya. The medic says you'll be fine…eventually."

"What? When is eventually? Mother, I am covered in a rash—"

"Listen, it's imperative that Donovan returns and takes the human back. Every minute she is here on Rubia is sixty seconds closer to our demise."

I felt my head trying to shake. My mother was going to leave me to fend for myself. All she cared about was the plan she and Ceci had set.

"He's not in the room right now, but I will tell him." It was all I could say. The only thing I wanted to do was hang up with my mother.

"Be sure. The jet is ready, and we need to make haste."

"Okay." My response was weak and feeble, but between my body at war and acknowledging my own mother didn't care, neither did I.

"Does that feel okay?" Donovan called through the half-closed door. I'd had sex in several different positions with the man, fallen asleep naked in his arms, and here we were—shouting between the bedroom and bathroom because I was naked in the tub.

I was currently in a lukewarm bath with baking soda sprinkled in, per a text from Caro. She'd poked around the medic's office and stole a book off the shelves outlining what to do for shock-induced hives. We weren't sure if it would work, but at this point, what could I lose?

Donovan had spent about five minutes grumbling over Caro finding the information and no one warning me, while murmuring *what the fuck?* I wanted to know all the answers to these questions, especially *what the fuck.* My skin felt like it was molting off.

I'd started to sit up and Donovan took the hint and called down to the kitchen asking for baking soda ASAP and told me he'd run the bath. After a few minutes of his flying around, I'd managed to stand and start walking toward the bathroom.

It was only when I crossed the threshold to my room that I felt weak and started to buckle in my knees.

"Shit," I whispered before leaning into the wall. Of course Donovan, in his heightened state of anxiety, sensed my suffering and hurried out of the bathroom, lifting me. "This is absurd," I argued. "You're not carrying me. I can maybe crawl?"

"Shut up" was all he said and then the doorbell rang.

He set me on the bed and ran for the baking soda, threatening me not to dare move.

I was trying to take my dress off when he reappeared and said, "Let me do that." I glared at him, and he'd told me, "Now's not the time to be shy."

He gently lifted the dress over my head and hauled me into his arms again, taking me to the en suite bathroom, placing me gently on the vanity. I unhooked my bra and kicked off my panties. "I need to go to the bathroom, and I do *not* want you to lift me on the toilet. I have to draw the line somewhere."

Thankfully, he listened to me, holding out his hand, and I took it without looking behind me in the mirror. I could only imagine my skin red with fury, my hair not combed, makeup smeared all over my face.

"I'll be back," he noted when I sat down, and scurried out.

I did my business, and in a moment of defeat called for him. There was no way I trusted myself to get up and then lower my body into the sunken tub.

Which was how we came to this moment, me soaking in a gross baking soda bath, Donovan on the other side of the door.

"It's cutting down on some of the itching," I told him. "But there are more by the minute." With nothing better to do, I watched the tiny red welts multiply on my skin.

"Should I text Caro?"

"No," I said weakly. "She will get in touch when she knows more. In fact, when I get out of here, you should go back." Running a damp hand through my hair and pushing back the strands lingering on my forehead, I thought back to Christmas when I'd dressed to impress Donovan. "My mom insists you get Valerie and bring her back here." I spoke softly, wondering how I would function on my own, unsure if this was the worst of it.

I hadn't mentioned the small tremor I got in my left hand every couple of minutes; I kept balling my fingers to cover it up.

"I will do no such thing." Donovan appeared in the bathroom, not bothering to knock. "I did what I was told to do, 'chaperoned' you here." He said the last part with air quotes. "I supervised the transfer of feelings, which rendered you sick, and I need to own that."

He leaned his butt against the same vanity I'd been sitting on when he brought me into the bathroom. When he crossed his arms over his chest, I couldn't help but stare. At some point he'd changed out of his suit and put on a T-shirt and shorts, his biceps bulging. Under different circumstances, I might have been curious to see more.

"I need to fucking own that," he repeated.

"Please don't feel guilty." I finally found my words. "I did this. I had to do this. You know the play of power with Ezza. She says to jump, and I do it."

His voice came out hoarse with emotion— "No, I should have asked if there were risks, what could happen. I never bothered to consider that or imagined they actually knew something like this could."

Closing my eyes, I dipped a tad deeper into the water, covering my shoulders. I wanted to get out, and I also never wanted to leave this bathtub. "You underestimated them. It doesn't matter—go and get Valerie. They're going to make her miserable, and all she's doing is being near her daughter. I will heal. I hope." I tried to argue, never opening my eyes, the end part coming out faint.

"I refuse to leave you." Donovan pushed off the counter and padded toward the tub.

My eyes were fully open now, watching his chest heave with conviction like a tiger after his prey. A tear fell down my cheek, and I managed to croak out, "My throat hurts." It was yet another new symptom, except it wasn't why I was crying. I realized the momentary chill I felt when Donovan was near was missing. Our special yin-yang connection he knew nothing about had disappeared. And I wondered why it did, along with wanting an explanation for how it made me feel so bereft.

"Let's get you out of the water and into a robe. I can order some soup or tea?" Donovan grabbed a towel and held it up before bending to lift me out.

There was no arguing left in me. I couldn't imagine bracing myself with my trembling hand or standing on my limp legs. All I could do was hope I got better.

And the little girl inside me, the one who'd watched the snowfall from the window, wishing she was outside playing in it rather than listening to her mother, moments before her power showed, pined for the boy this time. Could he be hers?

CHAPTER
TWENTY-THREE

Donovan

I t was late, and the sidewalks were flooded with people out for a raunchy, sensual, hot, exciting, or whatever type of night. I sped past lovers holding hands and groups of women celebrating birthdays and bachelorette parties. My feet hit the pavement with a ferociousness I'd pay for in the morning, but I couldn't bring myself to care. My body was strung out on fatigue and hungover on scotch and my mother's bitching.

Earlier, I'd helped Tulya out of the tub and into a robe, tucked her in bed and fed her some soup. She didn't know I saw her hand trembling, and I could tell she wasn't up for discussing it. But I'd clocked it long before she went into the bathroom.

It had been more than twenty-four hours since she lost consciousness, and her symptoms were not abating. In fact, they were gaining momentum.

With sweat dripping down my back as I ran, I knew it didn't matter how many miles I completed; I would not forget the way she'd swallowed the tea—as if it was sandpaper on the inside of her throat. To be sure it wasn't a virus, I'd felt her forehead, and she seemingly had no fever. But Tulya's body was unforgiving when it came to what her own mother tasked her to do.

I'd tried texting the medic and he only answered with a curt: *It will pass.*

I replied: *What the fuck? She needs help.*

He didn't respond to my venom, only wrote: *Examining Blake and making sure she's settled.*

Lord…it was his way of letting me know I had to deal with Valerie, or he wasn't helping with Tulya.

Turning back toward the hotel, I ground into the pathway along the beach, cursing my brother with every step. I wasn't sure when I became Magnum's keeper, maybe always, but I didn't like that it cost Tulya pain. And my power was to put agony on others; what a strange dichotomy in my life.

I could've run all night, but I wanted to get back to Tulya. I needed a shower and some food. I wasn't thinking of myself, only the woman asleep in her bed, who needed me. She'd mumbled something about my deal and going to Hawaii, not to put that off for her. But Christ, she could be permanently damaged because of my brother.

Slowing my pace, I drafted a text to him, stomping around in a circle and breathing heavy.

Then, I deleted it. Fuck him, he didn't have the strength to man up and handle his business when it came to my mother. Fooled around and fucked up and made a clusterfuck of a mess…that was Magnum.

Deciding to walk, allowing the ocean breeze to run through my damp hair, I felt my pulse starting to normalize.

My phone buzzed, and I almost ignored it until I saw it was Caro.

I knew she and Tulya had always had their differences, but the sisters appeared to have one another's backs. Caro had limited powers if I was correct—she could bestow tranquility—which was useful at times but only lasted so long. Most of the time, she relied on her electric personality.

I answered. "Caro, tell me something promising."

"Hi, Donovan, it's actually Prim."

"Oh, hey," I said to Tulya's best friend. Everyone knew those two were close.

"Caro said I could call. I'm so worried—I haven't heard from Tuvy since she went to the States other than Merry Christmas. At first I was worried she was falling for you, but now I hear she's sick. And it's crazytown here…with *the human*…and your brother's kid…a *kid*." She screamed into the phone and my head started to hurt. She picked right back up at her rambling. "And Caro was saying—"

"Prim, slow down," I demanded. She was hysterical, and I got it, but I didn't have the patience right now.

"I can't help it. Your brother—"

"Listen, I know, he's a class A dick, but I'm trying to care for Tulya."

"Tuvy," she corrected me. "She likes Tuvy. Not Tulya."

"Not when it comes to me. She prefers Tulya." I didn't know why I felt the need to set Prim straight. It wasn't as if this was going anywhere with Tulya…

"Oh" was the response I got.

Prim was getting the picture though. Which, who knew if that was right or wrong in this moment. "Prim, there is a lot going on right now, but the most important is Tulya. She needs the medic. Can you ask Caro to go see him?"

She started whisper-sharing what I was saying to Caro in the background.

"She did," Prim reported back. "He says it will pass."

"In how long?"

She asked Caro and then stated, "No clue. The whole island is up in arms over your niece. Half the place is ecstatic, and the other half—well, not so much. Mostly, no one is happy about the human."

"Her name is Valerie," I grumbled. Despite not adoring her, she was a person with a name, and the mother of my niece.

"Rumor has it you let Valerie come here, and the shit has hit the fan."

Standing still on the beach pathway in front of my hotel, I'd never wished harder to not be Rubian. Hawaii was on the horizon, and I wanted nothing more than to separate myself from my own family. "Again, there are many moving pieces at the moment. Put Caro on," I told Prim. She was too far gone in an emotional state to help me.

"Tell Tuvy I love her" were her final words. Then she added softly, "I would come if I could."

Yeah, I was getting the picture: no one was leaving Rubia to help Tulya until I restored order. Meaning plucking Valerie away from her daughter.

"Donovan, I'm trying," Caro now said in my ear.

"Try harder. What the hell is wrong with your mother?"

"Hey, don't take this out on me. Yours isn't much better, and I'll clue you in, Ceci is on a bender. She's running around our house, muttering quiet prayers, and saying shit about one son messed up but you won't. How you'll be home soon to marry your betrothed."

"Enough! Go to your mom and let her know I will come and deal with Valerie as soon as the medic gets here. I will do her bidding, but on my terms. She needs to at least pretend as if she cares for her daughter."

"I'll tell her. But I'll warn you, she doesn't do others' terms well."

"That's obvious," I added and hung up, rushing up the path to the hotel, thinking I'd been gone too long.

CHAPTER
TWENTY-FOUR

Tulya

I woke up in a jolt—a bad dream where I was standing at the altar waiting for Donovan and he never showed. Squeezing my eyes closed, I willed my heart to slow and tried to take a swallow, but the back of my throat burned like a four-alarm fire. No wonder my mouth was so dry; I'd been shallow breathing all night. I glanced at the clock reading a few minutes after seven and noted the sun peeking up through the blinds.

Looking up, I saw only Donovan. But not the version I'd dreamed of as my husband or the man who jilted me. He was sleeping in the chair in a pair of athletic shorts and no shirt. I was wondering how long he had been in here when the itching picked up again. With a trembling hand, I started to run my nails along my forearm, wondering why they felt wet. Lifting the sheet, I saw a mix of bright red blood and caked-over welts. I couldn't help the gasp I let out.

"Shit." Donovan sat up quickly, swearing a few more times. "Are you okay?"

"Sorry, I didn't mean to wake you. I'm…bleeding. The welts," I explained.

He stood and walked toward me, lifting the sheet himself, appraising the situation. Shaking his head, he cleared his throat. "I'm going to have to go out and get supplies today. Some first aid, ointment, gauze…" He was speaking aloud, but more to himself than me. "I can't keep calling the lobby. I don't mean to keep taxing the staff and there's no need to bring attention to what's happening."

Trying not to scratch, I brought one of my hands under my hair on the nape of my neck and felt my temperature. It was normal to the touch, but my hair was a greasy mess.

"You can go. I'll be fine. I need to shower. I don't think a bath is good for me with all these open sores."

"What? You cannot shower while I'm out."

Thinking he was probably right, I didn't say a word.

"You know what? I need a shower too. Let's go." He bent over, threw off the blankets, and scooped me up.

"Don—" I only semi protested because I really wanted to wash my hair.

"It's not sexual... I mean, I've thought about it, but not right now," he joked before setting me on my feet in front of the toilet.

"You've thought about it?"

That was what I was asking, while standing in the bathroom in a rumpled, bloody robe, covered in head-to-toe welts, my hair a literal rat's nest and my face likely marred with sheet marks.

"Of course I've thought about it, Tulya. I've gone over a lot of scenarios of you in my head, and none of them are G-rated. But that's for a different time. Now, use the bathroom and I'll be back to shower."

He left without any other pomp and circumstance, leaving me there to do my business.

When I was done, I held on to the wall and shimmied toward the shower, turning it on full blast.

"Wait for me," echoed behind me, and I did.

In five billion years, I'd never dreamt of Donovan caring for me when I was sick. Yet here he was, slipping my robe off my shoulders and letting it fall to the floor. With nothing underneath, I stood there bruised and weak as he shoved his shorts and then boxer briefs down.

Taking my hand, he guided me under the stream of water, propping me up as I let it fall all over me.

"Feel good?" Donovan's voice was strained as he held me with a strong arm.

"Mmm," I answered, and it was delicious.

The rainfall showerhead was just the right amount of pressure. I leaned my head back and allowed my hair to get drenched as I felt Donovan bring a bar of soap to my skin, rubbing ever so gently. He washed me as I continued to let the water cascade over me. It was the most comfortable I'd been in two days.

Finally, I murmured, "Shampoo," and while keeping me steady, Donovan began massaging some into my scalp.

We repeated the process with the conditioner, Donovan never stopping to take care of his own bathing needs…let alone, I couldn't help but notice, he was half aroused.

When my eyes traveled there, he said, "I'm willing it to go away."

Part of me didn't want him to, but I was in no shape to do more than be held under a shower spray.

"Sit." Donovan guided me to the bench in the shower once I was clean.

He made quick work of washing himself as I sat close to lifeless, the welts on my skin swelling to the surface again. I focused on the water raining over his six-pack, funneling through the vee and down into the area between his groin and thigh. I'd spent some time with my hand caressing that exact meeting point, and wondered if I wasn't so sickly, if we'd ever do it again.

He did a fast tussle of his hair under the stream and shut off the water, demanding, "Stay still."

He proceeded to hop out, wrap a towel around his waist, and snag one for me. He bundled me in the soft terry and guided me back to bed. I was walking but allowing my weight to fall into Donovan's frame.

Seated on the side of the bed, I whispered, "I hate to ask, but can you get me my comb? It's on the vanity."

"Please stop. Tulya, I *will* do whatever you need. Let me get you a fresh robe first. I didn't wear mine. Looks like the bleeding stopped," he noted.

I nodded, and replied, "I have to try not to scratch. Combing my knots will keep my hands busy."

With a fast knock of his chin my way, he ran to get a robe and was back in moments, unwrapping me from the towel and depositing me in the robe. Then he padded to the dresser and perused the surface, my own eyes continually drawn to his body.

Comb in hand, he looked at me with an eyebrow raised. "Do you want me to help?"

"Do you have experience?" It was the first time I'd joked in days…

"Can't say that I do."

"Here—" I held my hand out, waiting for the comb.

He gently placed it in my hand, and rather than turn around, he sat down next to me. I started to use the comb to pick at small knots at the bottom of my length, wincing each time I got the bristles through a mess of hair.

"I'm sorry," Donovan said.

"About my hair?" I refused to look at him while I said it.

"No. You know what." His voice was hoarse with gravel. "This," he explained. "You being sick, what might have been with us, and wanting more time to explore what we found. Magnum and his fuckup affecting you. And of course, your hair being knotted."

My heart ached over what we'd found and what could have been… "My mom would prefer I be a spinster, I'm pretty sure. At her beck and call, you know?" It was all I could come up with.

"Well, my mother is going to tighten her already strangling grip on me after this debacle. Magnum's trouble has become my problem. And I know it sounds weak for me to give in to what she wants, but my dad would've wanted that. Magnum once told me that Valerie made him stronger. And I argued with him, but I can see now what caring for someone does to the soul."

"I understand you're a man of honor, Donovan Malachite. You told your father you would take care of your family and that's what you're doing— Shoot!"

I dropped the comb to scratch my forearm where a new patch of welts began appearing.

"Damn," I muttered. "Here I am, trying to say something kind, and I ruin it." I tucked away any questions I had about what Donovan meant by caring for someone.

Donovan began shaking his head. "You're perfect. Now, let's get you comfortable."

I didn't know how he did it, but he managed to get the itching to halt with a baking soda paste. And then, while I laid back, he gently worked his way from side to side, detangling my hair. I never wanted the moment to end, and for a hot second I reconsidered thinking I was meant to live life alone.

Except, when I woke up he was gone.

CHAPTER
TWENTY-FIVE

Donovan

"I know. The deal is happening. Family matters interrupted, but all my financing is lined up and I'm ready to go." I spoke into the phone as I climbed down the staircase.

I stomped off the plane and my boots hit the snow, making a crunching sound all the way to my car.

"We weren't worried. Only checking in. You're A-plus in my mind," Charles responded, his deep voice filling the phone.

"Ha!" I hoped he didn't hear the snow under my feet. "I had to help my mom back east," I semi-lied to the investor selling me his property in Hawaii. Of course, my family had used a shell company with an address in Atlanta for all of our business dealings. My hotel project was no different.

"That's what I like about you, Donovan. You seem like a real family guy," Charles said to me.

"Thanks, Chas." I called him by his nickname as he'd instructed me to do. "There will be no delay, I can guarantee that. I should be with my gang here for a few days and then on my way to sunny skies and sandy beaches."

"See you then," he said, ending the call.

The beckoning of a better life away from all this Rubian crap should've felt great right about now. But with every step away from the plane, my chest ached more. In the last ten hours, every action that took me farther away from Tulya seemed to inflict a pain I'd never experienced before.

Maybe it was the way I'd taken a peek at her sleeping, knowing she wasn't rebounding and that I had to go back and fix my brother's millionth fuckup.

She'd said it: *You're a man of honor, Donovan Malachite.* And I was honorable. To her, only she didn't know this was about her.

Perhaps it was the manner in which she'd captured my heart in a way I'd not acknowledged. For years it had been attraction and what I'd cast off as mild caring for the woman. Now, the extent to which I cared for her was a punch to the gut. It couldn't happen between us, shouldn't have even started. Or the worst—it wouldn't have occurred except for this godforsaken mission.

The truth remained: Tulya was worsening, and I knew the two bitchiest mothers in the universe wouldn't send help without my taking care of Valerie.

Who, ironically, was a decent mother. She didn't want to leave her daughter to chance, the way Ezza hung Tulya out to dry.

Earlier, as Tulya slept, I watched her hand tremor. And it became clear that I had to go and fix everything. Admittedly, the feelings swelling around my heart were the reason I fled without saying good-bye—if I stayed, it would become harder to go. I wanted nothing more than to care for Tulya. Truth was, I couldn't nurse her back to health myself.

Back in Rubia, beeping the locks on my car, I recalled the last time I'd driven to the airport with Tulya, her eyes glancing at me, wondering what was in store for us. She'd had a feeling this wouldn't go well for her, but her own mother and the medic knew it wouldn't. And now those fuckers were MIA.

Damn straight, I was a man of honor, and my allegiance at the moment was to Tulya.

As soon as I decided to come back, I'd called Marley, Valerie's mom. It was a split-second decision, but I didn't have anyone else. It was also crystal clear that neither Caro nor Prim was allowed to come help.

Marley knew what had taken place and had a vested interest in my smoothing matters over with Valerie and the powers that be in Rubia. She agreed immediately to come and watch over Tulya in exchange for information.

My hands gripped the steering wheel as I drove toward home, my heart becoming more agitated by the moment. It had snowed in Rubia, fresh white powder covering the roads, and I tried to think happy thoughts. Did Blake like seeing the snow? Had my brother taken her out to play in it?

Swerving into the driveway, I caught a glimpse of Magnum standing outside, not doing any of the above but swirling a tumbler of brown liquor.

Barely stopping before throwing the car in park in front of our family's main house, I jumped out and stormed to where Magnum was standing.

"Asshole," I grumbled, punching him in the chest and knocking him unsteady, the tumbler falling into the snow. "I'm back here to keep fixing all your questionable shit, and you're out here drinking, not even being with your daughter?"

"Don, how's Tuvy? She's better?"

The bile rose up my throat, and I was thankful I hadn't eaten in the last twelve hours. "No, she is not at all better. Do you see her? No. Because she is sick beyond belief, back in Florida, and not one single fucker from here will send help. Do you know why? Let me tell you. Since you decided to bring Valerie back to Rubia, they will not send the medic."

"It's her kid—"

"Shut it," I interrupted. "I know damn well. Of course she wanted to be here. But you couldn't smooth shit over and call this a visit or whatever the hell you needed to do to keep her from getting on the plane. Tulya is lying there sick and alone in Miami, did you hear me?" I said the last part through gritted teeth.

"I tried to tell them it was temporary, but Mom is carrying on that nothing is temporary, following me around, watching every move I make. That's why I'm out here having a drink that you now spilled."

"Dude, I know you're not stupid." I kicked the snow, trying to find the right words. "You had an affair with a human. Then you had a baby and made promises to bring that person here. All the while, Mom promised you to Cinder, a match Dad blessed and wanted for many reasons. And now the real kicker—apparently, you carried a lot of dormant power because your half-Rubian daughter is the one to be feared the most."

"Watch it," he threatened.

I couldn't help myself; I sent a zing of pain up Magnum's spine. I needed him to own up to the absolute shitstorm he'd created.

"Don't fight dirty," he tossed my way.

"I'll do what I want."

"The hell you will—"

"Uncle Donovan!" Blake's light and airy voice filled the air around us and Magnum abandoned his threats.

The small child ran up to me wearing the coat I'd bought her and a pair of small snow boots, Valerie following behind in jeans and a parka.

"I got to see the snow, and it's so cold, especially on my tongue," Blake rambled.

"It is cold, sweetie." It was impossible not to fall for this kid. None of this was her fault. She was an innocent bystander in this mess of people. "Valerie," I greeted her mother. "We need to talk."

On the way back, I'd decided to make a deal with the devil in order to help Tulya.

"I'm not leaving my daughter" was her answer.

I nodded. "Let's talk, somewhere private."

"Not if it means your mother is watching Blake." With venom in her dark brown eyes, I realized how poorly the last few days had gone.

"No, Magnum will stay with Blake."

"What? No way. You are not speaking to V without me."

On his muttering of her nickname, Cinder and Ceci appeared, both wielding daggers in their expressions.

"Hello, son." My mother greeted me with an icy peck on the cheek. "I see you've returned to do the right thing. Good boy."

I knew better than to use my powers on my mother, but I sure wanted to make her feel a sting like I was experiencing. "I'm not a good boy. I'm here because Tulya needs help, and until I deal with everyone else and their mistakes, no one will go to her."

My mother served me a deadly stare.

Hours later, after settling Valerie in a room with Blake, making sure she knew I was on her side when it came to her daughter, and Cinder being occupied by Ezza, I sat at my desk. It was the only space I felt comfortable discussing the matter; my office was both private and a room I called my own. My mother was seated across from me, Magnum next to her, and the Minister on his other side. The single reason they'd agreed to this arrangement was because they knew I was the only one with a vested interest in removing Valerie. When it came to my brother, it was apparent he would be fine with her never leaving.

I cleared my throat, gave a chin nod, and waited for Ceci to go first. She was always better operating under the illusion of having the upper hand.

"Thank you for chaperoning Tuvy," my mother opened with. She could be as skilled at warfare as me. "But we have a problem. The human has to go. It's bad enough we have a leak and have been outed."

Leaning forward, I narrowed my gaze on Magnum. "Obviously, this isn't my problem seeing as how I didn't start the leak."

"But they always call you in to control me," he rebutted.

"Enough!" Elon, the Minister, his salt-and-pepper hair slicked back, sat cool as a cuke in his navy pinstriped suit. "The human leaves, the child stays. Period. After it's settled, someone will pay the human and her family a visit. They will get regular updates on the girl as long as they keep quiet. You take care of this, and the medic goes to Tulya, who is my niece by the way, suffering every minute you waste."

"And visits." Two words. I allowed them to settle.

"One visit to make sure the human and her family understand the circumstances. It's not your business to know this, but once before this happened, and that woman was exiled to Alaska with her ailing father—"

"No!" my brother stood and shouted.

"Sit down," Ceci demanded, and he obeyed like Pavlov's dog.

I put a pin in all the secrets that had been withheld and the craziness in which we lived, making a note to get out as quickly as I could. Living a life alone would be better. I then clarified, "I am not talking about the visit to see Valerie, the human. I mean Valerie will be allowed visits with her daughter."

"Absolutely not."

"She will. I plan to handle all this in exchange for the medic going to Tulya and Valerie having visits. No one will learn of us. Blake will live here and be raised Rubian. My mother can get her wedding. Period."

Elon threatened me with a glare. "You don't call the shots."

"I do, considering Valerie's mother is sitting with Tulya, doing us a favor and privy to everything that has happened and will happen."

"Do you want the serum?"

"What? What serum?"

"The one that will flush Tulya's system of the negative effects. The medic has one from the last time a Rubian used their powers beyond their realm."

I stood and spoke to the Minister in a way no one ever dared. "Fuck you."

I watched my mother's eyes bulge and thought *good*. I wanted her to know I would not be following her rules when it came to an arranged marriage.

"Careful, son, you seem to be showing a hand I don't think I like—"

Ignoring her threats, I turned back to the Minister. "I want that serum and the medic on a plane as soon as I depart with Valerie, you hear me? I will let her mother know she is coming back but arrangements are being made."

"Get her out of here. If she wants to see her daughter, it's best for her to go now."

"Gladly," I stated, thinking I'd won this round, but I wasn't foolish enough to think there wouldn't be many more.

I barely had my keycard on the door before Marley opened it herself, looking haggard.

"Thank you," I breathed out to the woman who had been considered an enemy only a few weeks ago. "Valerie is home. And she's not happy, and I feel sick about it, but the Minister didn't give my brother a choice. He banished Valerie, under the guise of having one-on-one time with Blake. The plane was ready to go as soon as my brother figured out how to get Valerie to acquiesce. I'm not even certain what he promised. I do know that she is aware I'm going to work on her being able to go back and forth to Rubia as soon as Tulya is well."

Marley nodded. "She's not good. Her hand, it's mostly a claw at this point."

On the plane, Marley had texted to let me know about Tulya's hand. I wanted to scream, but I was already dealing with a broken Valerie and the nicest pilot on all of Rubia, going out of his way to get us to the States as fast and safe as we could fly.

Now, all I could do was nod to Marley. I knew it had to be bad for Marley to text me. She was Team Valerie all the way, but she wasn't going to watch Tulya suffer either. And I knew she didn't want to bother me in the state I was in.

"I can't get into many details now. You know they're not giving up Blake, but there is no way I'm allowing them to sever her from her mother. And that goes for you too. I will make sure your visits are negotiated. You deserve to see Blake raised and grown—"

"I am putting a lot of trust in you and Tuvy to do right by us. Right now she needs you and Valerie needs me, so go." Marley shooed me toward the bedroom.

I patted her shoulder and she was off. I was sure she was happy to go see Valerie for a much broader report on the current state of affairs. I hoped they were ready to fight; knowing them, they were.

Quietly opening the bedroom doors, I found Tulya sleeping, curled on her side. I forbade myself from telling her how long they'd known there was a serum or how I'd gone absolutely batshit when I found out. I knew the woman in front of me, and nothing warranted drama in her mind.

"Hey." She stirred and looked at me standing over her.

"I'm here" was all I could say, sitting down next to her, making sure to be gentle.

"I see that. And so deep in thought... What were you thinking?"

"About the Tulya Conundrum." The words slipped out of my mouth before I could stop them. Another reality when it came to the redheaded beauty. She wanted me to be a better man, and while I knew I never could be, in the moment I strove to be.

Her voice gruff, she asked, "The Tulya Conundrum?"

A quick nod from me and I took her arm and brought her mangled fingers into mine, rubbing them. "Does it hurt?"

"Not when you touch it, but in general it's a dull ache I can survive."

"See, that's the conundrum. You don't like to upset anyone around you. You'd rather survive a shitty hand that's limp and crippled and can't do a single goddamn thing than speak up and cause chaos. It's both endearing and aggravating."

She wrestled her bent fingers free and ran her knuckles over my forearm. "I can use my hand."

"Stop. They're coming. The medic is on his way. Of course, the Minister ruled he couldn't leave until Valerie touched down in the States. I'm done with this shit."

She nodded. "Marley said. I tried to call Caro, but she didn't pick up."

I swept my hand through her loose hair, pushing it behind her ear. "If I'd known...the messing with humans would do this...holding the pain inside you for mere minutes...I wouldn't have allowed for any of it... But if they had revealed there was a serum… Christ, they were withholding it! You know what that does to me, Tulya?"

"This is my mother. You have to know by now. *This is her…*"

"And mine. It was my own mother who kept your mom from sending the medic. That's my burden to bear."

We stared at one another for a beat. I imagined both of us silently wishing for a different time, under other circumstances, where we could explore us.

It didn't exist. Not for us.

CHAPTER
TWENTY-SIX

Tulya

I sat alone in my room, waiting for the medic, rubbing my itchy thighs together underneath the sheets. Between the hives and the gnarled hand, I didn't blame Donovan for retreating from me, but it felt more about him. I'd wished for him to come back, maybe prayed a little, but he seemed distant. A small tremor traveled my hand as I thought about his concern and words, but he didn't hold my sore body, lie down next to me, or make any sweeping promises. I had to consider if he saw his fiancée back home. Had they exchanged rings? Did he say anything about me? Would he fight to be with me?

My mind was a train barreling through the night, errant ideas and thoughts steamrolling the ones I should have been focusing on.

Of course, no, Donovan is not fighting for me…

Closing my eyes, I wondered if he was still going to Hawaii, or if he had told anyone. I didn't want him to give up his dream, but sometime in the thirty-six hours he was gone, I'd become convinced he could be mine. It was now obvious that I was wrong.

I must have dozed off, then I heard a commotion in the main room of the suite. Next came a knock and the medic appeared.

"Tuvy." He said my name with a gruff tone. "Sit up," he barked.

I used my non-mangled hand to push up on the bed and did as he asked, a fire raging in my fingers.

He approached swiftly, lifting my damaged appendages without asking, surveying the appearance with a raised eyebrow.

Donovan spoke up from behind the medic. "Don't you speak with her first? Ask her how she feels? Say you knew this could happen?"

"Silence, Donovan. I'm here to take care of Tuvy. And looking at this hand, it will be a few days or weeks until this trauma passes. It's time for you to go back and deal with Magnum. Go." Abraham turned and looked at the only person protecting me.

"I will not be banished." I gazed up and saw Donovan staring down at the medic.

"Go, or I will leave. You put Magnum in his place and he is very unhappy. Something must be resolved with the human. Now."

"Donovan, please, do as he says. He will help me now." I willed the lone tear forming to retreat but it didn't listen.

In that tiny moment where it filled my eye and everything looked as if I was underwater, only the glint of Donovan's Rolex caught my gaze. Focusing, I saw he was pulling up his sleeve and looking at the time.

"I will be back" were the last words he spoke before he turned to leave.

As emotion clogged my throat, I tried to focus on what Abraham was saying.

"Let's take a look at your vitals…" He stuck a thermometer in my mouth while checking my pulse. "No fever, which is in line with you being a little sluggish. Your body isn't fighting this as aggressively as it should be."

I wanted to jest. *You don't say?* But I kept my sarcastic thoughts to myself.

He picked up my crippled hand and turned it over to see my fingers curling in, and asked, "How long did you hold the feelings in without allowing them to dissipate?"

Tension built in my forehead. "A few minutes. There was a lot of commotion, and Valerie knew what was coming so she was prepared to fight me. Not physically, but with some emotional walls. I had to really send it—you know?"

It was only lingo a true Rubian would understand—sending powers. These things didn't just happen, they often took a lot of mental fortitude.

A tremor stilled my thoughts, my whole body shaking with the force of it.

Abraham glared at me, watching my limp form shivering. "You didn't send it all, did you?"

I focused on the ceiling and didn't answer.

"Tuvy, look at me," the only person who had the knowledge to help me blurted out.

My head shook side to side, but I refused to make eye contact.

His chilly blue eyes piercing me, he gritted his teeth and spoke. "What did you do? Tell me, Tulya."

It was the secret I thought I'd never have to share, but when I fainted or went unconscious, my plan backfired. "It doesn't matter," I stated.

He stood and paced. "The hell it doesn't. What did you do? You were told to make the transfer. Am I wrong?"

My skin turned clammy, and I was reminded of how it used to feel when Donovan was near—the ice-cold ripples that would run down my spine. I missed them.

"I was at risk, no matter what, and my mother still sent me to do the transfer. That's why it doesn't matter what I did or didn't do. She didn't say what could or might happen to me. Neither did you." My voice came out hoarse, a combination of emotion and tiredness.

"We are not meant to use our capabilities on humans. That doesn't mean we haven't. It doesn't always go as planned, but when we force our powers to perform in a way they were not meant to—which you were already doing by holding them back for what should have been seconds, not minutes—it alerts something in our nervous system."

A fresh batch of tears began to roll down my cheeks. "No one told me any of this." I knew what I chose to do was putting myself in jeopardy, but I hadn't even been made aware of the overall risk. "Like I mentioned, there was a lot of commotion with Cinder and Valerie and Blake being inside...and I had to make certain it was all going to plan." I tried to find my voice. It was apparent that if I didn't stand up for myself, no one would.

He ran an aged hand through his salt-and-pepper hair and gave me another look of death. "But what did you do?"

I ran my healthy fingers over the ones atrophying and stared at them. Without making eye contact with Abraham, I spoke. "After capturing Cinder's feelings, I held on to them, channeling my energy to send them to Valerie. Then I began to transfer them. Slowly, a little bit at a time. Truthfully, I was shocked how much control I had over the whole process."

"We have tremendous faculties. You especially haven't even begun to understand your capabilities. The Rubians are a species not to be messed with."

Here I was, lying like a pile of bones, and Abraham was waxing poetic.

"I felt my knees go a little weak, but it was the force of the exchange. I'm used to taking on the pain and immediately allowing it to dissipate."

"I know what you are used to. I'm still waiting for what happened. It was more than the transfer." He leaned against the wall across from me and waited like he said he would.

"I thought about Blake, and how much she relied on Valerie. You see, Valerie isn't just a human. Despite the way everyone keeps calling her *the human*, Valerie is a person, a mom to a Rubian child, and this has to be an extremely hard time for Blake and her. I couldn't give her all the pain; she didn't deserve it. So, I decided to hold on to some and then allow it to dissipate later, seeing as how I had so much control...when I held it in."

"*But.*" He said the one tiny word with gritted teeth. "You went unconscious because holding on to the pain yourself wasn't the task at hand and you short-circuited your own damn powers by trying to control them in a way they were not meant to be controlled. Lord, Tuvy, you really messed up. Do you understand that when you passed out, those emotions funneled in and out of your veins? You stopped the natural process in the transfer, but then when you didn't send it all to the human… *Christ!* This is why the tremors started up and the hand is shriveling."

"I didn't know it would all go down like that. You have to believe me." There was no denying that panic had set in. Would I get better? Would I ever be the same?

Yet I had to defend myself against what I had done. Valerie might be angry with all of us, including me, but she was Blake's mom, and cared. More than my own mother, for sure.

"If you had done what you were told to do, I wouldn't have to be here. And I'm going to promise you one thing, Tuvy. You will be the one to explain to your mother what you actually did. Not me. And not because I agree or disagree, but Ezza is Ezza."

Sucking back fresh tears, my intact hand running over my handicapped one, I stared at Abraham. "If you haven't noticed, my mother isn't here."

He stepped forward, each footfall filled with malice. "No, she is dealing with Valerie, who you have somehow become attached to—"

"Whether we like it or not, we will have a lifetime of Valerie. No matter how much we want to deny it, she is Blake's mom."

"Listen, I've said all I will say. The serum will help with the hives. But as for your hand and the tremors—those may be irreversible. There is a higher power to what we can do when it comes to blatantly defying orders. *You take on pain and let it go.* Whether it's sending it to someone else or allowing it to scatter, you did neither fully. Your body is punishing you."

He set the serum on the nightstand, turned on his heel, and left without another word.

With Donovan gone, Marley rightfully back with her daughter, and my friends prohibited from coming, I did my best to slide over to the nightstand and pick up the serum. Staring at the label on the bottle, I read the instructions.

TAKE TWICE A DAY FOR FIVE DAYS TO INHIBIT HIVES FROM INAPPROPRIATE INTERACTIONS WITH A HUMAN.

It included a dropper to pull the correct dosage, and without waiting, I popped a dose full in my mouth and closed my eyes, allowing myself to feel the cool liquid travel down my throat.

I knew soon I would have to get up and pee and get a drink, maybe order some food. I had to start thinking about myself. As Abraham said, my hand might not heal, and the tremors might not cease. I was alone on a figurative island, and by the time I was allowed to return home, Donovan would likely be on an actual island.

Like I told Prim weeks ago, I was meant to be alone…and I sure was.

PART III

CHAPTER
TWENTY-SEVEN

Tulya

"Thank you for everything. You didn't have to do any of it," I said softly, kissing Marley on the cheek.

"Come on, sweet girl. What you did, even if you didn't spare Val the whole lot of it, I'd have done it."

It had been four months since I'd left Rubia. A new year had come, Valentine's Day passed, and I watched the Easter egg hunt by the pool from my balcony. I'd had two calls from my mother and one from the medic, all three only to check on my progress and to scold me for taking the human's side.

"Seriously, you didn't have to, but I'm forever grateful to you."

Taking my semi-healed hand in hers, Marley looked at me. "You will let me know how Blake is...?" She still got choked up every time she mentioned her granddaughter.

"Of course, and I will call with her on the line. It can be between us."

I knew from Caro—who checked in every few days—that Blake was living with Magnum and loving the attention from everyone in Rubia except for Cinder, who had taken to the role of wicked stepmother very easily.

"I'm going to work on having Valerie visit. That's my first order of business when I get back."

Marley closed her eyes and a tear fell. Her daughter had slid into a deep depression after being forced to leave Blake. She had no way of returning to Rubia without one of us taking her, and so she was stuck waiting…and waiting. It was a pain I didn't get firsthand as a caretaker, but I did understand as someone who'd held on to memories for months, hoping Donovan would return.

"Your first order is to keep getting better and take care of yourself."

I'd never told Marley about my love affair in Florida, but she suspected. Many times, she'd commented, *You look like you're wishing someone would walk through that door.*

Of course I never admitted a thing. To Marley, or to Caro when she called or texted. Not once had I asked about Donovan. She'd told me he came back to Rubia and fought with Magnum. The whole place knew there was bad blood between the brothers, but she had no idea what transpired. Cinder was carrying on as if she and Magnum were in love and to be married immediately. I'd heard Blake was going to be a flower girl.

This was also information I never shared with Marley when she would come to check in and sit and have room service tea with me.

Mostly, I told her about Rubia and our customs. She wanted to know what it was like where her granddaughter was living.

"I'm fine, or as good as I'm going to get." I never thought it would take this long for the hives to disappear, but I'd finally been hive-free for two weeks. My weak hand still tremored several times a day. And while my fingers had loosened a bit, they didn't work very well.

With nothing better to do, I'd taught myself an app for dictating my voice to text so I could write when I got back home. I wasn't sure if my powers still worked—Ezza had asked several times—or if I should be using them, but chances were high my mother didn't care.

I slipped a cardigan over my black tank top and flowy khakis, all internet purchases while I recovered and spring hit Florida. I didn't leave my room much other than sitting on my balcony, but I felt the need to still look better than good.

Oh please, I know the reason. Except he never came back.

"I will call tonight, and let you know I arrived safely," I said to the woman who had become my only friend. Placing a small kiss on her cheek, I squeezed her arm with my decent hand and sucked back a cornucopia of emotions.

"When you have privacy, honey. Don't rock the boat, ya hear me? We gotta get Val to see her daughter and at least pretend to play by the rules."

I nodded, knowing Marley cared for me but also prioritized Valerie. It was okay. I admired how much the mother loved her child.

"I'd better go."

She nodded and I was off. A black SUV waited for me downstairs, courtesy of the concierge, who had become a close acquaintance of mine. He thought I'd come down with a viral infection in my muscles, and thanks to another lie—my family's big Grand Cayman money—I'd stayed for months.

He'd arranged for my transportation to the private airstrip for my presumed flight back to the Caribbean.

With a quick wave to the staff, I was securely sitting in the back seat of the giant SUV, my fate unknown.

I'd dozed off for the flight, and my whole body startled when the flight attendant tapped my shoulder. "We're here," she said softly.

With a quick nod, I stood, grabbed my tote and purse, and made my way to exit the plane.

Outside stood my mother, Caro, and Ceci. It was an interesting combination, and not one I would have picked, but I had no choice other than to go see my welcoming party.

"Tulya." Ezza breathed my name and pulled me in for a limp embrace. "Good to see you are all put back together." She said this without even tossing a glance at my hand.

"Tuvy." Caro yanked me close. "I've missed you. I never knew how much you were the yin to my yang."

"Missed you too, Car." I used my good arm to hug her tightly.

"Hi, Ceci," I added when I let go of my sister.

"No one else on the plane?"

All of a sudden, Ceci being there made sense. She wanted to make sure I didn't bring Valerie.

"No, only me," I said without any emotion, but I couldn't help but think what a bitch my mother's best friend was.

"We have made it clear that no one but Rubians are welcome here."

"Who is *we*? Are you in charge now?"

Caro glanced at me as I sassed Ceci.

"*We* are your mother and her brother, the Minister."

I started to walk toward the waiting car, and I couldn't wait to be alone in my cottage. "Then why are *you* telling me?" I had to stop and ask Ceci. "If you're not part of the we?"

There was no surprise when my mother stood up for her friend rather than me. "Tulya, leave it be. You know the rules, so what does it matter?"

"It matters because the last time I checked, Ceci was no longer in charge of ordering me around. I did your bidding once." I squinted at the woman I used to sort of like and started walking again.

I didn't care what she said. I knew all the reasons were rooted in Valerie not coming back.

"Because my granddaughter is here now. To stay." Ceci closed the subject. "Welcome home to you."

There was no parade, not even a thank-you.

Inside the car, I stared out the window, counting the minutes until I was home. I felt Caro's gaze on me as I remembered the ride to the airport with Donovan. We'd been star-crossed enemies with a crush. Then, we became lovers and confidants for a brief time. And now I'd likely never see him again. Which left me heartbroken.

Sadness washed over me as the driver stopped in front of my cottage, the snow all melted and my tulips beginning to rise in front of the stone façade.

"Abraham will be over later to check on you. Your uncle will see you tomorrow for a full report of what happened. And later you will visit with Magnum and Blake, welcoming her to Rubia."

That was it from my mother. I didn't expect much more than a laundry list of tasks. In her mind, I was back to do her bidding as if I'd never left.

CHAPTER
TWENTY-EIGHT

Tulya

"Court asked me out." Prim sat on my couch, holding a mug full of tea, legs crossed, the fire burning across from her.

I was puttering around the kitchen, making myself a latte and trying to feel comfortable in Rubia again. It had been a long two days since I returned. Prim had been a mainstay for most of yesterday and it looked like it would be the same for today.

"When?" I turned to face my friend, mixed emotions roaring inside me. Part of me desperately wanted to be alone; the other half craved company. Although, if I was being honest, Prim wouldn't have been my first choice. I loved her, and appreciated her being with me in this moment, otherwise I'd be crawling out of my skin. But still…*the mind wandered.*

"The other day, right before you got home. I ran into him at the gym. Ugh, of all places. I was so sweaty and stinky, and of course he wasn't."

"Even if he was, would you care?" I raised an eyebrow.

"Probably not. I swear, he's been smoking hot since he was five."

We'd both thought Courtney Wellington had been gorgeous since forever. He'd never so much as glanced at me, but Prim was fun and sexy. I was neither— certainly not now.

I sat down in the armchair across from her, careful not to spill my coffee. For the last forty-eight hours I'd tried to hide how much my weak hand had deteriorated. It made me long for my lonely hotel suite and the occasional visit from Marley.

So I tried to move the conversation into brighter pastures... "Are you going to go?"

She looked away. "I'm busy with you right now. This is my priority."

Swallowing my own bullshit, I spoke. "Prim, look at me." She did as I said. "I'm fine. There's no reason for you to hide out here. Especially since Bruno never comes by—you know that. I haven't even seen him since I've been home."

"I'm not hiding," she said, barely audible.

"You are, and we both know it. Bruno is broken; he's never going to be fixed. And if he was, my mother is never going to allow it to be by you. You should say yes to Court."

She pushed a stray strand of hair behind her ear. "I don't want to say yes to Court..."

I tried to subliminally beg her to go for it.

Except my neck began to get hot, and I couldn't help the "No, no, no" escaping my mouth. I wasn't sure how I felt about my powers returning, but if Prim was experiencing this type of heartache...

"Bruno and I, we had a thing. That's why," Prim began to say.

I nodded, and whispered, "I heard."

Then I got up, despite knowing better, and moved next to my friend. Why? Her feelings had me burning up.

"Don't touch me," she stated matter-of-factly, her gaze boring into me. "I want the pain." She brought the tea to coral-painted lips and took a sip.

I watched as she swallowed and debated what to say. "Why? Bruno is not equipped to be with someone. I would blame it on Shelby having a fit many moons ago, but it was all my mother. She forced him to end his engagement with her, and he had no other choice. I've experienced Ezza's sheer ruthlessness firsthand, and she is like an ice pick tearing into soft flesh on a good day. You don't want that or him. He's broken because of it."

Closing her eyes, she spoke. "I do only want him. I love him. I've always felt this way since I was a little girl. And on New Year's, I stopped at his place to wish him a good year—"

I couldn't help but interrupt. "Prim! You did not!"

She smiled like the cat who ate the canary. "Anyway, I know this is weird because he is your brother, but he asked me in for a cocktail. And, well, one drink led to a few more. It was the most blissful night and morning I've ever had."

I reached out to take her hand in mine but she pulled back.

"I will not allow you to touch me. If you take the pain, it will stop me from remembering what I want. So, it's a no. I love you too, as my closest friend, but you cannot fix this. I'm going to."

I wanted to admit how much I admired her for going after the man she wanted, paying no mind to the roadblocks in front of her—starting with their age difference and ending with my mother—but I didn't. If I did, I would have to explain why. How I fell in love with someone also not attainable. How my heart suffered, and there was no way to shirk the feeling.

Instead, I muttered, "Okay, but no more details of that night. Sheesh, I cannot listen to that."

Prim gifted me with a soft giggle. She gulped more tea, and I walked back to my chair and my cooled latte.

"You know, there were some rumors that you and Donovan had a thing." She spoke to my back, and when I turned, she mirrored my raised eyebrow expression.

"Who said that?" I tried to keep my tone even and expression schooled.

"It was just a rumor. When Donovan returned, he was completely agitated and gone for someone to go help you. He practically dragged the human—"

"Valerie," I corrected my friend. "Blake's mom."

"He spent about twenty-four hours scowling at everyone but his niece. And then, from what I heard, he told *Valerie* it was enough, you needed help, and they were not going to send anyone until she left. I don't know what he promised her, but when he grabbed her hand, she went with him to the plane."

"Well, none of that has to do with me." I shielded my face with my oversized mug. "I did need help. It was nice of him to advocate for me. And truthfully, the help wasn't that helpful. A day late and a dollar short, if you know what I mean."

"I know. Really, I'm glad you are alive, and healed as much as you are. I'm only warning you that after Donovan left, there was a groundswell. You know Rubian imaginations run rampant. There was speculation that you two fell for one another. Cinder denied it, and Ceci put an end to all the whispering."

"That's good" was my response. More than anything, I wanted this conversation to end.

"Emelee held back the tears, especially when Donovan took Valerie home. When he came back a second time, Ceci met him and explained he would be married by next Christmas. Emelee appeared out of nowhere, and Ceci furnished a ring to give her."

I couldn't believe none of this information made its way to me.

Standing, I took my empty cup to the sink, busying my hand, trying to keep any tremors at bay. "Wow," I admitted. "I didn't know any of this."

I turned back toward Prim, and she hurriedly looked away. "Most are now considering you a sympathizer with the human—Valerie. You are not considered to be in the inner circle."

I wanted to say *good*, but I held back.

"I care for Blake," I explained instead.

Like taking my next breath, I did and didn't want to know about Donovan and Emelee.

"Yes, she is a sweet little thing. I get why Donovan was so in love too. Not just because she is his niece. Anyway, a fight broke out when Donovan returned home and Ceci had moved Emelee into his quarters. And he left...and hasn't been back since."

All of it was too much for my heart to bear. I longed to share sushi and feel his green gaze on me. There was only so much I could imagine his touch.

The sad reality settled in my veins. I'd either never see him again, or if I did, he would be living with Emelee. Both options made my body burn with rage and pain, and I wondered if this would be what finally broke me.

Maybe, I hoped.

CHAPTER
TWENTY-NINE

Donovan

"Look what I can do!"

Blake performed a cartwheel over FaceTime as I watched and tried not to smile like a silly kid, but I did anyway. I'd never imagined myself a kid person, yet here I was, acting like a goof.

These calls with my niece had become my favorite part of the week.

She did another cartwheel and then popped into a handstand. It was truly incredible how resilient she was among such family strife.

"Looks like we may have a gymnast in the family," I told Blake, and she grinned from ear to ear in front of the camera.

Despite bad blood between Magnum and myself, I was one hundred percent smitten with this tiny creature. She was the sun and moon...in a very dark time...at least for me.

"Prim taught me," Blake said excitedly. "Do you know Prim? She's so cool!"

Sadly, I couldn't mirror her enthusiasm when it came to Prim. Because if Prim was visiting Blake, I assumed she was going with Tulya.

"Of course I know Prim," I finally answered. If she was picking up on my sour mood, Blake wasn't letting on.

"Did you know sometimes Tuvy picks me up from school? And Prim comes! Did I tell you that Tuvy is back? I forgot."

She continued to rattle on, and my heart did this strange pinging thing when Blake mentioned Tulya being home. I tried to demand my body not react that way, but when it came to Tulya, I was learning I had no control.

Coming back to Blake's barrage of questions, I nodded while picking up my whiskey. It was close to three in the morning in Hawaii, but early in the morning at home in Rubia. Blake had made a habit of calling me when no one else was awake. Now I worried Tulya would pop over to pick her up. It was slightly overdramatic, but still...

I knew Tulya was back home. Magnum had told me she returned and was mostly better, but not one hundred percent. Of course, he added the fact of her being on his side. Apparently she was sniffing around for a way to bring Valerie back. If I knew Tulya, she would succeed, even if it meant breaking ties with her mother and uncle.

My brother thought he was getting one over on me by aligning himself with the mission, but I agreed that Valerie belonged with her daughter.

Blake's voice fell into a whisper when she said, "Uncle Don..."

"Yes, sweetie." I responded quietly too.

"Tuvy's going to help me see my mom again, but she said not to tell anyone. You won't tell, will you?"

I nodded again, emotion clogging my throat as eyes the same color as mine stared at me from the screen. "I know you would like that. You know what? Cinder is not going to replace your mom. You understand that, right, B?"

It was a sentiment I'd reiterated over the last few months. In my mind, if I shared this enough, maybe, just maybe, Blake would embrace some sort of relationship with Cinder.

Gah—if I wasn't on FaceTime, I'd slap myself. I still couldn't believe how dirty my mother did Tulya and me, and here I was, trying to make her happy by promoting Cinder.

It was Blake's turn to nod, and then she asked, "When are you coming back? I miss you."

"Soon," I lied.

"I hope so."

"Miss you." I was repeating her earlier sentiment when the door to the common area opened and I heard, "Who do you miss?"

I quickly blew my niece a kiss and hit end. I wasn't certain how much Blake knew, but I didn't need her telling Prim or Tulya that Emelee was in my hotel living room in Hawaii.

Fuck, I'm still in a hotel…which is a separate issue.

The woman behind the question was not to be stopped—she slithered onto the couch across from me, wearing a black silk nightgown, acting coyly. I was unimpressed.

"Who do you miss?" She unnecessarily repeated herself. "I'm right here, so I don't know who you could possibly be talking about."

I swallowed down the remainder of my whiskey, allowing it to burn my throat, wishing for something stronger—whatever that might be.

"Not that I have to answer to you, Emelee, but it was my niece. I have work in the morning, so good night." I stood and walked across the room to the second bedroom.

"If you're not going to come home, I'm going to stay," she countered from her seat on the sofa.

Emelee had showed up two days ago, out of the blue. Against my wishes, she'd been living in my quarters in Rubia. And I guessed when Tulya returned, she came to lift her leg and pee on me. Yeah, I'd heard the rumors about Tulya and myself having a fling, but I never suggested anything happened. My mother had throttled into fifth gear on Emelee and me getting married, which wasn't happening. Another reason why I was stuck in a hotel instead of moving into something more permanent on the island. No way I was allowing Emelee in any of my personal business. She'd decorate and never want to go.

"I'm not a violent man, so I won't force you to leave. But this is as good as it gets for us. You can stay or go, but we are never going to be what you want. Good night, Emelee."

I turned to walk into my bedroom and my brain felt cloudy. It was Emelee's power—to create confusion in the mind. We were two negative force wielders so we matched, according to my mother. Funny, the only way we synced up was when we went toe-to-toe in our abilities. I sent the scantily clad woman a shock up her spine. She looked at me in horror.

I glared, hoping she got the message.

"Don't ever do that again," I stated firmly and didn't wait for a reply.

As I laid down on my bed, I wondered what it would have been like if I'd asked Tulya to come with me. I'd heard from Marley, who I also kept in touch with on the down-low, that Tulya had never fully healed. Did that make her disposable to her mother now?

My thoughts were a runaway train in the dark. In an effort to get them to stop, I began to formulate a way to send Emelee back—maybe a house project? She could think it was for the two of us.

Although I knew I was never returning to Rubia. Or Tulya.

A few days had passed and Emelee was still traipsing around the hotel room. I went out daily for business meetings and prayed to every god I could conjure up that she would be missing when I returned.

My attitude had deteriorated substantially over the last seventy-two hours. I'd even avoided Blake's FaceTime yesterday.

"No, I will not be coming back," I barked through the phone to my mother who called under the guise of having some good news. "Emelee can come back and do whatever she likes in my wing of the house. I'm doing what I need to do here—"

"This is why your father never wanted to own hotels."

"And it's why I do." We continued to spar over the phone until I said, "Is that it?"

I'd finally made it back to my room and wanted to change and go downstairs for a steak. And a whiskey...maybe a double after I found Emelee in the common living area getting a massage.

"I found out people have been speaking with the human. I don't know who. Maybe multiple. Surely your asshat of a brother and maybe that tart who didn't do the full transfer—"

Stomping toward my private bedroom, I growled, "Tart? What the hell? That's your best friend's daughter."

I ripped my tie loose and toed off my loafers, the phone lodged in between my neck and shoulder. If I carried on like this for much longer, I'd need a massage.

"She only did part of what we asked. If she'd transferred all the pain, the human would have been mad or angry and tucked tail and retreated. Instead, she is working behind the scenes to come back."

"Who is your information from?" I had no idea who my mom's source was, but her network was far and wide.

"My stinky little rug rat of a granddaughter. Little girl was blabbering to someone on the phone that she was going to see her mom soon."

Slamming my fist into the hotel's bureau, I was furious. My FaceTimes with Blake were no longer safe or sacred. "That's her mother. Of course she wants to see her."

I walked into the en suite bathroom and turned on the shower, allowing it to steam up.

"I don't care. You know the rules, and since you and Ezza's daughter broke protocol, it's up to you to fix this."

I didn't question her referring to Tulya as Ezza's daughter; it was better than the Tart. "I'm out of the fixing business. Send Magnum to speak with Valerie and try and get her to acquiesce again."

"Boy, who do you think you're talking to? You will not defy me. Magnum will bring that human right back here to his side. This is up to you, and you will not go against me."

My blood boiled in this moment, but I had one card to play, and that was what I did. I had called Abraham late last night under the guise of wanting to know if Tulya's hand could be fixed. I'd played dumb when asking how she was coming along. I'd mentioned the possibility of me zapping her hand, wondering if that would help. He'd let on that while I was grasping at straws and pondering why, it seemed as though some of my zingers made their way into Tulya during the transfer, which gutted me.

"I will come back and help with this if—and it's the only way I will do this—if you end this agreement with Emelee. I did some digging..."

When I'd begun pushing Abraham on how he knew this could happen to Tulya's hand, he fessed up. He'd been in love with a human woman and was forced to let his feelings go. At the time, a cousin of his used his power to trap his lover in the house, while Abraham traveled back to Rubia. The length of time he had to use his power caused his leg to go rigid. I'd held on to this information and then told the medic he owed me, allowing me to chaperone Tulya on a mission that carried this risk.

"You see, Mother, I called in a favor and had a quick look at Emelee's medical records. She's not able to have children. A complication from when she was a teenager. I know this is a painful subject and not a valid reason to not choose a partner, but considering you forbid me from partnering with someone who would dilute or affect the power lines, why Emelee?"

"What?"

"The medic told me. Emelee cannot have babies. There will be no biological heirs from me if I marry her. We could adopt..."

"If you're telling the truth, I will ruin her. She didn't tell me."

"Ask her yourself."

"You know what? This opens up another possibility. You and Emelee can raise Blake."

"Mother, she is my brother's daughter. I'm not taking her away from him." Her mind worked overtime, finding a solution to everything, but this wasn't a viable one.

"Get on a plane, Donovan, if you know what is good for you" was all she said.

I couldn't wait to return the woman she'd sent to shackle me, get a glimpse of Tulya, and then tuck tail and run back to Hawaii. If heading to see Valerie in Miami was my cost of doing business, so be it. I had no plans to interfere with Blake seeing her mom. She should be with her every day.

CHAPTER
THIRTY

Tulya

"There, yes, there," I murmured, sliding my hand down to touch his cheek while his tongue devoured me…below. I was pushing him to go harder, deeper. Honestly, I wasn't sure what I wanted. I only wanted and wanted…

He turned his head to the side, leaving my most sensitive spot barren and aching, while he took my finger in his mouth, using the most perfect amount of suction.

My eyes were closed, but I felt them roll back in my head. Every nerve in my body pounded and throbbed. Desperation and neediness left me moaning.

I wanted his tongue back on me, and my hips wiggled and thrust in his face, neck, anywhere I could try and send the message.

I was right there, ready to explode and come apart. I'd never wanted anything this badly as he swept his tongue over my already primed areas, my body arching off the bed. Somewhere in the distance I heard the fire crackling as Donovan went to work, taking me there, my mangled hand on the couch and my working fingers now pulling on his hair, pushing him closer.

I couldn't get enough. I felt my whole-body gyrating, grinding—

And then poof, he was gone. My body froze, back lifted, sweat running down my spine, yet goose bumps littered my skin.

It was a dream. My phone's blaring ring had woken me up.

"Shit," I mumbled, sitting up on the sofa, my entire body now ice-cold, despite the fire crackling in the middle of springtime. I noted that thinking about Donovan now brought back the chills, which to the average Rubian would be strange, but not me. Heat was a negative vibe for me, and freezing was my pleasure center.

My phone, which I had forgotten about, started ringing again, knocking me out of my hazy state.

"Hello," I said, seeing it was my mother.

"Tulya, it's time to get back to what you do. And not the easy version you have been practicing. It's time to test your outer limits, moving forward."

It was a direct order, and one that brought an elephant-sized amount of tension to my neck. I knew better than to think my mother meant get back to my writing, which I was desperate to return to. "I don't know…"

"You will do what you were gifted. The Minister would not have it any other way, and you know when I'm in that position, I will be even less tolerant of disobedience. It's time to practice for my reign and this is a snapshot of how I will be."

I wanted to argue or get back to my sex dream, but I knew neither would serve me well.

Inside, I prayed to never have to do a transfer or work with humans again. Speaking of humans, I thought about Valerie. Blake had told me yesterday that her dad—Magnum—said her Uncle Don was going to see her mother. I tried not to beg Blake for information; she was just a little kid.

"Ceci needs you again. Her sons give her more trouble than any duo I've ever witnessed."

I smoothed my hair at the mention of Cici's sons and wondered if it was Magnum or Donovan she was speaking about.

"They may have gobs of money and brilliant business minds, but they are a shit pair of children."

Now fully alert, I asked, "What does Ceci need?" I tried to calm my voice, but if I was honest, anything to do with that woman made me anxious.

I imagined Blake. Somehow, the child had almost become a meditative thought to me. So caring and innocent. For whatever reason, she didn't hate me for what happened with her mother.

"Donovan," my mom said with authority.

My body went limp. There was no way I could touch Donovan and take pain from him; I was certain it would kill me. I wasn't sure how or why, but it would.

I thought about when we were intimate, our abilities lying dormant while we only made one another feel good. In this case, our innermost workings would be at war—I'd be pushing, and he would be pulling, or vice-versa.

"That witch, Emelee, lied to Ceci. That's all you need to know. The arrangement is over and it's not my business to share why, but she's back and she needs to move on to another love interest. Take her pain and send her on her way."

"That's it?"

"Yes, that's it. What else do you need to know?"

For starters, I didn't have to touch Donovan. Second, I needed to know if Donovan was back. I didn't dare mention either to my mother.

"Nothing else. I haven't used my powers in months. I hope it works."

"Don't breathe a word of that to anyone. Emelee is on her way over with Ceci. Take care of business. Then, Prim is coming over with some dresses for the Spring Ball. Or did you forget about the occasion?"

I had wanted to forget, but clearly that wasn't an option, and now all I wanted to know was where Donovan was.

"Thank you. I will look forward to the ball." That was all I could come up with.

I decided I looked a mess and needed to make myself presentable for Ceci, so I scurried off the couch and willed myself to not think about her son for ten minutes.

There was a soft rap on my door, and I didn't have to ask who it was. When I opened it, Ceci stormed through, dragging Emelee. For a quick moment, I prayed this was the last time Ceci barged into my place with another female in tow.

"Tulya!" She barked my name and then looked at Emelee. "She lied to my son, and now she is banished from my house."

A tear rolled down Emelee's cheek, taking some dark mascara with it. Her wavy black hair was down, shielding her face from more inspection, but judging by her wrinkled white blouse, she was tired and not happy.

I only knew Emelee to recognize her. We weren't friends. She was a year older and ran with a popular crowd.

"I'm sorry," she seemed to say to Ceci.

"I don't care. You should not have lied," Ceci answered in return.

"I wanted us to be happy, and there were other choices. Using Donovan's—"

"Cut it," Ceci interrupted, seemingly with zero fucks left. I didn't know what was going on but it felt heavy.

The nape of my neck was on fire, and I couldn't help feeling badly for Emelee—it was in my genetic makeup. Much like Cinder, Emelee, who I didn't know well, trusted Ceci to do right by her. But Donovan and Magnum could not be told what to do.

I tightened my cardigan around my body, keeping my lesser-than hand by my side, hoping no one noticed it. Moving toward Emelee, I didn't ask any questions. Partly because I didn't want to know—maybe I couldn't handle it—

and I wanted to get this over. It would be a test of my abilities, and I needed to make sure everything worked.

Stopping by her side, I wondered what her power was. I knew most of everyone's capabilities as a result of being my mother's daughter, but not Emelee's. It was my assumption that whatever she could do matched up better with Donovan's skills. Otherwise, they would not have been promised to one another.

Forbidding myself from asking, I brought my strong palm to the side of her cheek and let my body do its thing. The floodgates opened and I felt her vitriol and sadness flow through me. With nothing to do other than allow the magic to happen, I didn't interfere. It was a relief to feel everything working and, as the anger and emotions fled my body, a large weight lifted off my back.

Emelee started to slump, and I let go, using my hand to guide her to sit down. It was safe to say the process had worked and she was feeling empty.

"There you go," I was whispering to Emelee when my front door banged open, a murderous Donovan standing in the frame.

"Mother, have you not learned your lesson? Stop bringing all your messed-up mistakes to Tulya. She is not your private servant."

His words came out curt as his green gaze jolted around the room.

"I'm sorry," he said to me, walking toward the sofa. With an arm linked under Emelee's, he helped her off the couch, steadying her when she stood. "Time to go home," he told her.

I wasn't sure if he would take her or send her with Ceci, but when he left my cottage with her on his arm, without another word, I got my answer. And when I felt the tears start to fall, I shied away from Ceci seeing me.

"You can go, it's done," was all I said to the woman who had been making my life miserable. "I can't promise she won't need it again though, with the way he left with her." I didn't know if it was wishful thinking, or what. What had I really thought—that Donovan ran to my house so he could choose me? To declare his undying love?

Of course he didn't. He came to protect Emelee, despite whatever she'd lied about.

My life would be void of any such scenes orchestrated for me. A life of isolation was my destiny.

CHAPTER
THIRTY-ONE

Tulya

"Did we have to go out?" I spoke a touch above a whisper to Prim, who was sitting next to me in a maxi dress and gladiator sandals, looking on top of her game.

"We did. I know you're a homebody, but there is only so much sulking one can handle." She stared at me, presumably taking in my skinny jeans, black tank, minimal makeup and my hair down rather than pulled back.

I didn't respond to her comment or perusal, instead I took a sip of my Malbec. It had been a long day with the whole "Emelee's feelings" situation.

"You're not still upset over what happened with Bruno? You had to know it would happen eventually. I've been pining for him since we discovered boys. And let's be honest, he needs someone who loves him for him. I'm good for the man."

Another sip of Malbec as I looked around The Toasted Onion. It was one of a handful of taverns we had in Rubia. If I had to go out, it was my favorite place to go, which was why I suspected Prim chose it. It was lined with shelves filled with books and knickknacks, and chandeliers made of candelabras hung from the ceiling. It was Beauty and the Beast meets shabby chic.

I smoothed an imaginary stray hair; I'd straightened my red hair to within an inch of its life and left it down. I felt naked without my bun. "If Bruno is the hill you want to die on, go ahead. My mom will never allow it, and you know that. I hate being brutally honest, but there is no other way to put this."

"Look, you're clearly in 'don't mess with me' mode." Prim addressed my mood but not my dose of reality. "Tuv—I'm your friend, and you need to talk with someone. Choose me. Caro is your sister, but her loyalty to your mother's social standing is her weakness. I'm not in Ezza's camp of favorites…as you just highlighted—"

I interrupted. "Nor will you ever be."

"You said that already, but we can't help who we love." She tucked her own hair behind her ear, her diamond stud twinkling at me. Leaning in, she spoke again. "So, if you're not upset with me, what is it? Writer's block? You've been totally absent since returning. I don't care about your injury." Waving at my hand, Prim hit on several of the elephants in the tiny tavern bar, but not the main one.

A third gulp of Malbec was in order.

"You can't keep hiding behind your wine. Something is going on. You're back, and not the same, and I don't believe it was only the transfer. Although I know it was hell, but that's not it. Period."

My eyes swept the room, searching for a diversion. "I'm writing, a little. I mean, it's been a whirlwind since I got back, but I'm trying to settle into it."

"Tuv—spill it." It was the second time she'd shortened my nickname. I knew she meant business.

"There's someone." Two words came out on a whoosh.

Prim stared at me wide-mouthed. "Who? What? When?" Her questions came out in short bursts, her expression somewhere between shocked and incredulous. "That was not what I was expecting." Her hand dug into a bowl of nuts sitting in front of us. She rolled several cashews in her palm, and I chalked it up to nervous energy.

I tried to let her down gently. "It's not going to be anything."

"Why?"

"Stop with the questions. Seriously, put your excitement to bed." I waved my hand in front of her mouth, hoping she understood I meant for her to be quiet.

"I will do no such thing."

"Can I get you two another round?" For one moment, luck was on my side as Milly, the bartender, interrupted the discussion.

"Put a pin in this," Prim sadly told me and then turned to Milly and said, "Yes, two more rounds."

"Two more?"

"We can call Bruno to get us," was her response.

"Umm, I'm nowhere near that stage of acceptance when it comes to you two—"

"Hush" is what she told me.

A small tremor hit my weaker hand, and I stuck it under my leg. I still tried to hide any lingering reactions I had to the transfer. I'd successfully helped Emelee, putting me back in my mother's good graces. Truthfully, I was unsure why I wanted to be there, but I did.

Maybe it was all I'd ever known.

"Back to you." Prim brought me out of my haze. "You've been busy since you returned?" She raised her eyebrows.

"Stop, shh," I pleaded.

Milly slid our drinks in front of us, taking us seriously, leaving two apiece.

"It was while I was in Florida," I said. "It shouldn't have happened, but it did, and now it's complicated."

Prim's eyes looked like they were going to bulge out of her face. "Donovan?"

I nodded.

"I told you he liked you. At the party."

The nape of my neck started to burn, and not because Prim was feeling any sort of sadness toward Bruno. This was all me. I'd started to react to my own shitty feelings.

Sliding a delicate elastic off my wrist, I tugged my hair into a low ponytail and wrapped it tightly. "Maybe we've always had some sort of weird crush. I don't know, but it can't be, or whatever. I'm a yin to his yang, but it's not allowed, if that makes sense."

Prim took a long sip of her martini. "Is this some book crap? Fiction you made up? Yin and yang usually work. He pulls, you push."

I felt my head shaking. "No, our powers are opposite and both strong forces. We don't sync like that. Mixed together, we're not a match. That's what our mothers would say." It was the most I'd talked about Donovan, and a wave of relief washed over me.

"But you had a tryst?"

I couldn't help the laugh escaping me. "No need to be so dramatic. We had a few nights, some tender moments, celebrated Christmas. Maybe that's why— we bonded over the holiday, nothing more."

Her eyes flew to my ears. "Oh my Lord. I thought those were out of the ordinary for you to choose."

"What?"

"The earrings."

Again, all I did was nod.

"This is why he came back guns blazing, dragged the human—Valerie— out of here. He was beside himself over the medic not going to you. There were rumors, but I thought this was all born out of guilt."

"No, he brought the medic and that was that. The end of the line when it came to me. I'm a delicate piece of glass and he's a hammer; that's how much we don't fit." I was sucking down Malbec number two, and all of a sudden happy to have number three waiting.

Prim grabbed my hand and squeezed. "This is absurd. You're not listening to your mom. Look at you, a woman who's smitten."

"I have to. Plus, he won't go against his mother."

"Nonsense. He's a grown man, and you didn't see him when he returned. We took it as maniacal warrior, but it was man in love."

"Not love," I quickly interjected.

"Oh? Want to bet?" Prim batted her eyelashes at me and then tossed her chin up.

I didn't tell her there was no need to alert me to Donovan being here; my entire spine was chilled, goose bumps running up my legs. Judging by how freezing I was, he was close.

"Ladies," I heard.

Prim looked like a cat who ate the canary and was in hot pursuit of a second one. I wanted to tell her to wipe the grin off her face, but Donovan was standing by my side now, and imaginary icicles were forming in my undies.

Prim spoke first. "Hey, Donovan."

"Prim, how are you on this lovely evening?"

"Tuvy and I were just getting all caught up." She winked, and I wanted to smack her.

"Is that so, Tulya?" Donovan turned toward me, using my full name, differentiating himself.

"We haven't seen one another in a long while," I said, hoping to end Donovan's visit.

"Yes, it's been great, but we were just about to call Tulya's brother to get us. Maybe you can drive her home?" Prim tossed the suggestion out there as if it was a normal one.

"Of course. Now?" Leave it to Donovan to pick up what she was putting down and take advantage of the opportunity.

Jerk. Not to mention, Prim would get alone time with Bruno now.

"I'll settle up." Prim shooed us off and Donovan didn't waste any time.

"Let's go, Tulya." He tugged on my stool and waited for me to stand, his hand resting on my lower back as we made our way out.

Judging by how cold I was in the middle of late spring, I was in big, big trouble.

CHAPTER
THIRTY-TWO

Donovan

"She's my friend," Tulya said without prompting as we got into my car.

"I know" was all I said.

"I'm allowed to talk with who I want."

I didn't reply, only started to pull my car away from the curb, the bar shrinking behind us.

"Were you meeting someone? You don't have to leave."

"It feels like you want to argue with me, Tulya. Do you?"

"No, I don't want to argue with you or anyone." Her voice was soft, as I knew the rest of her body to be. She yanked her hair out of her ponytail and allowed it to cascade in front of her face.

"I was going for a cocktail to clear my head. Something drew me to the Onion. Maybe it was you."

"We are not connected like that." She spoke firmly.

I drove toward her house, not under any impression she'd invite me in, so I took my time. "I'm beginning to think we are. My orbit is constantly circling yours."

"Stop. Seriously. Why are you here?" She set her hands in her lap and kept her gaze out the front window.

I'd never seen this side of Tulya—argumentative, sullen, stubborn, and maybe a dash cynical. "I went to see Valerie."

"Oh? Working on whose side? Your mother's or Blake's?"

I knew this would get a reaction out of her.

I turned into the main driveway of Tulya's childhood estate. "My mother asked me to go, but I diverted from her perceived mission."

This got me a side glance. "Blake wants to see her mom."

"Is that what you were filling Prim in on?" I couldn't help asking, even adding a wink.

"No. If you must know, I told her what happened between us. I don't care if you're mad."

I came to a stop in front of her house and waited to see if she finished her thought.

"I am sorry if you are upset or hate me… Actually, you have every right to, but so do I. Your mom paraded Emelee through my place today, and you came in to rescue her."

"I didn't rescue her," I tried to explain.

"You didn't protect me."

"You know that's bullshit, Tulya. I jumped through hoops for Abraham to come and see you. You have been the only person on my brain since this all started. I went from shamelessly flirting with you at the holiday party to falling in love with you… And Emelee was another pawn in my mother's games."

Rain started to ping around us, droplets falling on the car. For a brief moment, I thought I'd stuck my foot in my mouth and Tulya would jump from the car despite the weather.

"You love me? How? Why?"

"You can't wonder how or if it's true. I started falling deep when I came here after the party, seeing you in your surroundings, wearing a robe, more stunning than ever, and ready to do whatever was asked of you—"

She started to open her door.

"Where are you going?"

With her hand on the door, rain seeping in the small crack left ajar, she turned to me. "You can't say that. You pushed, then pulled, and then left. Look, I knew it was always your plan, but shoving it down my throat now with falling for me back then, and then coming to Emelee's aid? I mean, what do you want me to do?"

She didn't leave me time to reply, just jumped out of the car, running in the storm toward her door.

Without thinking, I did the same. Chasing her to the front alcove, I put my hand on the door as she was closing it. "Stop," I said, demanding her attention. It was gruff but necessary.

She allowed me to step inside, likely to protect her floor from the wrath outside. We stood there dripping wet, and I took her in—

"You're more beautiful every time I see you." I started to encroach on her personal space, and she stuck out a palm to stop me. I abided.

"I asked what you want from me."

"What I need is for you to love me back. It's more than a want or a desire. I've come to realize it's a necessity."

"What?"

She could have backed up, run to another area of the house, but she didn't. Her feet planted, she stood staring at me.

"My mother doesn't rule me. Being without you, and seeing what Mag is going through, being forced to live with someone else when he is in love with Valerie and his daughter, to get this. It took me a while, but I got there."

She looked at me, her hair matted against her forehead from the rain, her lips inviting me—although I would wait for a more formal ask.

"But Emelee was there with you. And then pained? And then you came? And—"

"Shhh," I said, taking a step, narrowing the small gap between us. "May I?"

She nodded and I gathered her in my arms. My lips met the top of her head, and I allowed them to linger there a while. "Emelee just showed up, and I had to bide my time. When I was finally able to send her off, it was under the direction of my mother. I know, I have to stop listening to her…but I need to help Blake when it comes to Val."

"I understand. I want her to be with her mother," she whispered back, her hand holding steady on my waist.

"And I need to fix this for Magnum. I did him wrong. I should have listened to my own brother… I'm ashamed of what I've done."

"We were both only doing what was expected of us, even if it was wrong. This is how we were raised to be."

I hated how she was making excuses for what I did. "Don't try to pardon what I forced you to do, and how I chose my mother over my brother."

"You didn't force me to do a thing. My mother would have set this in motion with or without you."

With one hand, I tipped her chin to look at me, not letting go of her with the other. "That's why I rushed over and grabbed Emelee. It's not your place to do what Ceci or Ezza ask of you anymore. You've done enough."

"But?"

"But I couldn't tip my hand and show how I felt for you—just yet—in front of my mother."

"Maybe never." Her two words didn't come out much above a mutter.

"That's not going to work for me."

"Donovan." She breathed my name, and I had nothing more than a kiss to reply with—my mouth melded with hers and it was over.

Wet clothes started falling to the floor, and I knew that if it was the last thing I did in Rubia, it would be to set Ezza straight.

I deepened the kiss, my tongue colliding with hers. I felt her hand grip my waist and I moved her back against the wall. A soft moan escaped from her lungs as my palm grazed her rib cage and over her side cleavage. I made quick work of snapping off her damp bra, allowing it flutter to the floor. Letting go of our kiss, I lowered my mouth to her nipple, sucking hard, extracting a deeper mewl from Tulya.

"Donovan," she pleaded.

I didn't hurry, or rush, like she wanted. I took my time, giving equal attention to each breast before dropping to my knees. Her skirt had come off at the door, and I yanked her panties to the side before throwing all caution out the window and ripping them completely off. My tongue sought her heat, making contact with her most sensitive spot, her back bowing off the wall.

I felt her fingers claw through my hair and I kept pace, eliciting the most delicious purrs from her. She pushed into my face, her hips grinding, and I couldn't get enough of her taste and reckless abandon.

"I'm…" she began to murmur, and I said, "Let go," while humming against her. In a whoosh, her hand gripped my hair so hard I thought it might come out, and she huffed my name through rapid breaths, dampening my face and squirming like she wanted more.

I was ready to go again, to draw another orgasm from her, but she dropped to her knees and without caring, began kissing me with ardor.

"Do you like your taste?" I asked and she moaned, nodding her head. "Tulya, I am falling for you—"

"Take me to bed." She interrupted my sentiment, and who was I to argue?

I stood swiftly and lifted her into my arms, walking down the lone hallway. I'd never been in her bedroom, but as soon as I stepped foot inside the room with the doorway open, I knew it was hers. Soft ivory carpet, a pine canopy bed filled with a million throw pillows, and fresh flowers on the vanity. Laying her gently on the lace bedspread, I couldn't dwell on her decor because Tulya was spread out naked in front of me. Quickly shrugging out of my pants, my shoes long off, I shoved down my boxers and crawled over her, keeping my weight on one elbow.

Her palm ran the length of my back, and I noticed she only used her "well" hand. Taking my own fingers, I grasped her "broken" hand and wove it with mine. "I'm sorry this happened."

She closed her eyes, but whispered, "Kiss me."

"Anytime," I said back, following her orders. Our mouths mashed as our hips grinded, every body part seeking some sort of friction. Our powers were quiet in the background, no sign of them emerging. There was only tenderness between our hearts, and skin on skin when it came to our bodies.

Our need funneled between us as if it was palpable.

"Inside," she muttered.

"Without anything?"

She nodded.

I didn't need any help. We fit together like we were made to do so, and I began a slow and steady pace of drawing in and out, our lips staying mostly fused other than sounds of ecstasy.

"Feels so good," I told Tulya while doing my own body scan. Being with her made me feel numb to all the shit around me, but also there was now a low hum of something, a different power. This was something new—a type of control—and it almost felt as if it was in a throttle position. An intangible string, keeping my ability at bay, not allowing it to ignite in the presence of Tulya's.

Could this be happening? Some weird bond between our abilities as our feelings for one another grew? An unspoken agreement between the forces that both bound us and pushed us away?

I made a note to ask the medic, but came back to the moment, picking up speed, pushing into Tulya as deep as she could take and gliding out. Her foot came to rest on my ass, forcing me to stay at a fast rhythm.

"Deeper," she begged, and I went as far as I could. "Oh God," she added after a few pulls.

"Fall, Tulya. Jump off the cliff," I instructed her. I was right there, and ready to dive after her. As soon as she began to come undone, shaking in my arms and pushing up to meet every one of my thrusts, I began to climax.

It wasn't dark yet, but stars lit my vision. Whatever dreams or goals I had were set aside, whether I wanted them to or not. My home was with this woman, and as I cleaned her off and she dozed off in my embrace, I began to formulate a plan.

CHAPTER
THIRTY-THREE

Tulya

I woke to my favorite smell, fresh brewed java, and for a moment I wasn't sure where I was.

I considered if it might be the hotel in Florida, and Marley had ordered room service. I remembered that happening on several occasions—it was a highlight of my time there after Donovan left.

But today, after taking in my surroundings, I noted it was my very own bedroom. Burrowing a touch deeper in my blankets, I took a beat in order to appreciate being home. I'd missed my cottage while in Miami. It was my sanctuary.

Except I didn't recall ever having someone make me coffee, and I never set a timer on the complicated barista-like machine. Stretching my body, feeling the delicious soreness from head to toe, I finally knew who was awake before me. The same man who had left me feeling every nerve ending, each joint and tendon, and all of my most sensitive spots, while forgetting the pain I'd endured the last few months.

Donovan Malachite.

He'd shown up at the bar and brought me home from the Onion. I had no idea he would be there, but I felt him as soon as he entered. Later, when he'd said my mom had *done enough*, I experienced a wave of relief or understanding I'd never felt before.

Of course I'd quickly fallen into bed with him, and we'd made love. But was it love? Could it be?

For a fast second, I thought about calling Prim. She must be pacing, wondering what happened last night. Either that or she was in bed with my brother. The latter brought a frown to my face, but I decided it was the most likely.

I made a mental note to go see Bruno and clarify what was happening with them. Later, of course, because Donovan was still here, apparently brewing coffee. I started to swivel out of the sheets, looking forward to wrapping my arms around the man of my dreams and breathing him in. Maybe he would stay for a while? Or maybe he had to work? Several scenarios ran through my mind...until I heard voices in my kitchen.

A warm current hit my spine, and not the pleasurable kind. I worried someone was here for me to take away their pain, heating up my entire body. In a hot second I desperately missed the chills associated with Donovan. I took a long inhale, listening more intently, determining it was Donovan's deep tone mixed with...my mother's shrill voice.

I stood faster than I should have, my head feeling tipsy, and rushed to grab a robe, ignoring the urge to pee. The idea of the two of them discussing anything, let alone the reason for Donovan being at my place in the morning, made me sick to my stomach.

"You will do no such thing. Your mother warned you long ago, and I know you're not one to listen to orders, but you two do not go together. I will not permit it." Ezza was in the middle of the kitchen, staring Donovan down.

He stood there defiantly, shirtless, in a pair of boxer briefs, not even trying to hide what we'd done. "I am a grown man, and I will care for and adore who I choose. Your daughter is my priority, and clearly not yours," he spoke back to my mother, and I refrained from gasping. No one stood their ground with

Ezza. Not ever.

"You will not speak to me like that. My brother is the Minister, and you will bow down to power," my mother ranted.

"Never again. I did your dirty work, and your *daughter almost died*," he spewed back.

Typical Ezza, she ignored Donovan and turned her wrath to me. Instinctively I pulled my robe tighter as she glared at me with venom in her eyes.

"You will get yourself in line, Tulya, or your uncle will burn this household down to the ground. He will bring the torch and watch it disintegrate into smithereens, banishing you to a public apartment and a lifetime of nothingness. No more riches, young lady. We are a family of rulers, and not women who chase after men who are wrong for them. We grow and finesse our powers. We do not diminish our capabilities." She spoke from the back of her throat, each word coming out deeper than the one before.

I couldn't help the fire licking at the base of my spine when she mentioned the torch. It was reserved for the worst offenders. The elaborate candelabra sporting a flame sat in the corner of the Minister's office and was regarded as the most wicked tool in all of Rubia. It was the equivalent of a hanging in early America. It was the one power no one wanted to fall victim to.

"To suit who? Who do you cultivate your powers for?" Donovan piped up and asked, back to staring my mother down. "No, don't answer. Let me guess. You? Who else? Rubia is going to be around with or without the advanced powers. Why can't we live our lives how we want? Even more, why do you act like such a fucking elitist? The torch—you have to be kidding me! For falling in love." He continued to poke and prod my mother in a way I'd never witnessed anyone do.

My head pinged between the two of them. I couldn't bring myself to utter a word. I knew I'd eventually meet Ezza's wrath, and while I appreciated Donovan sticking up for me, a small part of my mind knew he was making it worse.

"It is our legacy, Donovan Malachite. The advanced powers. You know better than to question it, you fool. Both you and your brother will fall in line, or should I remind you of your own elitist roots? Your daddy built an empire based on elitism, and thankfully he had the brains to back it. But I'm starting to worry about you, my dear boy… Buying a hotel outright against your daddy's wishes, with his money, leads me to question your own intelligence."

"We will not fall in line, as you say. We've done enough of that," Donovan growled back, his fists balled at his side. "And don't you ever question my intelligence. I know exactly what I'm doing, and I'm my own goddamn man, for the record."

I'd cocooned myself deep in thought, wondering how I'd forgotten about the torch and burning houses down. There hadn't been one since I was little; I didn't even know why the Minister did it back then. It had seemed random, if I recalled.

"Tsk, tsk. You will fall in line," my mother threatened.

That was when she turned and started to walk away, then stopped and waited a beat or two before facing back to us. She rolled her hands together, creating a swirling image of my cottage on fire, my screams echoing out from the imaginary glass ball forecasting the worst.

"Then that is the future," she noted.

I couldn't help but stare wide-eyed. I'd never seen my mother use this power before. There were rumors she had extra abilities she'd honed over the years, but this…

"See, when we use our strengths and grow them, doing good for our people, we are gifted enhanced advances. My brother will see that you are stripped of yours and destroyed."

When she turned away this time, she didn't say a word, only strode right out of my house, leaving me there still speechless.

I couldn't move. My feet stayed planted on the floor, my eyes centered on the door—

"Tulya, don't worry," I heard whispered in my ear. I felt Donovan running his palms down my arms over the sleeves of my robe.

"I have to. We can't, you know?"

"We can," his lips said along my neck. He placed kisses all along the path from my clavicle to my cheek, coming to face me. "It's going to work," he said to me before his lips met mine.

I allowed myself the moment, thinking it might be my last before my cute cottage no longer existed.

When he broke free, he stated, "I made coffee," as if the entire scene with my mother hadn't happened.

And that was exactly how we had our cup of joe, without a care in the world before Donovan left to work and fix the problems of Rubia, in that order.

CHAPTER
THIRTY-FOUR

Donovan

I paced my office, knowing my pounding the carpet would not help a single damn thing, but I did it anyway. Slamming my hand onto the desk, I stilled before sitting down and popping open my laptop. I needed to quiet my mind in an effort to think straight when it came to handling Ezza.

I made sure the hotel was continuing to operate at a six-star level, checking in with the manager, asking if there had been any issues. Only one, where a teenager got hurt at the pool, but a quick trip to the emergency room showed he was okay, and the parents were happy with a free night and five-course dinner.

My breathing started to regulate as I perused financials, seeing that I was in beyond good shape when it came to that area of my life. My mind even wandered to another resort I'd been eyeing, before coming back to the scene at Tulya's from this morning.

Fuck Ezza and her throwing my dad at me; I'd taken what he'd built and multiplied it several times over. I was my own fucking man, like I'd told her, and my brain operated just fine.

Screw her. I could take care of her daughter in every way possible, and she knew it. We would figure out the powers, and I wasn't worried other than Ezza threatening the torch. What a bitch... She was still sour over Bruno's messed-up life. And who the hell threatened to set her daughter's house and life on fire? Only Ezza, and maybe my own mother. Those two deserved one another.

I'd been deep in thought, tapping my fingers on my desk to an easy rhythm and calming my overactive pulse, when there was a soft knock on the door. It was open, so I had no fucking clue who it was until I looked up and spied Emelee.

"Hiiii," she said, leaning against the doorjamb.

"Everything okay?" I asked the question, despite not being up for whatever situation was unfolding.

"Yeah," she responded in a whisper, approaching my desk. Taking note of her slip dress and hair sleekly brushed, I couldn't help but wonder what was going on. "I wanted to talk."

I leaned back in my chair and watched her sit on the corner of my desk. "I guess I don't have to ask how you got in… I never asked for your key back."

"I want to make this work."

That was her answer instead of addressing what I'd specifically asked. I continued to eye her acting like a woman in love, and the hackles on the back of my neck rose. "It's not going to."

"When you came to rescue me at Tuvy's, I knew we were meant to be together."

God, why is everyone getting the wrong idea over that?

"I didn't rescue you. It was enough of taking advantage of Tuvy."

"Tuvy, Tuvy, Tuvy. That's her role. Ask her mom," she said, standing and sashaying in front of me, dropping to her knees.

"What are you doing?" I tried to stand but she'd firmly placed her hands on my thighs, and I wasn't in the habit of pushing a woman off me.

She traced a path up my leg to my groin area, where nothing was happening, but she still made a play. "We could be so good, and we could help with Blake. Cinder needs it—"

"Emelee, get up," came out on a roar, and this time I did stand and let her gently plop to her butt. This reeked of my mom.

"You were promised to me." She stayed on her knees, pouting.

I decided to go with, "And you lied."

"So did you. You cared for someone else. But I was falling for you, and you were letting go of your feelings for Tuvy—"

"You don't know anything about my feelings."

She finally stood, and I'd hoped she was leaving but she came close to me as I stood against my desk, my ass hitting the edge, arms crossed in front of me.

"I know you fought with her mother, and I was told to make it right between us. And I have no problem doing so because I love you, Donovan Malachite. There is no you and Tuvy."

My green eyes must've been turning red, I was so pissed. How dare she do Ezza's dirty work and taint my feelings by even discussing Tulya and me? "Get out, and never say that to me again. In fact, I'd better not hear Tulya's name come out of your mouth."

That was when the tears came, and I knew she'd convinced herself she would have me again. Her feelings were back.

Without any notice, she draped herself over me and wept into my shoulder. "You can't say that."

As I was trying to disentangle myself, there was yet another soft knock at my office door.

"I see you two have worked things out." My mother's shrill tone echoed through my private chamber. She strutted into my quarters like a peacock, fluffing her feathers.

"We have not," I said a bit gruffly, extricating myself from Emelee's grasp.

"Well, that simply won't do. Will it, Em? We have new plans for Blake, and they are perfect." My mother addressed Emelee as if she hadn't just banished her from my life. Then she glared at me. "I made a mistake. You were promised to Emelee, and I thought it was because of what you learned about her condition that you didn't want to pursue the relationship. But I was wrong. Those silly rumors about you and Tuvy are all I thought they were, rumors. Why would I believe you would tangle yourself up with the one person you are forbidden to? I was also wronged—and Emelee can't be blamed for something that isn't her fault. She will love Blake as her own. With that magic she has, you'll be able to hone her."

Emelee tag-teamed with my mother and stated, "We can fix us, and make it right."

She threw her arm around my neck in a dramatic way and clung to me again, making me want to shoo her off, especially when Tulya showed up in my doorway breathless.

She'd never been to my area of the house before, and I presumed the housekeeping staff had let her in and showed her the way. I took in her chest rapidly rising and falling.

"Donovan," she choked out, her eyes scanning the scene before her.

"Tulya, what is it?" This time I did wrestle free of Emelee and walk straight toward the woman who held my heart. "What happened?" I didn't know why, but I grabbed her weakened hand and held it tightly, absorbing the tremor running through it.

"My mom… She said…this," was all she got out. Her eyes zipped around the room, taking in the scene in front of her.

"Donovan, you heard your mother. You're promised to me," Emelee said, slinking up to my side.

"You're not. I'm my own man," was my response, to which she started crying.

"Ceci, you said—"

"Maybe I should leave?"

My grip on Tulya's hand tightened. "No, you're the only one not leaving," I said.

Granted, this wasn't how I imagined Tulya's first time in my space. I had to temper my thoughts; I would show her around later after I dealt with this fiasco.

"Mother, listen. I made a mistake in siding with you against Magnum. He should love who he wants. Our family's legacy will still go on. Look at Blake—she has greater powers than most. The House of Malachite prevails no matter what. We are stronger than this."

She looked like I'd put a gun to her temple. "You don't believe such a thing."

"I do, and I should have a choice too. I want Tulya for me, and she picks me. We are good together, better than good. Amazing."

"You will do no such thing. The woman who cares for you is by your side." She motioned toward Emelee who was still clinging to me. "Tsk, Tulya, you know you can't. I always told your mom she babied you."

I shook my head. "Tulya, I need you to take Emelee's feelings away. I know I shouldn't ask, but I need this all to be done with her. She's confused by my mother's words and has fallen for me all over again. But I'm not Ceci's to promise to anyone."

Emelee started backing away, but Tulya stepped forward, letting go of her connection with me. She brought her strong hand in the air and was close to Emelee's cheek when the room darkened, the lights dimming in the Minister's presence.

Looking up, I found he and Ezza had joined our miserable party.

"I will have you know I did no such thing," Ezza told my mother with a glare. "I heard you, and I did not baby Tulya. She is at my disposal."

A small gasp left Tulya's mouth, and it wound its way up my spine, making my chest rage with anger.

"Emelee is with Donovan, and you're to back away," Ezza said to her daughter.

"She will not," I barked back.

"Tulya! You will do as I say."

I watched Tulya take in her mother and look back to me and then glance at her uncle.

"You're being taken advantage of, sweet Tulya," I said, standing up to them. "They're always telling you to use your powers, or not to, and even have subjected you to being hurt while exhausting them on humans. And yes, I asked you too, but it's time for us. I've had enough of this bullshit."

"No! *I've* had enough, dear young Malachite," said the Minister. "Ceci, your boys have made a mess in Rubia, starting with your younger one and ending with this malcontent." He pointed at me. "We have risked everything, and at the very least, Donovan is right that Tulya was injured helping you with Magnum."

"I'm abiding by Rubian law!" Ceci tried to argue with the Minister, but it was to no avail.

He raised his hand in the air and the room went black. Then he produced a mirage like Ezza had done earlier, except this time it was of the holiday party. Tulya and I were having a conversation. She was saying she had to go, and we parted ways easily and seemingly forgot about one another in that moment. Magnum was making his way toward Cinder and gathering her in his arms. It was the way the evening should have ended for the four of us. Tulya and I separated, and Mag and Cinder leaving together.

"We will go back to this," he said in a deep tone, looking at the mirage. "To a time when there was peace and my ruling prevailed and you both listened to your elders, coming and going from parties with whom you are meant to. I am in charge of Rubia, only me, and I demand due process."

Emelee fled the room, yelling, "Bye. You know what? I don't want any part of this," clearly scared of the Minister.

My mother was busy rocking on the balls of her feet, praying and begging for forgiveness, and for the second time recently, Tulya went limp and nonresponsive.

The only positive was the Minister's mirage went up in a poof of smoke, evaporating before our very eyes.

"Was that supposed to happen?" I asked as I bent down on the floor and lifted a limp Tulya.

The Minister's silence told me all I needed to know. No—it was not. We were stronger than his bullshit mirage.

Good, I thought to myself before grumbling, "Get out. Your magic is not working here, with us." I stared at the three assholes in my office, waiting for them to go, then heard myself yell, "Get the hell out! I need to revive Tulya for the second time in six months."

Finally, they listened. In the moment, all I cared about was my sweet Tulya, shoving all thoughts of the Minister torching my house to the back of my mind. His mirage had evaporated, so it was clear Tulya and I had some collective worth. But first, I had to figure out why she collapsed again.

This time around, Tulya recuperated from the incident in my bed, where she belonged. My mother was banished to her side of the house—no one would dare force me to separate from Tulya now or ever, moving forward, after the immediate action I took. First, I knew Abraham loved a human, so my brother wasn't the only one. This type of scandal was not exclusive to our family. Second, I gave more thought to the Minister's disappearing mirage and came to a big conclusion. I called Ezza, who wasn't happy to hear from me, but I didn't care.

"Her abilities are greater than yours" was all I said.

"I'm still her mother," she replied, knowing exactly what I meant. Tulya's potential was grander than her own.

"Together we could either cancel one another or double the powers, making our houses the strongest collaborative house."

"It wasn't meant for you two…"

"Bruno! You wanted it to be Bruno!"

"It still could be."

Rolling my eyes, I couldn't believe what I figured out. "You don't want to be overshadowed by your own daughter. Screw you, Ezza."

I hung up before she could reply, not caring she could be my mother-in-law. I'd uncovered her weakness, and she wouldn't want it revealed.

I did text my mother and let her know Ezza and I had come to a mutual agreement. When she asked for details, I left her unanswered. Let her ask her friend.

For two days, I didn't leave Tulya's side, holding cold compresses to her forehead, running ice along her lips, kissing her shoulder, and making sure she appeared to be comfortable. I couldn't stop worrying as to why this happened again, and refused to tend to myself other than taking calls right outside the bedroom door. I hadn't showered in forty-eight hours, and my feet had traced a permanent path in the carpet. That was exactly what I was doing when Abraham showed up without being summoned. Shock and relief ripped through my body in equal measure.

"What do you want?" I greeted him without any pomp and circumstance, thinking I should be nicer, but I wasn't in the mood.

"A little thank you, maybe? I was the one who shared the information with you regarding Emelee's medical diagnosis, allowing you to make some progress with Ceci."

I felt myself nodding. "Yeah, sorry. Thank you for that, but that sort of backfired. Anyway, that's on me. Been a lot going on here." I spoke in short, choppy fragments, waving my hand at Tulya in my bed, her head propped on the pillows, her arms tucked underneath the blankets.

"That's why I'm here. Ezza visited me—"

"That bitch. She's the reason this is happening. *Again.* She doesn't have her daughter's best interests at heart." I didn't mention my reasons or the torch, unsure if I should or not.

"Shh, we know Ezza is only about Ezza. But she is worried about Tulya, so I'm here."

"She's only worried she won't be able to use her daughter's power." *And she's afraid of me.*

"That's true," he agreed. "But here's the thing, every time Tulya gets overwhelmed with anger, her abilities are shorting out. This isn't about Emelee's feelings making her go unconscious. It's about her own aggravation at the situation."

"With Ezza too?" I couldn't help but ask.

"Ezza, Emelee, you and her... And yes, she caused additional problems when she held the feelings before and after the transfer, but I believe it was coupled with her being mad about the scenario with Blake. We know she's come to care for the girl."

I felt myself nodding, wondering where Abraham stood on the issue.

"So, I thought about it and casually mentioned to Ezza that she would get a lot more use out of Tulya if she allowed her to be happy."

"Wow," I said, not believing what I heard. "You did?"

Abraham patted me on the back. "I did. You're a good man and an even better Rubian, Donovan."

"I don't know," I mumbled, still thinking about the torch but schooling myself. I could only worry about Tulya in this moment.

Abraham interrupted my black hole of bad thoughts. "More on all of that later. I have ideas on fixing it all, but let's get your lady better."

Quickly, he pulled a syringe out of his pocket, and I sat down next to Tulya on the other side of the bed without prompting. Touching her, in case she needed to know I was there.

I couldn't help but take in the aging medic, dressed in a navy suit, hair graying at the temples, and wondered if he could advocate for Blake too. Surely there was no one better to do it than him with his age and wisdom. I was drawn away from my thoughts when he pushed the syringe into Tulya's arm, now exposed from the sheets.

And then we waited, both of us tracking up and down my carpet path.

CHAPTER
THIRTY-FIVE

Tulya

My throat was dry, and I could feel my lips cracking as I ran my tongue along them. My body felt like a bag of bones, but I willed myself to open my eyes.

Of course I was met with a sparkling pair of green eyes staring at me, small crinkles in the corners as if he hadn't slept in a while.

"Hi," he whispered, his palm reaching out to smooth the hair off my forehead.

"What…" I tried to form a question but my voice crackled and croaked. Immediately, Donovan stood and went to pour me a glass of water. I noted the vanity was stocked with several cold beverages, coffee, and fruit, and my gaze landed on a bowl of bananas.

"Want one?"

I shook my head. "How?" I managed to get out another word.

"The staff," was all Donovan said.

He brought me a lowball full of ice water and held it out for me to take a sip. I didn't know if my hand was ready to grip the glass, so I allowed it.

"The fighting, or whatever you want to call it, is over," Donovan said when I finished a long gulp, whispering the words in my ear.

Unsure why he was whispering, or which fight he was referencing exactly, I leaned my cheek into his face. My unwelcome, big, sloppy tears plastered his skin.

"Shhh," he crooned, holding me tight, setting the tumbler down.

I felt my head shaking against him.

We were in a bedroom, but I wasn't sure whose—a guest room or Donovan's—or how long I'd been sleeping or out cold again, like back in Miami. My body was failing me regularly.

"We can't do this" was the first string of words I murmured, moving my arms under the blanket, wiggling my fingers—making sure they were all working—not asking where we were. My heart took a beat at all ten of my digits accounted for.

"We can't do what?" Donovan took my chin in his forefinger and thumb and tilted my face to look at him, his deep green eyes searching mine.

"We can't be together." I brought my mostly recovered hand out and set it on his shoulder. For a quick moment, I wished he wasn't wearing a shirt. Being skin to skin with Donovan was my weakness. I'd hold those memories for a lifetime.

Instead of flat-out arguing with me, he brought his free palm to the nape of my neck, helping me to rise until his lips covered my own. The kiss started out soft, making its way deeper and harder. We were one breath, a single soul, in this moment…until I broke free.

"My breath," I mumbled.

He had the nerve to laugh. "Seriously, that's what you're worried about, sweet Tulya?"

I wasn't even sure why Donovan was still in Rubia, let alone here with me, sitting on the edge of a bed and giggling like a schoolgirl at me.

"Don, don't mock me."

This got me a wide smile. "Never."

"Please." I pleaded for his serious side. "You heard my mother…the

Minister… They all said we are not meant to be. Our powers mixed are bad. Their swirling is yin and yang, or oil and water, gas and a match, yada, yada," I rambled, afraid to meet his eyes again.

"I don't care. I spoke with your mother."

"What?"

He caressed my cheek. "I realized something when the mirage went up in a little poof. You are destined to be more powerful than your mother, and she doesn't like that. Especially because you *want* to be with me. So the vision of us not being together disappeared."

I felt my head shaking, unable to take in what he just said.

"And Abraham is on our side. He was here," he countered, smoothing my hair behind my ear.

"He was?"

"He revived you, with a serum. Your mom sent him."

"She did? Why?" I didn't know what was wrong with me—all I could formulate were one-word questions.

"It doesn't matter. Maybe she is worried I will out her. What is important is Abraham showed up and helped, and then he told your mom you have demonstrated incredible control over your powers. More than anyone ever thought was possible. You can hold them back in a way Abraham didn't know existed. You held Cinder's anguish, and you didn't send it all to Val—"

"Look where that got me," I interrupted, whipping my mangled fingers from under the blanket and waggling them at him.

"You beat that episode back. Abraham didn't believe you could, and then this latest one showed him you are actually reacting to the anger hanging in the air around you and not the discipline you are using."

"What?" My head felt hazy and confused. "You and Abraham really got tight," I added, trying not to sound like an idiot. "And my mom, she just listened to you?"

"Look at me." His voice sounded hoarse with emotion. I turned my gaze like he requested. "I don't care what anyone says anymore. Not my mother or yours. I should have listened to Magnum when he said love makes a person stronger. He didn't get a chance to make it happen with Valerie, and I'm sorry for that. More than you know. But we can make us work. Your mom can't stand in our way; you have all the power and control. We would do it even if she didn't know. Abraham agrees we need to do it. He has his reasons and will do what he can. He may not be your uncle, but he does have influence."

Fresh tears streamed from my eyes. "What are you saying?" I had no clue what reality I was in as the question came out of my mouth. "I almost took Emelee's pain away for the second time, this go-round against your mother's wishes. I would have done it for you. Because you asked. I wanted you to get back to your life in Hawaii. Your big dreams." My voice floated off on the last part when it occurred to me this was how true unconditional love felt. A constant hum of caring for a person living in your veins, but a whisper, maybe a touch above one of their own desires and wants and needs.

Donovan turned my chin for the second time, placing his lips on my forehead and kissing me there for an eternity. He didn't speak or let go, only let the touch live on forever.

I tried to get his attention. "Donovan, are you listening to me?"

"My sweet Tulya, I asked you to use your ability on Emelee because I want that chapter of my life to be closed. My dream is to be with you. No way I'd have you risk your health so I could run away. Or unless it meant we could start our life together."

"Why? The whole episode started a feud of epic proportions. Ceci, Ezza, the Minister...for once, they didn't want me to take someone's pain away." Donovan scooched in close to me, wrapping me in his arms. I couldn't believe what was unfolding. He blanketed me in his comforting silence. "But why? They seemed hell-bent the first time." I couldn't help but ask, mumbling my words into his chest.

"It's not my place to say. I don't like secrets, but this is something I shouldn't say other than Emelee isn't well-suited to be a lifelong partner."

"Unless the other choice is me?" It hurt to say it, but it was the truth. "Then, your mother is willing to pick Emelee."

"Yes, my mother wanted anything but this, us. Except this isn't her choice. It's mine, and I want you." His fingers intertwined with mine, his thumb caressing the side of my palm. "Look at me, Tulya. This isn't Ezza's pick either," he added. "She cannot tell you what to do. You are your own woman."

"The Minister has a say. That's his role."

"The Rubian way is strong in you. Years of living under your mother's thumb makes you think that, and I agree we must play along with it. That's why I consulted with Abraham. We have him in our corner. He is willing to vouch for us, saying we can couple…" He waggled his eyebrows. "If you get my drift."

"Emelee can't have children," I blurted out, and Donovan looked utterly shocked.

"What? You have known? How?"

"First, my heart breaks for Emelee. That's no reason for her not to marry. But how did I find out? Blake told me. When she met Emelee, she used her powers to feel her out. Apparently she has been doing that and not saying anything to anyone. She wants to know who her allies are. Anyway, she sensed this with Emelee mostly because she had a strong inkling Emelee empathized with Valerie. God, don't be mad at sweet Blake for sharing with me. She is just a young girl with these extraordinary powers and is walking around with an incredible amount of information, in a new place without her mother."

I'd lost count of how many times his lips caressed my forehead, but this time they made their way across my cheek. "I would never be upset with Blake. She is a child, and my niece. She was moved here, separated from her mother, and expected to act as a Rubian. That's part of the issue with Emelee. My mom started to think I could raise Blake with her."

"No!"

"Right, she belongs with Magnum, not me."

I nodded. Donovan was a softie when he wanted to be.

"But remember when we made love in your bed and it felt like our powers were suspended? I know you felt it." Donovan changed subjects like a toddler.

I nodded again. This time slowly.

"Abraham said we are stronger than we think. We've served Rubia well and our capabilities are expanding. He sees no reason why we cannot be together—forever."

"We can?" I heard myself asking, hope coloring the two words.

"Especially since I revealed your mom's secret agenda. So yes, my sweet Tulya, we can be us." He gathered me closer, if that was possible. "Abraham is going to tell your uncle his revelations, and your mom has backed down after I called her out. Not to mention, she's afraid not to have the medic's support in her own Minister campaign," he added.

"Oh," I breathed.

"I love you," he stated, turning us front to front, my body melding to his.

"I love you too…but what about Hawaii?" Panic settled in my chest for the umpteenth time. "I don't want to steal your dreams, but I live in Rubia." I hated to admit it, but this was all I'd ever known and it was my home.

"Babe," he muttered, cupping my cheeks, "I can go back and forth. I'm not my dad. And he wouldn't want me to be a carbon copy of him. That's what my mom wants. But I'm me, and I can own a hotel and live here. Plus, it's a decent place for us to visit when we need a break."

The tears started falling, and Donovan gently wiped them from my cheek with his thumb.

"It's all going to be fine after you say yes."

"What?" My throat cracked as the same one-word question I kept asking came out.

"Yes, to marrying me." He looked at me dead center. "I can't get down on one knee because I'm lying here with you and I don't want to move. Also, I clearly don't have a ring yet. I've been busy, but I need to know."

I swallowed every last excuse, and said "Yes" as quickly as I could. I was foolishly and helplessly in love with Donovan Malachite.

We'd started to kiss, our hips looking for friction, cold waves filling my spine in only the way Donovan could make happen, when I stopped suddenly. Pulling back, I said, "But we can't have kids... You know what our mothers said. The powers mixing."

"We can," he said, placing his lips on my temple.

"But...what if our kid is evil? Or has no ability? We will be shamed by everyone, further angering Ezza and Ceci."

"We are not going to allow either of those scenarios to happen."

"How?"

"You want to talk about this now?" His hand smoothed a hair off my face.

"I have to know." It was the best feeling to be able to speak freely with Donovan.

"Abraham has some ideas, but mostly he thinks IVF and growing the fetus outside for a little bit will allow him to make sure it has a Rubian capability."

"So, not the real way? I mean the traditional way. You know, sex?" I felt myself blushing despite having been naked with Donovan several times.

"There is no real way, Tulya. Plus we can have all the fun practicing and role-playing. Like how about now?" He wiggled his eyebrows and a laugh barreled up from my chest, breaking the moment.

We went back to making out, and I was in the middle of a long moan as we were in the process of yanking each other's clothes off when a panicked pounding echoed through the house.

"Don! Don!" we heard from outside, and I could tell it was Magnum.

Donovan threw on his shirt, leaving it unbuttoned, and ran to the hallway where I heard Magnum shouting.

I found a robe and tied it around me like when my mother was at my place, and walked out to find Magnum on his knees, face in his hands, begging Donovan.

It was a sight I wouldn't forget.

"Bro, I need you. You have to get Valerie. Please?" His voice was tight with apprehension and hoarse from sobbing.

"What happened?" Donovan asked authoritatively.

"Mother and Cinder. That's what happened. They got a hold of Blake and told her she could forget seeing her mom again. She's locked herself in her room and all I hear is crying outside her door. They're breaking her."

Magnum had been reduced to a small child weeping on the floor, and my heart broke for him.

"Not on my watch," Donovan declared. "We stood up to Ezza, found a loophole of sorts. I'm going to fix this, brother. I know some other information that's not mine to divulge, but it will help us. Trust me, that's my vow to you." He turned to me. "I have to go. Maybe you can go to Blake? She might see you? Comfort her?"

I felt myself nodding furiously. "Go, and yes I will, my love." I couldn't help but add the ending. I wanted him to know how I felt before he bolted out.

Donovan stopped, and turned to me, kissing my lips, his tongue lingering on the precipice of entering before he stopped himself. He broke free and said, "I love you." He did nothing more than give me a quick kiss on the lips...and then ran out the door.

Which was how I ended up kneeling next to my lover's brother, Magnum, rubbing his back and wondering if both of them could have a happy ending...

THE BROTHER MALACHITE

SNEAK PEEK

THE CALL:

"*I love you, V.* I'm not going to let anyone come between this or us. I miss you… Gotta see you or I may not survive," he breathed into the phone from somewhere far off.

I tried to imagine it, but it was a place of only imaginations. I wasn't even sure it existed. No one knew of it; at least no one I could ask. His voice was hushed as always, keeping our communications private.

"Mag." I matched his tone, whispering his name as if it might be the last time I ever muttered it. If it weren't for the nature of the news I had to share, I might have convinced myself he was a figment of my mind.

"Babe, listen, I promise soon," he said, thinking I was going to complain about his absence.

We hadn't seen one another in two months. He'd been on a string of trips for his family business, filling in after his father passed. Apparently his brother was left at the helm of the company, but he was second-in-command. Which was why his father had sent him to the States a little over a year ago to take a business course. He knew this day was coming and wanted his son prepared. If only his dad knew…

"Donovan is sending me to Atlanta to meet with some investors, and then I'm going to visit for a few days. We can stay in a hotel and make a staycation out of it, yeah?"

I felt myself nodding while running a hand over my belly. I'd known when I saw him last, but he was so broken up over his dad, I hadn't shared.

"I have to tell you something before you see me." I didn't want him to notice before I mentioned the situation.

"Did you dye your hair?" He laughed as he said it. I adored the way he joked with me. He'd told me he wasn't that way with others, only me. I believed him; he had a serious side.

"No…ummm, Magnum, there's no easy way to say this, but I'm pregnant." I blurted the words out before losing courage.

"What? Babe? V?"

I hurried to answer questions he hadn't asked. "I didn't mean for it to happen, or trick you. And there's only been you."

"V, stop. Don't act like I'm that guy, who would accuse you of setting me up. How far along? You've been dealing with this without me." His voice was a bit deeper, and I could hear him pacing, the swish of something under his feet.

"A little over four months."

"Hmm." I assumed he was doing the math. Actually, I knew he was pragmatic like that.

Panic started to creep up my spine. He'd told me all he could about his roots, more than he should have. I would never visit his land or meet his family. If I ever spoke about their existence or special powers, he'd lose his place on their secret island. How was this going to work? A baby!

"I should have taken care of things," I quietly said. "I couldn't though."

I felt tears prick in the corner of my eyes and was furious with myself. This wasn't me; I was tough inside with a hard exterior. My mom didn't raise me to be a pushover or the sentimental type, yet here I was, on the brink of crying.

"I'm going to fly there tomorrow. I'll make up an emergency meeting. I don't want you to be upset for one second until I get there. We'll figure this out." He spoke quickly, authoritatively, and it seemingly calmed my nerves for a millisecond.

Then I started to think about telling my mom why or how we couldn't be a real-real couple. *Mom, I'm in love with a paranormal person. An alien. And oh, we're having a baby...*

"Magnum! I need you," I heard his brother say loudly in the background, and I knew our call was coming to a fast and furious end.

"Tomorrow, I will be there. Love you, V," he said, and disconnected the call.

His family didn't even know I existed. My mom believed he was a human male. Laughter bubbled up my throat at the thought of it all.

I didn't even know if we would have a normal child. I'd asked him once if there were dragons where he lived, and he'd let out a hoarse laugh. *Of course not*, he'd said, but he didn't explain any further.

When we'd met, it had been instant attraction and not only physical. He didn't wait long to reveal his abilities to me and explain why he came and went. He cared about me that much. That was what I'd told myself.

My God, I'd fallen so hard that I didn't care if he wasn't like me or couldn't marry me or even live with me. But could I raise a baby this way?